I0675050

TWO FOR THE ROAD

ALEXA MILNE

Two for the Road
ISBN # 978-1-83943-873-8
©Copyright Alexa Milne 2019
Cover Art by Cherith Vaughan ©Copyright January 2019
Interior text design by Claire Siemaszkiewicz
Pride Publishing

Published in 2020 by Pride Publishing, United Kingdom.

Pride Publishing is an imprint of Totally Entwined Group Limited.

TWO FOR THE ROAD

Dedication

This story is dedicated to my brother, who sadly died, way too young, last year. I hope my sister-in-law will forgive me for using a line from a letter he wrote to her. I had no idea my brother was such a romantic. His words made me cry then as they do now. I love and miss you, little brother.

I would like to thank Cath for putting up with me and reading every word as usual, as well as C.F. White, Tanja Ongkiehong and Rebecca Baker, my editor, who gave me some wonderful suggestions and made my words so much better.

Chapter One

Riley tapped his fingers on the wheel of his BMW, glanced first at his watch then up the steps to the door.

"Where the hell is he?" Should he get out and knock on the door? *Why did I agree to this? Giving lifts is never wise.* Riley already knew the answer. *Because his father was my best friend. Because I'm lonely. Because...*

The black-painted door flew open and a tall, gangly red-haired youth — in Riley's eyes — rushed down the steps, attempting to push one arm through a coat sleeve while holding a piece of toast in the other. He stuffed the toast in his mouth, somehow managed the coat then turned around and ran up back up the steps to collect a bag from his mother. He flung open the passenger-side door and jumped in, placing the bag on his lap.

"I'm sorry. I've no excuse. I need to take a clock into the shower. I won't do it again, I promise. Dad's already torn a strip off me."

Riley smiled. He'd never admit it to the young man at his side, but timekeeping had never been a strong point of *his* youth, either. He recalled his father dragging the bedding from over him, then slammed shut the memory.

"Try not to make a habit of it." He adopted his firm but fair tone, the one he used with clients making impossible demands. Glancing sideways revealed Dylan hadn't changed much. Always skinny with a head of bright red hair and now matching beard, Dylan had been a smiling toddler when Riley had moved to London and a thin brooding teenager of fifteen when he'd last met him.

"I won't," Dylan replied cheerfully to Riley's admonition. "Should we get off? It's my first day, and I need to make a good impression."

Riley turned on the engine and slipped the car out of brake into gear. He checked in all directions and pulled out into the traffic. A light drizzle began, typical weather on the north side of Pendle Hill. The village of his childhood, and his home for the last twelve months, nestled on the side of the hill famous for its witches. He negotiated his way out of the village and onto the motorway. The drizzle turned to rain pattering on the windscreen.

"Thanks for agreeing to give me a lift. I hope it's not too much of a pain, and I'll try not to be irritating."

Riley didn't reply, hoping to stop the conversation. He was used to quiet journeys accompanied only by the radio or a CD if he felt so inclined. He'd expected Dylan to pull out his mobile, stick in headphones and amuse himself. Dylan, however, didn't take the hint.

"You doing this is such a relief. I panicked when I got the job, but beggars can't be choosers these days, and I'm lucky to have one at all. Dad said he'd sort something out for me, and he did, thanks to you. You and him go way back, he told me, but you left to live in London. I remember you visiting a few years back?"

Riley had no chance to reply.

"I've only been once, you know, to London. I bet you know all the good places, theaters, restaurants, museums, clubs? I didn't plan to come back here, but I got the job in Preston, so here I am. Hopefully, I'll be able move out of home to somewhere nearer, or with a railway station when I've saved enough. I went to Durham University, but I expect you know that."

Riley did, but only because Tony had come to his father's funeral several months back. The meeting had been awkward. He'd been back six months already at that point, taking care of his father as he gradually faded away. Any guilt he'd felt about not reaching out to his oldest friend had disappeared when Tony hadn't contacted him, either. He nodded, knowing Dylan would continue.

"I loved Durham, but there weren't any jobs there. I miss my university friends, but we're determined to meet up. I bet you got up to all sorts at uni in London."

Ah, the past. Riley sighed. He'd never be able to stand this onslaught every morning, especially if it came accompanied by twenty questions. Perhaps it wouldn't be for long. He reached over and turned on the radio, hoping Dylan might get the message without him having to be rude and ask him to shut up.

"Oh, I love this one. You hardly ever hear Living in a Box on the radio." Dylan proceeded to join in, singing and dancing in his seat.

Did I ever have such energy? Riley felt every one of his forty-two years weighing him down.

Dylan nudged him. "Come on, don't let the side down. Join in. Didn't you and Dad used to play this together back in the day?"

Riley couldn't resist smiling and humming along. How long had it been since he'd played? His guitar lay gathering dust in one of the spare rooms. Dylan had a good voice.

"We did, but how do you know this song?" he asked. "You weren't even born."

"I bet you know all the Beatles' hits," Dylan replied.

"Yeah, but everyone does, don't they? My father was a fan. He saw them play at the Cavern Club in Liverpool." This fact had always surprised him. He couldn't picture his staid, conservative father in such a venue.

"And so, *my* dad still plays his stuff from the eighties. They say you never forget the songs you listened to in your early teens. I grew up with his stuff, and..." He leaned forward and whispered, "Don't tell Mum, but I liked it more than Dylan. She still plays *his* stuff all the time too."

Riley chuckled. "I remember her and your father discussing what to call you."

"And, Mum won. Still, it could be worse. At least she wasn't an Elvis fan. Can you imagine having to spend your life as Elvis Hargreaves? Do you still play guitar?"

Riley smiled at the memory. Their band hadn't been anything special but had still played at every school concert, even when he'd moved to the local grammar, due to a music teacher desperate to have acts willing to perform. "I haven't for a while, but I expect I could strum out a tune. I was never as good as your dad. He played lead. I was the silent, hardly moving bass player."

"Cool. I play sax. I took music at A level. It always surprises people I did math and music, but they go together somehow — chords, intervals, progression — all math. And I've always been good with figures. Some people think accountancy is boring, but I've always loved being able to manipulate numbers and see patterns. Music is the same, isn't it? The best songs use certain intervals between notes to hook you in and chord changes and sequences. If you study it properly, you can see how a song is constructed and pull it apart."

Riley pressed the accelerator to overtake the lorry on the inside lane. "You know, I've never thought about music in that way." There was certainly more to Dylan than met the eye. "I just like how it sounds. Do you still play sax?"

"For myself, but Mum worries about the neighbors complaining. I might look for a group to join. Not driving is a pain, though. Once I start getting paid, I'm gonna save up for my own car." He ran his hand over the dashboard. "Nothing like this beauty, though. I bet it even has heated seats. Good to know my arse will be nice and toasty in the winter."

Riley didn't want to think about Dylan's arse, or any other part of him. That part of his life was well and truly over.

"Maybe you and I should get together and play with Dad. Mum still sings, you know, and Kayleigh plays keyboard, though she didn't get beyond grade five. She hated having to practice, and I doubt she'll be home from university much. She can't stand living here."

"But you're all right with it?" Riley asked. Over twenty years ago, he'd had the same feelings.

"I guess so, and this way I get my food made and washing done. I know you're supposed to go to university, have experiences, develop a network and find someone. Well, I found lots of someones, but no one special, and even though I loved Durham, I've found I quite like being home too. Mum and Dad are great, and I have my old mates, Matt and Dan. With any luck, I'll meet new people at work. Are you planning to stay in the village? Dad wasn't sure, with all the memories. Looking after your father those last months must have been tough."

"It was." The last conversation he wanted to have was about watching his father fade away as the cancer took the man who'd always been so strong. He hadn't decided what to do about the house, but he couldn't return to his old life. Taking the partnership at his father's firm now tied him to the area and gave him a reason to get up every day. A face from his past flashed into Riley's mind. He pushed it away.

"Sorry, sometimes I open my mouth without thinking. Please tell me if I blather on. I'm not good with silence and tend to fill it with words. See, I'm doing it again, babbling on. Feel free to tell me to shut up."

"It's fine," Riley lied. Maybe if he let him, Dylan would get all his words out in one trip. "Truth is I haven't decided what to do with the house." He stared into the distance.

"Mr. Ormerod."

Riley braked harder than he intended, realizing the roundabout at the end of the motorway was coming up. They were both thrown forward. "Sorry about that. And please, call me Riley. My father was Mr. Ormerod." He pulled up at the first set of lights.

"D'you need me to stop at the town hall? It can sometimes be busy at this time of day. I have a parking space at my office just around the corner. I could drop you off there instead. With your long legs, it shouldn't take you long."

"Sounds good to me. Now, what about tonight? I'm supposed to finish at five. Shall I meet you at yours, or hang about outside? I could go to the library if it's raining, or there's a café opposite, if you're going to be late, or as it's flexitime, I can leave a bit later. Give me your phone, and I'll put my number in so you can call me."

This was the bit of the arrangement that had worried Riley as much as the noise, but after several solitary months, Tony's call out of the blue, asking if he could give his son a lift, had provided him with a lifeline, and Sue, his father's carer, had encouraged him to take the olive branch.

"Remind me when we get there. I usually try to finish around five, but it depends as some clients can't get to the office during the day. Most of what I do is paper, not people, but meetings can happen any time." He pulled up yet again.

"Bugger me, there are a lot of lights on these roads since they made all the changes and pedestrianized the shopping area," Dylan said. "And cameras everywhere. Dad hates driving in Preston."

"At least they've finished updating the roads around the station and built the new entrance," Riley agreed. "They've made a real effort to improve the place since it got city status, with lots of modern buildings, and it's such a big university town now — you should feel much more at home. Riley glanced across at Dylan again. He looked much more like Lori than Tony. "You know, it's funny. Of all the jobs I thought your father might do, I never figured he'd follow your granddad into his shop in Clitheroe. He hated being dragged there when we were young."

"I guess people change. He loves the place now he sells what he wants. And it turned out he has a nose for an antique. When Granddad had his stroke, Dad took over. He used to take me with him on trips to find new items. You never know when you'll get a bargain, he'd say. He's like a pig in muck at a house clearance. He's at the big auction place in Clitheroe today. By the way, I'm supposed to invite you round for dinner one night or Sunday lunch to say thank you."

Riley turned into the narrow lane behind the high street then into the car park, grateful not to have to reply. It had been tough and lonely, coming back home and caring for his dying father, a man he'd never been close to. He hadn't only come back for the man, but for himself, having nowhere else to go.

"We're here," he said, pulling up in front of the sign declaring Whewell and Ormerod, Solicitors. "Give me your mobile and we'll sort out the numbers." He exchanged numbers and gave Dylan back the phone.

"Ring me when you're ready," Dylan said.

Riley tucked the phone into his jacket pocket. "Good luck on your first day."

"Thanks. I'll see you later." Dylan clambered out of the car, threw his bag over his back and hurried off through the narrow back lane between the buildings. Riley sighed. Had he ever been that young? If he had, it was a lifetime ago.

"Bloody hell," he said, staring in the rear-view mirror. "You're forty-two, not ninety. Your life is not over." Willing himself to believe his own words, Riley picked up his briefcase, stepped out of the car and headed for the office with a spring in his step.

Chapter Two

Once out of sight of Riley's car, Dylan stopped and leaned against a wall, despite the damp. He needed to get his act together before he turned up at work. Checking his hand, he held it out in front of him — nope, still shaking — and his heart felt like it was pounding out the rhythm to *Agadoo*. Maybe wangling a lift with the man he'd crushed on for years hadn't been such a sensible idea after all. But he'd been so close to him. Close enough to smell the aftershave or shower gel Riley used. Close enough to note the small patch of gray hair at Riley's temples, and those deep blue eyes. Okay, the overall look and demeanor had been slightly grumpy, but Dylan could work on changing that. After all, he'd got Riley to hum along, hadn't he? So what if he had no idea about the man's sexuality? There was just something. He recalled his friend's words from the night before.

'You do know you're off your head, don't you? He's twenty years older than you, and you've no idea if he bats for your side.'

Dylan had refused to give way. He'd stuck out his lower lip. There might have even been some pouting. *'Anything's possible. There's never been any mention of a woman in his life.'*

'Or a man either, according to your dad. Perhaps he's not interested in either, or he's a workaholic. You're most likely on a hiding to nothing.'

Matt didn't understand. For seven years, his memory of Riley, immaculately dressed in an expensive suit, had fed into Dylan's dreams. He grinned as the sun disappeared behind a large cloud. Spending forty minutes sitting next to the man had only confirmed his feelings. He *had* to find out. He *had* to know. He glanced at his watch and set off, hurrying through the morning crowds to the council offices.

The gray building appeared darker in the gloomy weather than it had in high summer at his interview. Low cloud seemed to sit atop the highest gabled towers. Dylan pushed through the wood and glass door, then headed for the stairs, taking two at a time. As a trainee assistant finance officer, he would get to experience working in several departments, but his first was in the local tax department dealing with council tax collection and distribution. He knocked on the manager's door and waited.

"Come in." His boss, Barbara Wilson, was an older woman who'd been on the selection panel. Dylan opened the door and entered.

"Ah, there you are, Dylan. Nice to see you're on time. You're going to be working with Oliver. He'll take you through the everyday stuff and find you a desk."

"Will I get my own, or do we hot desk?"

"Depends on space, and how busy we are. Oliver will show you. We're a friendly bunch, and you're the first new body we've had in a couple of years, with the spending cuts. You can learn a lot here about the practical application of your skills. But one thing to remember is that here we deal with real people's lives. We have to be certain and take care. A decimal point in the wrong place...well, I'm sure you understand."

The door opened behind him, and a face appeared.

"Come in, Oliver. This is Dylan, the trainee."

Oliver grinned at him. *At least he appears friendly.* He stuck out his hand. Dylan took it and shook.

"We may as well get started straight away, but first the tour." Oliver gestured for him to go out.

The tour lasted about thirty minutes as Oliver introduced him to too many faces around the vast offices. "And here you'll find our small kitchen to make tea and coffee, and the gents are across the way. Now, let's get you a desk, and I'll explain what we're starting you on. It's basic to begin with, but let's break you in gently. For now, everything will go through me."

"I expected as much," Dylan said.

The day passed in a blur of figures and people. He didn't have time to think about Riley or anything else. The last thing he wanted to do was make a vital mistake on his first day, so he triple-checked everything before passing it on. Oliver stopped at his desk every so often to glance at what he'd done so far and offer encouragement. At least he didn't appear to resent having to deal with the new boy. By five, Dylan was happy to be able to log off and look away from his screen.

"How was your first day?"

Dylan glanced up to see the woman who occupied the desk across from his standing next to him. He searched his memory for a name.

"Lucy," she said, clearly seeing his struggle.

Heat rushed into his cheeks. "Oh yes, I'm sorry. So many introductions. I'm Dylan, Dylan Hargreaves."

"It can be a bit intimidating being new, so I thought I'd introduce myself and mention that a few of us get together some Friday nights for an after-work drink if you fancied joining us. There's some great venues opened recently. We try to be a sociable bunch. I just thought I'd make the offer."

"I don't know," Dylan said. "I get a lift home, so I might not be able to manage it. I live in Pendleside off the A69. Do you know it?"

"I don't, sorry. I'm from Broughton, but there are a few people who live in that direction. I'll ask around and get back to you."

"That would be great." He didn't want to appear stand-offish. "Talking of lifts, I need to get off." Riley hadn't phoned, so Dylan assumed they would be leaving on time. "I'll see you tomorrow." He stood.

"I look forward to it," Lucy said. "It's been a while since we've had a new face around here."

At the entrance, Dylan undid his top button and removed his tie, carefully retaining the Windsor knot his father had attempted to teach him how to create that morning, before stuffing it into a pocket. He stepped out of the town hall into a light drizzle. So much for the promised improvement on the forecast.

"Damn." He reached into his backpack and pulled out his umbrella, put it up and skipped across the road. He didn't want to keep Riley waiting.

Dylan had asked his dad all about Riley when he'd arranged the lift. The way his father described him had created an image of some stuffy fuddy-duddy with no sense of humor. Could he have changed so much in seven years? Dylan hadn't sensed any of that in the car, just a certain reticence, and he liked to think he was good at people. He certainly thought Riley was still easy on the eye. Tall, dark and handsome without the slightest awareness of being so. The graying hair at his temples only increased his allure, in Dylan's mind.

He turned the corner into the car park to see Riley emerge from the rear door of his offices. Catching his eye before he got into that magnificent car, Dylan waved and hurried across the tarmac. Having already seated himself, Riley pushed the passenger door open.

"Jump in before the rain gets any harder."

Dylan shook his umbrella, closed it then climbed inside. "Um, what should I do with this?" he asked, not wanting to put the damp umbrella in his bag or on the seat.

"Plastic bag in the glove compartment. This is Lancashire. You always have to be prepared for rain."

Dylan quickly wrapped the offending umbrella. "It must have rained in London as well," he said. *Hell, we're talking about the weather already. So typically British.*

"It did, but I didn't tend to walk around much on a work day. And I didn't have a car like this. I used the Tube to get around, and my office was right next to a station."

"I can't imagine living there," Dylan said, as Riley put the car into reverse and turned it around.

"Hmm, Durham's tiny in comparison. It's a good university, though. Always had a good reputation in my day, even if, like Bristol, we used to think of it as the home for Oxbridge rejects."

"Yeah. There was a feel of that about the place. It was my first choice, though. I didn't want to go south. Where did you go?"

"UCL—University College, London."

"Did you ever think about training to be a barrister? They always seem to get the glory in the TV shows," Dylan said.

Riley eased the car into traffic heading out of the city. "No. I always wanted to be a solicitor. I'm not one for putting myself in front of people like that. Being a barrister is all about the performance. You slip on the wig and play your part. I've always been more of a details man."

Dylan sat up in his seat. "Me too. I love the nitty-gritty of sorting out figures."

"So," Riley said. "How was your first day?"

Dylan let out a long breath and leaned his head back. "Busy. Lots of people to meet. The department has been pared back to the bare bones because of cuts. I suppose I was lucky to get a job at all. I'd already met Mrs. Wilson—she's the chief accountant in my section—at the interviews. Basically, my current job is to check the figures for the collection and distribution of council tax. I'll get to move around departments as a trainee, checking figures, but it's more than adding up figures. There are the wages as well as tax payments, purchases, rent and benefits. In the current climate, we all need to be flexible. I guess you cover a variety of specialties as well in a place like Preston."

"I do. In London we did much more criminal work than here."

"That must have been exciting. Shit." The car lurched to a halt.

"Bloody idiot pushing in. I'd have let him if he'd asked. Sorry, it takes an age to get out of here sometimes. I need to concentrate."

Dylan took the hint and shut up. His mother said he could talk the hind leg off a donkey. Instead, he examined the profile of the man next to him. Riley's furrowed brow came down over his eyes. He had a longish, straight nose, slightly padded lips and a decent, strong-looking chin. It was a good profile. The lobe of his ear clearly, and rather surprisingly, revealed a pierced ear without adornment. Next, he checked out Riley's hands as they held on to the wheel. The fingers, long and straight, had no jewelry, although the skin on the third finger had a lighter band. Had Riley been married? His dad hadn't said anything. Mind you, his dad was the first to admit he'd only spasmodically kept in touch with his school friend. Dylan couldn't help wondering if they'd fallen out, or simply drifted apart.

'I thought he'd go back to London once his father was dead and buried,' his dad had said. 'He always hated this place. He and his father didn't get on, and he hardly ever visited, especially after his mother died. I didn't even know he'd come back to nurse his father through the cancer.'

His mother had suggested asking Riley for a lift. His dad had been reluctant but had never been able to argue with Dylan's mum. Dylan had crossed every finger and toe in the hope that Riley would say yes and thus allow Dylan to get to know him. He hadn't said much about his life so far, but Dylan intended to keep digging.

"That's better. The motorway's not so bad now," Riley announced as they passed the Blackburn exit.

"You were going to tell me about London," Dylan said.

"Was I? I don't remember saying that."

"It must have been so busy. I'm not over keen on crowds. Dad took me to Turf Moor once, and I had to be taken out."

"I can't imagine Burnley ever having such a crowd." Riley chuckled. The throaty sound hit Dylan by surprise. It was deep and raspy and, from the reaction of his cock, rather sexy.

"Hey, they're back up in the Premiership, I'll have you know." He wasn't much of a football supporter but felt duty bound to support his dad's team.

"So, you're a fan then, or do the crowds still get to you?"

"Truth, I'm not really into footie. Dad has a season ticket, but I only watch on telly to stare at their thighs. I couldn't explain the offside rule if I was tortured."

"Oh."

Had he said too much? Dylan didn't hide his sexuality from anyone. "Yeah, let's say I didn't have a certain tattooed Man United player on my wall simply because of his ability at taking free kicks. Are you much of a fan? Of football that is, not the player, or his thighs and tats."

"No. I prefer tennis, but I haven't played for a while."

"Did you go to Wimbledon?" Dylan had always wanted to go, but he didn't admit his admiration for any of the players this time.

"My firm had tickets every year, so sometimes we did get to the center court. I saw the Olympic final there in 2012 when Britain won gold."

"Awesome. I'm fairly rubbish, but if you fancy a game one weekend."

"Maybe, though it's not exactly the right time of year, and I would have thought you'd have had enough of me during the week," Riley said.

"More the other way round," Dylan muttered. Riley sniffed and raised his shoulders.

"Mum says I talk too much. It's usually when I'm nervous, but I find silence a little intimidating. Tell me if I'm annoying you. I wouldn't want to do that when you're being so kind."

Rain splattered on the windscreen again as Riley turned onto the A-road. They'd be home in a few minutes and Dylan noticed Riley hadn't said anything about his life in London. Still, there would be other times.

"Here we are," Riley said, finding a gap. "I'll see you in the morning bright and early."

"I promise I'll be on time tomorrow," Dylan said, climbing out. He waved as Riley pulled away. Something about the man intrigued him. Twenty years away and no one seemed to know anything of Riley's life in the big city. Had he spent all that time alone? Had there been someone in his life? So far, Riley was a closed book, but Dylan knew there was a story there and he desperately wanted to hear it.

Chapter Three

Dylan was sitting on the doorstep, eating toast, when Riley pulled up the next morning. He bounded down the remaining steps, once again leaving Riley wondering if he'd ever been that young. A vision entered his head unbidden. How he'd hurried down the steps of the lecture hall, wanting to speak to the barrister who had come as a special guest. How the same person had taken his hand, spoken to him for ten minutes then slipped a piece of paper into Riley's palm. He'd opened it later to reveal a telephone number. It had taken him several days to pluck up the courage to ring, much longer than it had for Nate to persuade him into bed. He'd been overwhelmed by the man's presence. Now, twenty years later, he found it harder and harder to remember the good times.

"Wow, serious face. I'm not late, am I?" Dylan slammed the car door and did up his seatbelt.

"No, just work. You know what it's like." Riley shifted the car out of neutral, checked his mirrors and pulled out. He loved the way the car almost purred. It had been his one treat for himself after his father had died, leaving more money than Riley had expected. With the rest of his inheritance, he'd bought into the practice.

"I don't really," Dylan replied. "Know what work's like. I did help my dad in the summer and work some shifts behind the bar while at university, but this is my first real job. One day, I'm hoping to work for myself, go freelance, you know. Local authority pay isn't brilliant, but the hours are all right. Dad says you're a partner, so does that make it your firm?"

"It gets my name on the door and the letterheads," Riley said. "Whewell and Ormerod, Solicitors. It has an auspicious ring to it."

"Your dad was a solicitor as well, wasn't he? Before he got ill. Must have been hard leaving London and coming back after so much time away. We're not exactly cosmopolitan here. There isn't even a railway station, or a secondary school. At least we have a pub and Mum has kept the post office and shop going."

Riley checked both ways before pulling out of the village. After what had happened, leaving London hadn't been a problem. Being home had been a different matter altogether. He'd never told his father anything about his life, never encouraged him to visit, or mentioned Nate. He'd been as guilty as his father for the distance created between them, and even after he came home, that distance had remained. Regrets — he had more than a few.

"London may sound glamorous, but it's not all it's cracked up to be." He didn't explain further.

"My boyfriend and I went down to a convention once. We cosplayed Captain America and Bucky. I was Bucky." Riley caught his downward glance. "I don't exactly have the chest muscles for Captain America. I dyed my hair and everything. It was huge, with so many people, but I got loads of autographs. I'll have to show you my photos."

Boyfriend? So, Dylan was gay and not afraid to tell people. Did his parents know? Tony had been as casually homophobic as many others in school. Riley said nothing but attempted to concentrate on Dylan's words. Like everyone, Riley had seen the trailers for the *Avengers* films. Did he admit to never having seen one? Dylan blethered on about who he'd seen and the costumes they'd worn. It was a different world. Riley let him talk until finally he stopped.

"I'm wittering on again, aren't I? Sorry. I told you it's a habit. I'm trying to be really careful at work to keep my head down and my mouth shut."

"It's fine," Riley said. He wasn't exactly lying. He spent too much time on his own. Occasionally, Sue, his father's helper, invited him out. It had turned out they'd known each other as children. Village life was like that, although Sue had gone on to a different school.

They'd got to know each other well over the months before his father died. She'd come in during the day, leaving him with the night shift. The cancer his father had left too long to treat had spread until finally it reached his brain. His common sense told him he should sell the four-bedroomed house he'd been brought up in. He had no need of so much space. He'd be better off buying somewhere nearer Preston. But six months later, he was still there. Sue had helped him give away his father's clothes, yet everything else remained to taunt him, especially the unopened diaries his father had kept from childhood. *Maybe I'll have my own bonfire on Guy Fawkes' night.*

"You will tell me if I go on too much, won't you?"

Dylan's words brought him back. He needed to concentrate. Luckily, the traffic tended to lessen after they'd passed Blackburn. "I told you. It's fine. Have you been to other conventions? I've read about them, but I fell out of the habit of watching TV and films — never had time with work and everything. I did watch *Star Trek Next Generation* as a teenager —"

"You *must* watch *Deep Space Nine*. It's my favorite version, though *Discovery* might challenge that. I could take you to a *Star Trek* convention, if you'd like. It's great to have gay characters in such an iconic show. It's about time they were more diverse, don't you think?"

Was Dylan trying to work out his view? Instinctively, he chose his words carefully. "I agree. After all, *Star Trek* is supposed to represent a future when mankind works together, but I'm sure you've got other friends to go with. You don't want an old fuddy-duddy like me hanging around."

"You're hardly old."

"I'm the same age as your dad, remember, and I bet you think he's old."

"Well, you've kept yourself in better nick than him, that's for certain."

If he didn't know better, he'd say Dylan was flirting with him. *Don't be stupid.* He wished away the warm flush spreading up his neck to his face and kept his eyes on the road. "I run," he said. "I used to go to the gym in London." *Yeah, and that's where Nate picked up his little gym buddies, all muscles and no brain.*

"I run, too," Dylan said. "Maybe we could run together. There are some scenic routes around here. And at least I can't talk and run at the same time."

Riley laughed. He hadn't been out for a while, and he was tempted. "Perhaps next week we can sort something out."

"Awesome. I thought I'd do a couple of miles twice a week to shake out my muscles after sitting down all day. I could bring my gear and change at yours, or you could change at ours, if you're not fed up with me already, that is.

"And I'll get those DVDs for you as well. You must see *Deep Space Nine*. Maybe we could watch together once a week. I'd love to discuss them with you. It's always more fun to watch with someone else."

Could he stand spending time with such an enthusiast? He'd grown annoyed with himself and practically turned into a recluse, according to Sue. He imagined her face if he told her about Dylan wanting to spend time with him.

"I have to bring work home a lot of the time," he said.

"Surely, you can spare one night for fun. All work and no play makes Riley a dull boy — you're sure you don't mind me calling you Riley?"

Riley smiled to himself. "I told you, it's fine." The journey had been quicker today and the lights on green. He turned into the narrow alley leading to the back of his office building. "Here we are."

Dylan climbed out of the car and stretched. "I'll see you same time tonight." He bounded across the tarmac, then turned to wave. Riley lifted his hand. He hadn't given Dylan an answer, but he did like *Star Trek*. What would be the harm of having some company?

Once inside, he popped into reception before heading to his office. As always, Ruth greeted him.

"Morning, Mr. Ormerod. Weather's brighter today." Ruth had been there for nearly twenty years and kept the place running like clockwork. "I've forwarded a few emails to you, and I'll bring the post when it arrives. Mr. Whewell is off today but hoping to be back tomorrow. Mr. Ali has the custody meeting at ten. Such a sad case, and Ms. Price is in court." The door opened behind him.

"Morning." Riley turned to see Katie, their most recent trainee.

"Are we still all right for our meeting this morning?" he asked.

She looked tired. "Yes, I've a few questions to ask about a house conveyance, just to make sure."

"The paperwork is in your in-tray." Ruth, as always, was one step ahead.

"Better get on then." Katie pressed the keypad to the inner offices and held open the door. He followed her past the conference room into his own space. It had been his father's office and faced the main road. He sat himself behind the large desk and started his computer.

The day passed like many another. He drank too many coffees and stayed sitting for far too long. He needed to get running again, but he wasn't sure he was ready to run with Dylan whose long, lean frame would no doubt outpace his own. There was also Dylan's dinner offer to consider. It would do him good to get out. It was time to decide. Except for taking this job, he'd let all other aspects of his life slide by. He placed the outgoing post into the out-tray, knowing Ruth would pick it up, and stood and grabbed his jacket from the back of the door before making his way back to reception. A group of people waited in the entrance, and Afzal appeared behind him.

"Problems with a co-owner in a shared house of flats," he said. Riley nodded as Afzal introduced himself and took them through to the conference room.

"Your young man is outside already," Ruth said. "He popped in and introduced himself. Seems like a pleasant lad."

Was Ruth digging? She was usually discretion itself. "I'm giving him a lift as a favor to his dad. We were at school together, and they live in my village. He doesn't earn enough to buy his own car yet. I'm hoping he'll find someone at the town hall to take over from me." He stopped. Did he sound defensive? Had he said too much?

"I'll see you tomorrow, Mr. Ormerod."

Riley mumbled an agreement and hurried through the door. He found Dylan leaning against the car, staring at his phone while he mouthed the words to unknown music. Seeing Riley, Dylan removed his earpiece and grinned.

Riley pressed his key fob and opened the car. Dylan jumped in immediately.

"Good day?" he asked.

Riley closed his door and pulled on his belt. "The usual. And you?"

"The same. I don't think you want to hear about my day checking endless columns of figures. Oh hell, we may have the two most boring jobs in the world after all. We could always pretend we did something more exciting. What d'you think? Ever fancied being a firefighter or a doctor, or a spy? Yeah, that's it. You could totally be James Bond in that suit. Do you like it shaken or stirred?"

How the hell do I reply to that? Riley reversed and headed out of the car park. "I'm not sure any of those jobs are as glamorous as they are on TV," he finally replied.

"Spoilsport," Dylan said. "And there was me thinking I'd look great in uniform rescuing damsels in distress and expertly handling a hose."

Riley spluttered and nearly ran a red light. He needed to bring this conversation back down to earth. "Before

I forget, I'd like to accept the offer of dinner. Tell Tony or Lori to choose a time. I don't have anything on in the evenings." He paused, knowing how sad he sounded.

"Great. I'll let them know. Did you get a chance to think about running with me? We could do a country run if the weather stays fine. There are some beautiful places to go, and we could stop at the pub after."

"You don't need to. I don't want to take up your time."

Dylan didn't reply straight away. "I want to. It's interesting having someone else to talk to."

"There must be some people at work. Everyone there is new to you." *Too defensive?* He had no idea why Dylan would want to spend more time with him. Perhaps Tony had asked him to ease things between them.

"There are, but I bet you've been to all sorts of places and met some interesting people. The firm you worked at had celebrity clients. I bet you know a thing or two."

Riley chuckled. So that was it. Dylan wanted some hot gossip to share with his friends. "I can't tell you anything much — confidentially."

"There must be something. Didn't you deal with the music industry?"

"Writing contracts, though we did get to go to some of the awards ceremonies."

Dylan edged toward him. "Go on, you must have a story from them."

"Okay, but no names." Riley told a few tales of drunken evenings leaving out who he'd been with. Nate had loved these occasions, rubbing shoulders with celebrities. As it turned out, that wasn't all he'd rubbed. Time passed, and soon they were heading back along the main road into Pendleside.

"How about we do a short run tomorrow?" Dylan said, before getting out of the car. "Just a couple of miles to get you back in the swing of things."

"I'd like that. I'll have to dig out my kit. See you in the morning." He watched Dylan take the steps two at a time as usual and grinned to himself. Such enthusiasm was clearly contagious.

Chapter Four

"Good day, love?" His mother placed a large mug of tea in front of him.

"You know, Mum, much the same as yesterday, just getting my head around everything. I miss real math, though."

His mother sat in one of the armchairs. "I've never understood where your love of math came from. I hated algebra and geometry. None of it makes any sense to me. Why would you have letters in math?"

"Pure math has such beauty and logic. Ah well, good job you've got me to do your accounts. How was the shop today?"

"Same as ever. I'm not sure how much longer I can keep it going. People complain if the local shop or post office goes under, but don't use it because it's too expensive. I'm thinking of leaving when we've paid off the mortgage in a couple of years. I could work in a supermarket for the same with fewer hours and less hassle. You'll be gone by then, and Kayleigh will have finished university, and no doubt be off somewhere, leaving me and your father. Anyway, enough of me. Met anyone interesting yet?"

Dylan sighed. His mum meant well, but her endless hints about settling down simply reminded him of his single status. "No, Mum. I'm only twenty-two. It's too early for me to settle down." He pushed away thoughts of Riley.

"I just want you to be happy and find a nice boy — "

"Man, Mum," he interrupted.

"All right, a nice man then. It's not as if there are lots of gays in this village."

He cringed. "Mum, please. Give it a rest. I need to concentrate on work for now and get myself established. With some experience behind me and working to get chartered status, I can set up my own firm."

"Are you sure that's wise? Working for the council is much safer. You'll be able to save for your own place or a car. You don't want to be dependent on Mr. Ormerod forever, do you? I mean, I know he's been kind after your dad twisted his arm. Did you remember to ask him to dinner to thank him?"

"I did, and he says he'll come."

"Good. I don't think he gets out much since his father died. He must rattle around in that big old house. Has he told you anything about London? I asked Sue when she came into the shop, but she's tight-lipped that one. Said she couldn't tell me anything because of confidentiality issues. I'll have a word with your dad and sort out a date."

Dylan swallowed a mouthful of tea. He needed to get his mother on to another subject. "What's for dinner? I'm starving." The front door banged.

"There's your father now. And we're having sausage, mash, peas and gravy. I got some of those pork and leek ones you like."

"Onion gravy?" he asked.

"Of course. As if I'd give you anything else." His father came through the door, carrying a nest of tables. His mother sighed. "Put them in the back room."

"Right, love. They need a bit of polishing, that's all. Got them for a steal of a price. Did I hear the word sausages?"

"Yes, love, I'll put them on now."

They had virtually the same conversation every night. His father regularly brought things home to restore or improve. His mother sighed. They'd been together since they were teenagers. "I knew the moment I first saw him on stage," she'd said more than once. Somehow, they seemed so much older than Riley, but didn't everyone think their parents were ancient?

Dylan sipped his tea and thought back to the time he'd met Riley seven years ago. His father had stopped to talk to a man. Only afterward had Dylan discovered they'd been to school together. Dylan hadn't had his major growth spurt then, and Riley, dressed in a pale gray suit, was tall, dark and handsome. Dylan had been aware of his own sexuality for some years, but he'd never felt the same longing as he did staring at this man. When he'd discovered his crush had moved back to Pendleside, he'd attempted, with little success, to accidentally bump into him. He might have hung around Riley's house. When his father had suggested he ask his friend Riley Ormerod to give Dylan a lift, his heart had leapt into his throat. Now, he'd get to spend nearly two hours a day in the company of the man he'd been dreaming of since that meeting.

"All right, son?" His father ruffled his hair. He smoothed it back down again.

"Yes, Dad. How was the auction?"

"Oh, you know. Win some, lose some. Did you ask Riley about the house? I bet he's got all sorts in there. I could make a killing at the right price."

"I didn't, but he's agreed to come to dinner, so you can ask him yourself. He said he still has his guitar."

His father grinned. "We weren't U2, but we had fun and got all the girls' attention."

"I bet Riley did. He's a good-looking bloke."

His father stared at him. Had he said too much? "Riley played bass and mostly kept to himself. He was always the strong, silent type who didn't say much."

His mother entered, carrying plates, and set them on the table. "Come on, you two. Tuck in while it's still warm."

Dylan smiled to himself, storing away that little nugget of information in his hope box.

That evening, Dylan half-watched the TV while texting Matt, telling him Riley had agreed to go running with him. Little steps, getting to know each other, discovering bits and pieces. Nothing he'd found out yet to put him off his stride.

In the end, however, the weather had been against them, and the run hadn't happened. It had poured with rain for the rest of the week, making the journey to and from work depressingly long, and conversation curtailed as Riley had to concentrate on driving through the spray.

Friday, Dylan asked, "Are you doing anything this weekend? Perhaps we could get a run in then." He wasn't sure how he wanted Riley to answer his question. Truth was, he felt knackered. The end of his first week of work had arrived more quickly than expected. Until Wednesday, the time had passed so slowly, but now a week had passed in the blink of an eye.

"I'm going to be busy," Riley replied. "My friend Sue has agreed to help me sort through my father's belongings. I've been putting it off."

"Oh." Dylan debated on how to reply. He hadn't expected Riley to be so candid. He rarely said anything personal. "Were you close? You and your father?" He thought of his own easy relationship with his dad. Riley didn't answer him.

"I'm sorry. You don't have to answer. It's none of my business." He noted how Riley gripped the steering wheel and stared straight ahead at the Friday-evening traffic.

"No. We weren't close. My father was forty-five when I was born. He'd married late in life. My mother was the daughter of the head of the practice at the time. She died when I was nine — breast cancer. We each withdrew to our separate parts of the house. I went away to university and didn't come back. I didn't want to be some provincial solicitor like him, doing conveyancing for a living. I wanted to be where the money was, and the prestige. The practice where I did my training took me on. I did well, brought them in corporate clients willing to pay a fortune to a lawyer who could work his way around the system. I had a fabulous flat, ate in amazing restaurants, met important people…"

Where the hell had all that come from? *So why don't you sound happy? And why did you leave all that and come home?*

"But it doesn't matter now. I made my choice. You only have one father, and he needed me, though he said he could manage. His sight had deteriorated because of a tumor pressing on his optic nerve. Sue was his carer."

"Will you keep the house? It would make sense for you to move nearer Preston. Not that I want you to, or I'll lose my lift."

Riley visibly relaxed, his grip loosened on the wheel, and he chuckled. "Of course, giving you a lift is my number-one reason for staying."

"I should think so," Dylan replied, attempting to lighten the conversation.

"And how about your plans for the weekend?"

"I plan on sleeping. I'm not a morning person. And at least Dad can't tell me to get my lazy arse out of bed to help him or Mum in the shops now I'm working myself. I'm meeting up with some people from school on Saturday night. There's a quiz at the Farmer's Arms, and the barman is pretty fit." If he'd hoped for a reaction, he didn't get one.

"I see. Well, good luck with the quiz and the barman. And make sure you're careful."

Dylan snorted. "Now you sound like my dad."

"I'm old enough to be your dad, remember."

"Age is merely a number in my opinion." *In for a penny, in for a pound.* "I've never thought age mattered whether you're gay, straight or any point in between. There are couples who've been together for a long time despite the age gap." He didn't give Riley a chance to comment. "There are some fanciable sixty-year-olds I wouldn't turn away. Age is a state of mind." He chose his next words carefully. "Anyway, don't they say sixty is the new forty? So, forty must be the new twenty."

"That logic would make you a fetus, so perhaps we need to get off this conversation."

"Okay, but my grandma, on Mum's side, says you're never too young to try something new. She's off to New Zealand with a friend of hers for Christmas. I think she's trying to show my granddad she doesn't care that he's gone off with a younger woman."

"I heard. Sue has a talent for picking up gossip. I always liked your grandma. Whoa, bloody idiot cutting in. Where's the fire?"

"Someone wants his dinner too much."

Silence resumed after the interruption, and Dylan stared out of the window as they negotiated their way into the village, until Riley pulled up in front of the house. "I'll see you Monday then. Have a good weekend."

"You too. I hope sorting your father's things won't be too painful for you." He put a hand on Riley's arm. "I'm glad you'll have someone with you. See you Monday. Perhaps we can get a run next week."

Without giving Riley a chance to react to his touch or words, Dylan hurried out of the car, then up the steps. Despite his speed, when he turned to wave, Riley had already pulled away.

* * * *

Riley poured more Merlot into his glass and stared through the French doors into the garden. The roses his father had loved still bloomed, creating a range of warm colors — oranges, yellows, reds. The grass needed cutting. Another job for the weekend. He swirled the liquid around and sniffed. Nate had taught him to appreciate wine along with many other so-called finer things.

He glanced around the room. Nate would be appalled at the house, with its clutter and dark 1970s decoration. The carpet, with its pattern of autumnal curls and leaves, would have been the first item out of the door. Nothing in the house had changed since his childhood. Every room needed redecorating. It could be beautiful with some work, and he could afford to make those changes, but did he want to stay? Dylan had been right about it being more sensible to sell up and buy somewhere nearer his office. He'd never liked the place after all, but if he put his own stamp on it...

Dylan — there was another problem. The bolt of electricity he'd felt when Dylan had touched him was surely down to lack of human contact, wasn't it? Maybe a night in Manchester would help, a trip to Canal Street, an anonymous encounter. Twenty years, twenty years of monogamy, twenty years since anyone other than Nate had touched him. Twenty years of delusion that he'd found perfect happiness only to have that illusion shatter into a million pieces, and Nate had sat there.

'I don't understand your problem. I always come back home to you,' he'd said, as if that was the answer to everything. *'You're my rock. I don't know what I'd do without you.'*

Find someone else. Along the grapevine, Riley had discovered some mid-twenties blond twink had moved into their flat soon after Riley had packed a bag and left. Somebody else who could cook and clean and wash Nate's designer underwear. He swallowed the rest of the wine. He needed to eat before he finished off another bottle. A black streak flashed across the garden. That cat had been hanging around for a while. Perhaps he should get a pet, a dog, maybe, to give himself someone to talk to, and a reason to leave the house every day other than work.

"Food." He rose and ambled through the hallway to the kitchen. The units in the London apartment had been steel, all gleaming and monochrome. Here, dark wood occupied all sides with cream-colored tiles and vinyl flooring. A designer could have a field day with the place, ripping it out and installing—what? He placed the lasagna into the microwave and watched it revolve.

"Enough, stop feeling sorry for yourself." He resolved to get out of the house in the morning and buy some proper food. He loved to cook, but most nights he shoved something into the oven and ate out of the tray. He added Parmesan to his dinner, carried it through to the living room then spent the rest of the evening checking out kitchen and bathroom designs, modern furniture, wallpaper and paint colors.

The next day dawned bright and warm with no sign of the rain of the previous week. Riley washed and dressed, then made his way downstairs. Seizing the moment, he took himself out to search the nearest DIY store for ideas.

Soon after he arrived back home, the front door clicked. "Hello. Only me."

"I'm in the kitchen," he called back. Sue's head immediately appeared around the door.

"Oh, excellent. You have some of the good stuff made." She poured herself a coffee, added milk and two sugars, then took the seat next to him. "You've been busy. Planning some changes at last, are you?"

Paint samples, wallpaper books, kitchen and bathroom designs and furniture catalogs were spread over the table. "I had a mooch around the shops this morning. I need to lighten this place up, bring it into the twenty-first century."

"I might be able to help you with that. I'm not usually one to sing the praises of my family, but Linda has a painting and decorating business, and her husband is a joiner. They'd give you a great price. Also, Jake, my neighbor, is a plumber and bathroom fitter. He turned our downstairs cloakroom into a wet room for Dad when his arthritis meant he couldn't manage the stairs any longer. And if you need a builder, there's Sid, but he is cash in hand, if you know what I mean. Oh, and Matt Lomax does plastering."

Sometimes, Riley forgot about the joys of village life. He couldn't imagine what they thought of him. No doubt all sorts were said about his return and how he kept to himself. He hadn't dared ask Sue, the font of all knowledge as far as the village was concerned.

"I'll keep everyone in mind," he said.

"Have you decided to stay then, or are you doing the place up to sell?"

"Not sure. It would make more sense for me to sell and get a place nearer Preston." But then he'd be back on his own again, away from the few people he knew.

"You could transform this place, and it's not as if you don't have the money, if you don't mind me saying. It's got central heating and double glazing already, but a new kitchen and bathroom would help. These dark units are so dated. I didn't say anything to your dad, but the carpets are hideous. You could definitely turn this house into something beautiful and keep all the features."

That much was true. His father had left him a substantial sum along with the house. He'd also saved for his own future, just in case, which was just as well as he'd walked out of his home with practically nothing. His home. How stupid had he been not to get Nate to give him a share in ownership, considering property was his specialty? He'd been so naïve and believed they'd spend the rest of their lives together.

"Done up, this place would be worth a small fortune—a four-bedroomed detached house, set off the road with land around and stunning views over the countryside, but near enough to good transport links. The estate agent's brochure writes itself."

He sighed. It would mean a lot of upheaval and having people in, but for the first time in his life, he could make something his.

"I'm sorry, I'm coming on too strong, aren't I? I worry about you, that's all. Your dad did, too. He worried about you being on your own and giving up your life in London. You know, if you ever want to talk about anything..."

Sue meant well, and he had no doubt about her ability to listen. She'd worked as a carer for years and took on his dad, even with his prickly personality. She'd even made him laugh at himself and others, which was no mean feat.

"Thanks for the offer," he said, without accepting.

"Oh, well then, on to other matters. How's the young tyke behaving?"

"Tyke?"

"Dylan Hargreaves, tall, lanky, ginger. You're giving him a lift. Has he made it on time of a morning yet? I used to see him every day hurtling toward the school bus or flagging it down, usually with a piece of toast in his hand. Good job he has those long legs, or he'd have missed the bus more often."

Riley grinned. "I know what you mean about the toast. He's managed so far. Seems like a nice enough lad. He's young, that's all."

"Got a sensible head on his shoulders, though. He's worked for his parents doing their books since he was a teenager and done the books of others around here, including our Linda. She says he's saved her loads of money working out what she can claim for. He might look like a giraffe with that shock of red hair and those long limbs, but there's a fair bit of brain power there. He got a first, you know."

Riley straightened up. "No, I didn't know." *He must have done some work in between the fun.*

"Do you know he's gay?" She glanced at him from under her fringe. Was she checking his reaction?

"I do, as it happens. We have time to talk on the drive there and back. Young people are a lot more open about these things nowadays."

"Aren't they? Can you imagine someone coming out in school in our time, even twenty-five years ago? My niece is bisexual. She has a lovely girlfriend."

He stood and placed his mug in the sink. "Should we start sorting?" He wanted to shut this conversation down. "I thought we'd begin with Dad's room."

Sue drank down the last of her coffee. "Right you are then. We'll need a bag for rubbish, a charity bag and paper to make a list of things to sell."

Riley collected everything required and followed her bustling form up the stairs.

Chapter Five

Riley surveyed the scene. They'd been through the drawers and cupboards of his father's bedroom one by one.

"Does anyone use real handkerchiefs now?" he asked, pulling out yet another box. "There are some here that haven't even been opened."

"I've no idea. Put them in with the charity stuff." Sue opened the wardrobe. She stared at him with a questioning expression.

"I told you I gave away *his* clothes from the wardrobe," he said in self-defense. "I just didn't do anything else. After that, I couldn't face this room again. Don't judge."

It hung there still, the item which had stopped him in his tracks those few months ago. Tucked in among his father's suits, he'd found his mother's wedding dress covered in clear plastic, a beautiful confection of silk and lace. Back then, he'd sat on the bed and gazed at it, remembering the woman who had gradually faded away, riddled with cancer. In the end, they'd attempted to keep him from her bedside for fear of upsetting him, but he'd crept in the night before she died, determined to stay at home, and had fallen asleep next to her. The carer had discovered him, still lying against her body. Even as a nine-year-old, he'd been happy his mother hadn't died alone.

Ignoring the dress, Sue picked up the three boxes in the bottom. She closed the door and lifted the lid of the nearest. Inside were lots of smaller boxes. Sue opened one.

"Wow, look at this." She held up a crystal perfume bottle to the light. Riley moved next to her.

"Mum collected them. Some of them will be valuable, I suppose. I should get someone in to check. I wonder what's in the other boxes. After the dress, I couldn't face finding out." He took another out and unwrapped the first object. "It's a pipe. I've never seen these before, and Dad didn't smoke. Maybe they were my grandfather's. He died long before I was born—heart attack. He was nearly sixty when Dad was born. Seems to have been a family habit, marrying when older."

"There's time for you yet, then," Sue said, chuckling.

"I'm not the marrying kind," he replied without thinking.

Sue wrapped the bottle up again and placed it on the bed. "So, you are gay then?"

"What?" He juggled the pipe which had slipped out of his hand.

"You said you weren't the marrying kind. That's usually a euphemism for being gay, though it doesn't stand up now gays can get married. Of course, it's none of my business. Forget I said anything."

What the hell did he say? He didn't want to lie. He'd spent all his life lying in this house, firstly to himself then to others. He sighed and placed the pipe safely back in the box. "I *am* gay."

"Right, well. I wish you'd told me, but I suppose you had your reasons. I assume you didn't tell your father."

"No. I never found the words."

"He missed you. Yes, I know he would never have said so, but he did. He once asked if you'd told me why you didn't come home more often or invite him to London."

Something squeezed his heart and held it tight. He needed to get out of there and find air and light, but instead, he stared out of the window, digging his nails into his palms, failing to stop the tears that flowed over his cheeks and dripped onto his shirt.

"I couldn't. I didn't want to disappoint him. I overheard him talking to another solicitor once about someone who had HIV. He called him a queer. He didn't exactly say the bloke deserved it for being a filthy pervert, but he might as well have done. I was thirteen. I already knew I was gay. At the time, being gay meant dying early, alone and in agony. I didn't want to admit it to myself, let alone anyone else."

Sue wrapped an arm around him. He leaned into her hug. "Oh, Riley. I'm sorry. I had no idea. Maybe it was a one-off. I certainly never heard him say anything."

"I couldn't take that chance." *I didn't want to see his face or hear those words said to me.* He wiped his eyes. "I met someone at university. We were together for twenty years —"

"Oh, my God. I'm so sorry. Did he have…? Did he die?" Sue squeezed his hand.

"No, nothing like that. It turned out he'd found a younger model, well, several younger models. Dad needing me provided the perfect opportunity to get myself out of a dire situation. I had money, so I left my job and came back here. I owed him that much. If he ever suspected, he didn't say anything. I thought about telling him then, but it wouldn't have changed the situation, so I kept silent. He talked a lot about Mum, and his career, asked about mine, but never about my private life. I was grateful not to talk about Nate."

"It must have been hard, splitting up after so long."

"It was. No one likes to be made a fool of. I'd forgiven him before, but I couldn't forgive him putting my health in danger by being reckless." Her hand clutched his. "I'm okay," he said. "I got checked immediately." Her hand relaxed.

"We need to decide what to do with this stuff." He waved at the boxes. "What else is in them?"

Sue stood and lifted the other boxes to put them on the bed. She unwrapped the first item and held up the china dog. "This one is full of ornaments. Look here's the pair."

Riley opened the last one and pulled out a plate. "These are Clarice Cliff, aren't they? I recognize the style from antiques programs." He unwrapped another and another to reveal a dinner set, all in the same pattern.

"Those will be worth a few bob," Sue said. "You need to get a proper valuation for this lot. I could ring Tony. He'd know. Why don't I do that now? I'm sure he'd sell them at Clitheroe for you or give you a decent price."

And make some money himself. "He won't want to be disturbed on a Sunday." But Sue already had her phone out. Riley listened as she talked.

"He says he can come over now, if you want."

"May as well get it over with," he agreed, picking up one of the boxes. Sue followed him downstairs.

Twenty minutes later, they heard a knock at the back door. Sue leapt up before Riley could. Tony came into the kitchen and behind him stood Dylan.

"Hope you don't mind I brought the lad with me. As you're giving him a lift, I figured it would be all right, and he's better at lifting the heavy stuff." He cuffed the back of Dylan's head. "Got to be useful for something, eh, lad?"

Dylan shrugged, then rolled his eyes. Riley guessed this was a familiar conversation between father and son.

"Sue thought you'd be able to give me some idea of the value and what to do with the items I've found."

Tony glanced around. "It's a while since I've been here, but I remember your dad had some nice pieces. I always admired the desk in his office. I could go through the whole house for you, if you want. I'd give you a good deal, or you could take them to the auction yourself. I doubt you'd get much more than my offer, though."

Riley smiled to himself at the obvious dealer spiel. "Let's start with the contents of these boxes. My father kept Mum's things as well."

"Righty-o then, as you like." Tony opened the first box of perfume bottles. "These will vary depending on the silver content mostly. Not much market in my shop, but the auction will get rid of them." He whistled, opening the next one. "Is this a full set?" He handed the Clarice Cliff teapot to Dylan.

"I think so. I heard they aren't as valuable as they once were. I remember the set used to stand on the dresser over there, but Dad removed them after Mum died."

Dylan stepped forward. "There's still a market out there. I've always loved the strong colors."

Tony examined the milk jug. "This is an early design as well—worth more. Why don't you show me round? I'll tell you what I'm interested in and what you could sell at the auctions. We'll get the lad to add everything up item by item and give you a quote. You could get someone else in, but as we've known each other for years…"

Dylan smiled at him and flicked back his fringe. "I'll make sure he gives you a decent price. I wouldn't want to lose my lift."

"Job's a good 'un then," Sue said. "I'll make us all a coffee."

Riley followed them around as Tony pointed out bits of furniture to Dylan who wrote down each piece and noted an amount.

"You can leave my room," Riley said. "There's nothing in there." Was that a brief look of disappointment he saw in Dylan's face? Whatever it was, Dylan quickly altered his expression.

After forty minutes, they'd finished the whole house except for his father's office. Tony ran his hand over his father's desk while Dylan stared at the shelves full of books and numerous diaries all carefully labeled year by year.

"This wood is beautiful, and this leather is original. A London shop would make a fortune on it. You can't use wood like this now—it must be from sustainable sources. Not sure I could do anything with the books. No one wants them, really. Charities take them sometimes. The green desk lamp is worth a few quid, though."

Dylan ran his fingers across the diaries. "Do these belong to your father?"

"Yes, he kept one from childhood onward," Riley replied.

"Have you read any of them?"

"No, it didn't seem right. I've thought about burning them but haven't been able to."

"I'm not sure *I* could resist." Dylan gazed at him. Riley found himself doing the same until Tony coughed.

"Good job I don't keep a diary," he said, glancing at Dylan. "This one always was a nosey bugger. 'Why' was his favorite word."

Dylan glared at his father, but his eyes twinkled. He winked at Riley. "If you don't ask, you don't learn. Riley knows that, don't you?"

Riley had no desire to get in between the two of them.

"Oh, Riley, is it? I hope you're not being disrespectful."

"I told him to call me Riley. I have to be Mr. Ormerod at work." It struck him Tony appeared much older. Maybe it was his lack of hair, or because Dylan was his son—the dynamic between them was different.

"Well, don't let this young whippersnapper annoy you. He can talk the hind leg of a donkey given half a chance."

Dylan shrugged again, his face clearly revealing his irritation. Riley needed to say something, "I've enjoyed having Dylan along for the journey." And he had. "He's a bright lad. You should be proud of him."

Dylan straightened up, his eyes widened and the furrows on his face smoothed out. "See, Dad?"

Tony wrapped his arm around his son. "Ah, take no notice of me. He knows I'm only teasing."

Taking in Dylan's face, Riley wasn't sure he did—fathers and sons. "If that's everything, I expect Sue's got fed up of waiting, and I, for one, could drink a mug of coffee. I've cake as well."

Tony hurried out of the room while Dylan hung back. "Are you all right?" Riley asked, placing a hand on his arm.

Dylan stared at him, then his hand. "I'm used to it. It's just his way." He opened his notepad and showed Riley a figure. "Don't take any less than this for your stuff. He'll offer below that amount, but this is a fair price."

"Thank you." Riley shivered as the hair on the back of his neck rose. No, he couldn't have feelings for this young man. He simply wanted to make sure he was all right, didn't he? But the way Dylan looked at him...

"We'd better go to the kitchen before your dad eats all the cake."

As Dylan predicted, Tony offered him less, but Riley held his ground until his old friend upped his offer. "You can't blame a man for trying," he said, grinning. "Let's shake on it, then we'll get these boxes loaded in the van."

Twenty minutes later, Riley was back with Sue in the kitchen. She stared at him.

"That lad fancies you."

Riley put the last of the mugs back in the cupboard after washing up. "Don't be bloody ridiculous. Why would he fancy an old fogey like me?"

"I don't know," Sue replied. "And I'm not going to flatter you by giving you a list of your many attributes. I just know he does. He couldn't stop sneaking little glances, and he hung onto your every word. He wasn't exactly subtle, but I suppose at his age, you aren't."

Riley sat back at the table. "No, but then again I remember a certain person deciding aged fourteen she'd found *her* man. Your Neil didn't stand a chance."

"Just a few pushes in the right direction, so he knew what was good for him. I was right, though. Twenty-eight years and two kids later, we're still together. Next year will be our twenty-fifth wedding anniversary." She hesitated. "Would it be so terrible, you and him? You're both gay."

"Really, Sue? You're going with the 'you're both gay' argument? I repeat, he's twenty-two and, if anything, maybe has a crush on me. *He* doesn't know I'm gay, and his father is one of my oldest friends. I can see how that would go down. Stop pushing. Imagine if it was your Michael or Shannon. How would you feel if some older bloke slept with him or her? I can imagine Neil's face. I can hear the words 'dirty old man' now. No, if he does have a crush, I'll let him down lightly." *Maybe I could find a woman to go out with for a while, but that wouldn't be right either. Damn, this could get complicated.* He needed to make sure he did nothing to encourage this infatuation or whatever it was.

"Okay, I'll admit you have a point, but it wouldn't hurt you to get out occasionally. You've hidden yourself away here for over a year. It's not good for you. What about Grindr? There must be some other gay men around here. Doesn't it tell you where they are?"

Heat rushed up Riley's neck into his face. "Not interested. Once bitten, twice shy, and no, I don't want to talk about *him*. I don't need the hassle of a relationship. Dylan will find someone his own age, I've no doubt, and realize I'm far too old for him. Now, don't you have a home to go to?"

"All right. I can take a hint." She stood and kissed the top of his head. "You must come round to dinner sometime. At least it will get you out of this place. And once you've decided about any changes, give us a ring and I'll get our Linda to give you a quote. Neil could show you some of the kitchen designs as well. This place would look lovely with white units and beech surfaces — much lighter than this old dark wood. You could knock through and have a proper dining kitchen — all the rage now."

"Yeah, I know, the kitchen is the heart of the home. I've seen those TV shows too. I'll see. I'm not sure I want to start knocking down walls."

"Well, the offer's there. I'll see myself out."

Riley glanced through the kitchen brochures. He agreed the Shaker style might suit the room. He needed to tidy his father's office after Tony and Dylan had removed all the items they wanted. Once there, sitting in his father's leather armchair, he stared at the many diaries lining the shelves. Dare he read them? Most of him said no, these were his father's private thoughts, but then again, he hadn't told Riley to burn them after his death. Riley wanted to know his father. It was true he'd cut him out of his life. It had been easier to blame his father rather than himself for the distance between them.

He picked out the volume for the year of his parents' marriage. His father had been forty, his mother twenty-five and so beautiful. He glanced at the wedding photograph his father had always kept on his desk. Flicking through the pages to find the exact date, he made himself comfortable and started to read.

Chapter Six

"Morning," Dylan said as he jumped into the car, toast in hand. Riley didn't answer. Instead, he stared ahead and put the car into gear. Dylan checked his watch. He wasn't late, but the mood in the car was as somber as the gloomy gray weather. Should he say anything? He decided against it and finished his toast, taking care not to get crumbs on the immaculate upholstery. Finally, once they were on the motorway, he could resist no longer.

"Are you okay? You're quiet this morning."

"I'm fine."

Even Dylan could translate the typically British reply into *I am not fine, but I don't want to talk about it.* "Can we have the radio on, then?" he asked, needing some sort of noise to fill the awkward silence. At least this way there was a chance Riley might be encouraged to join in.

"If you must," Riley snapped back.

Dylan instinctively moved back in his seat while Riley continued to grip the steering wheel. Every so often he tutted as another car cut in or moved out without indicating. Rain splattered on the windscreen, adding to the gloom. Desperate to fill the silence, Dylan turned on the radio and hummed along with the songs.

Every so often he stole a look at the man next to him. Gray streaks flecked Riley's dark hair. He'd not lost any, unlike his own father who now shaved what he had left. In fact, Riley was in remarkably decent shape for his age. This morning, he wore a dark gray suit with a mid-blue tie which brought out the blue in his eyes.

Dylan let his mind wander back to the day before. He pictured himself in Riley's bedroom — not that he'd managed more than a glance while Riley was occupied elsewhere — perhaps with his hands tied to the headboard, totally at the mercy of the man above him whose hair fell over his face, who kissed down his chest until he teased, rubbing his cheeks over Dylan's highly interested cock. Oh yeah, Dylan could get with those thoughts. He shifted in his seat, conscious of his arousal. At least he had some clear wank fodder now, picturing himself in various scenarios in that house.

"Busy day today?" he asked finally.

"What?"

"I asked if you had a busy day today. We're having a team-building morning, so I get to meet people from the other departments. I suspect we'll end up making bridges with straws like we used to on industry day in school. Or we'll have a production line making cardboard cars or some such nonsense. I'd rather add up a column of figures, to be honest, but at least there'll be some fresh faces."

"You sound as if you're not enjoying the job," Riley said.

"Oh, you know, work is work, and I don't mind the day-to-day stuff. I'm looking forward to audit time, and we've some procurement negotiations coming up, so hopefully I'll be involved in costing different bids and working out which gives us the best deal, which will be more of a challenge than dealing with council tax."

Riley yawned.

"All right, I know some people find it boring, but there's something satisfying about columns of figures. Then we have the wages challenge every month, making sure we get the payments, tax and National Insurance right. The council employs lots of people in so many places, and all need to get the exact amount, or the complaints flood in. You'd be pissed if your accountant messed up your finances, wouldn't you?" Dylan folded his arms and stared out of the windscreen.

"I'm sorry, I didn't mean to imply anything. I didn't get much sleep last night."

That might explain your mood. "Oh, okay. Sorry, sometimes I get a bit touchy. Do you often have trouble sleeping?" He tried to pull his thoughts away from Riley lying in bed, the sheet draped over his body, his chest slightly exposed. Dylan hoped there would be a smattering of dark hair, not too much, but he liked something to run his fingers through, leading down. He'd probably have stubble which would scrape against Dylan's face if they kissed. He swallowed hard.

"Sometimes." Riley paused as if debating whether to continue. "I started reading my father's diaries last night."

"Oh." What the hell else did he say? His brain scrabbled for words. "Do you want to talk about them?

I know I chunter on a bit, but I'm a good listener as well."

Riley's Adam's apple moved as he swallowed. "I read from when he'd met my mother to when I was born. I'd never realized how close she came to death giving birth to me. He loved her so much. He was my age when they first met at the hospital. She was one of the nurses who looked after him when his appendix burst and nearly killed him. She was fifteen years younger. He didn't think he stood a chance, but she asked him out and eventually discounted all his concerns about the age difference."

"Age shouldn't matter," Dylan said. Now was his chance. "If you love someone, who cares about age?"

Now off the motorway, they pulled up at a red light. Riley glanced across at him. Dylan tried to read his expression, but Riley simply shook his head before moving off again and staring forward.

"I suppose not. *They* made it work. Every word he wrote about her spoke of how much he loved her. Then she had me. He was worried he might be too old to cope with a baby, but she wanted children, and he agreed. She had a small stroke giving birth. I was fine, strong and healthy according to his description of this bundle. He was terrified he'd be left with a baby on his own, but Mum pulled through and recovered. I think if he could have sold his soul to keep her, he would have."

Dylan choked back the lump in his throat. He longed to reach out and touch Riley, to give some comfort, take him in his arms and hold him. "Not everyone is lucky enough to have a love like theirs."

"No, they aren't. It's funny. I don't remember much even though I was nine when she died. Dad thought it best to keep me out of the way so as not to upset me, but I used to sneak in sometimes and read to her. She loved romance stories."

At the noise of the indicator, Dylan looked forward and realized they were about to turn into the back of Riley's office. Where had the time gone? Riley parked in his usual space but didn't move. Instead, he stared straight ahead.

"She was younger than I am now when she died. My father hid himself away and my grandma came to look after me. He didn't write much for a while after. He said he had no words. I'm sorry. I shouldn't burden you with all this."

Dylan couldn't stop himself. He reached over and touched Riley's thigh. "I told you. I'm a good listener. If you ever need to talk, about anything, I'm here for you."

Riley glanced down at Dylan's hand. "There's no point dwelling in the past. It won't change anything."

"We don't always want to change what happened, just understand it. I spent ages trying to understand what had made me gay. Dad worried whether he'd done something. He actually said I was too tall, and I played football, and I'd never shown any interest in dolls, or watched *Sex and the City* or sung songs from musical theater."

Riley chuckled, low in his throat. The sound vibrated, sending shivers up Dylan's spine as the hairs rose on the back of his neck. Hell, he wanted to kiss the man and take away all his sorrow.

"Your dad was never the most sensitive man, but you know he has no problem with you being gay."

"I know. Sometimes he can be an idiot, but he and Mum have always supported me. They want you to come to dinner one night this week now Mum's off the evening shift at the shop. That house of yours is a big place to be in on your own with all those memories." *Have I said too much?*

Riley sat up and Dylan reluctantly removed his hand from his thigh. "Maybe, and I'd like that, coming to dinner. It was good to spend some time with your dad yesterday, and your mum is a great cook."

"She'll make enough for an army. She says she must have starved in a previous life as she always cooks too much. We have a freezer full of food. You will come, won't you?"

"Yes, I'll be there. Tell them thank you and find out what night suits. You'd better get off or you'll be late. I don't suppose you brought a brolly." The rain ran down the windscreen.

Dylan shrugged. "No, I didn't."

Riley reached under his seat. "Here, take mine. I'll see you later. Have a fun morning team building. I expect to hear all about it tonight."

Dylan opened the door and raised the umbrella. "Bye. Have a good day." He slammed the car door shut and hurried across the car park. When he glanced back, Riley was still in the car with his head in his hands, leaning on the steering wheel. He'd be counting the hours today. With that thought, he hurried out to the main street and the town hall.

* * * *

Riley put the document to one side, unable to concentrate. Sometimes the minutiae of contracts drove him mad, but his specialty had always been to make sure every possible loophole had been investigated and sealed. Maybe the fact that previously he'd been dealing with companies worth millions and now… He reached for his second coffee and mentally slapped himself.

He yawned. Reading his father's diaries had both soothed and upset him. The love his parents had shared shone out of every page. His mother's death had torn his father apart, but he'd never shown any emotional distress to his son. He clearly believed he needed to be strong and not give in to weakness. Men didn't cry. Riley had ached with frustration, wishing his father had been a different man. He'd no idea how to deal with his own grief, so he'd followed his father's lead, and the two of them had drifted apart, each occupying their own part of the house, not even meeting for meals provided by the housekeeper. Why had his father never told him how proud he'd been when he became fully qualified? From what he read between the lines, it seemed his father had deliberately pushed him away to a better life and career.

Should he return to London? He could sell the house and have enough to get somewhere to live in the capital. No doubt he'd be able to pick up where he'd left off. He'd had enquiries from firms he'd dealt with in the past. With video conferencing, perhaps he could combine the large with the small. He picked up the file again and his yellow highlighter, always preferring to proofread on paper rather than on the screen. His personal phone rang with an unknown number.

"Riley Ormerod speaking."

"Hi, Riley, it's Tony. Just thought I'd let you know I've sorted the stuff from yesterday. I've put some in the shop and some aside for the auction. I'll make sure to keep the receipts for you."

"Thanks, Tony. I appreciate your expertise." It was funny. They'd been such great friends in primary school. Only the band had kept them together until he'd gone off to university. He'd never had one of those close friendships some people managed, and thankfully he'd never fancied Tony, either.

"We should have a proper boys-only catch-up sometime. I thought you and I could have a round of golf, or maybe catch a game now Burnley are back in the Premiership, if you fancied it."

"I'm not one for golf." In fact, he couldn't play at all. "But I'm happy to take in a game when you want. Will Dylan be joining us?"

Tony laughed. "Oh yeah, but he has different reasons. He's more a fan of the footballers than the football, if you get my drift. Still, he understands the current offside rules, which is more than some. I'll sort some tickets for us. I know a few people. Perhaps an Arsenal or Chelsea game."

Riley noted how Tony obviously didn't care about Dylan's sexuality. A bolt of envy shot through him. "I'm more of a Spurs fan," he said.

"Spurs it is, then."

"Dylan mentioned Lori wasn't working late this week..."

"That's right. How about you come round for dinner this evening then? Lori's desperate to interrogate you about life in London. She keeps badgering me to take her on a long weekend, but with both the shops, getting away can be a problem. I'll give her a ring and let her know. We always have something in for visitors." He paused. "How are you anyway? We haven't really talked since your dad died." He didn't mention how Riley had kept everyone at arm's length. "I'm glad for both of you that he went peacefully at the end. Cancer is such a bastard."

"I'm fine. You know Dad and I weren't close."

"But he was still your father, and you gave up a lot to come back home with your important job down south, so he must have mattered, and at least you got to be with him during his last months."

Because I needed to get out of London as much as he needed me to come home. "Sometimes you just have to, but I'm glad we got to spend that time together."

"So, will you do the place up to sell? It's a big ole house just for you. Still, you're not too old to get married and fill the place with kids. Being an older dad seems to be all the rage. Not sure I could cope, though. I'm hoping to get both of them off our hands soon enough, not that they're bad kids or anything. Lori worries about Dylan finding someone special. She hoped he'd meet someone at university, but he's not one for putting himself out there, despite appearances to the contrary. He's always been a home-body. No idea where he got his brain from. Not me, that's for certain." Riley heard a bell ring in the background.

"Customer — better get off. Oh, she's looking at your Clarice Cliff set. See you later around seven. Fantastic. Looking forward to it."

Riley leaned back in his chair. Outside the rain tapped against the window. He swallowed down the last of his coffee and picked up the file, but, instead of him reading the details of the contract, his mind wandered toward thoughts of Dylan. He smiled. Dylan brought that out in him. His infectious enthusiasm for life warmed Riley's heart after the cynicism he'd lived with in London. There, only money mattered, who had it and who didn't. He couldn't imagine Dylan being capable of sneering at someone's choice of clothes or their choice of furnishings. Had he been so inclined himself? He hoped not. Material things hadn't mattered to him in the same way they did to others in his circle. He'd enjoyed what money had brought him. He'd been to beautiful places, enjoyed many great performances on the London stage, but, unlike many, he'd never put his hard-earned wealth up his nose or in his veins. Coffee had always been his drug of choice. The intercom buzzed. He pressed a button.

"Hi, Mr. Ormerod. Mr. Whewell has asked if you could see a new client this afternoon at two. He's buying an old cotton mill to turn into flats but has been having some problems. You have an hour then."

"Sure, Ruth, give me the details." He wrote everything down, then, with highlighter in hand, began to work once more.

Chapter Seven

Dylan stood leaning against Riley's car. His dad had texted to tell him Riley had agreed to come to dinner. The chance to spend more time with Riley had brought a distinct improvement to a frustrating day.

After the morning session, he'd concluded he didn't like team-building activities. It seemed to him that there was an 'i' in team for some people who simply wanted to assert their positions within the group dynamic. *Shit.* He was even using the bloody terms. He'd be blue-sky thinking before he knew it, or running things up flagpoles. The rear door to Riley's office opened, and the man stepped out. Hell, he looked good in a suit. Dylan's cock woke up, and he had to shuffle. Riley strode across the tarmac to the car. He never hurried, unlike Dylan who always seemed to be a few minutes behind where he should be.

"Have you been waiting long?" Riley asked, clicking his key fob to open the doors. "You should have texted me."

"No, just a few minutes. I've been enjoying the sun while it shines." Dylan opened the passenger door and climbed in, sliding down on the leather seats but resisting the temptation to make them squeak.

"How was your day?" Riley asked. "Is your team like a well-oiled machine now?"

"Is it buggery," Dylan replied. "I was right about making the bridge with straws. It was like being back at school again and some people simply bossed the others around and didn't listen."

"Ah. Still, at least it wasn't a day out on an assault course or sleeping in a tent." He shivered.

"Camping not your thing then?"

"No, we always stayed in hotels when I was young."

Dylan thought of the occasional holidays his family had managed. How he'd resented those bloody shops. "We used to get a few days away in a caravan by the sea if we were lucky, at Blackpool or Bridlington. Once we went to Anglesey. I bet you've been to some exciting places."

Riley stiffened beside him as he eased the car into the right-hand lane to get them into the correct position to head to the motorway. As usual the roads in Preston were busy with traffic heading out of the city. Had Dylan said something wrong? Riley seemed not to want to talk about his past, especially his time in London.

"A few," Riley replied, without further explanation.

Had he been with someone, Dylan wondered. Exotic places with glamorous people? Did Riley miss London? If he did, he didn't seem eager to return and no one had visited. He knew this because nothing happened in their village without the gossipers reporting it to his mother in the shop, and Dylan had asked some innocent questions to make sure. Something had happened, and not simply his father being ill, to make Riley return home. Of that Dylan had no doubt.

"I've always wanted to go whale watching off the coast of Alaska or Canada, or to those places where they have the huts over the sea and you can look through glass floors to see the fish, or to Machu Picchu, or even Antarctica."

Riley smiled. "That's quite a bucket list."

"Just dreams, really. Instead, all I've been to is Ibiza with the lads from university and the war graves of Northern France with school. All the lads wanted to do was get pissed then get laid."

"Not your thing then."

Dylan smiled to himself. "Oh, don't get me wrong, I'm a huge fan of getting laid, but I'm not one for meaningless encounters, and I'm not a big drinker. I've never understood the fascination for getting so drunk you don't know what you're doing and let anyone screw you. That might make me boring, but I'll take being boring and being safe. Too much out there to take stupid risks."

"You've an old head on young shoulders," Riley said, glancing sideways at him.

"I guess some people find different things addictive, be it sex, alcohol, drugs, chocolate or even power. I'm happy enough without much. I've never been one of these people who need to have the best of everything or need to be perfect. All I want is my independence and to have a business of my own."

"Sounds eminently sensible. Power and money can be a bad combination in the wrong hands."

If Dylan had wanted more, he didn't get it. One day he'd crack that handsome exterior and find out more about the man underneath. He decided to change the subject. "Dad texted earlier to say you're coming to dinner tonight."

"I'm looking forward to it."

"I hope you have some embarrassing stories to tell about Dad when he was young. I bet you and he got up to a few things. I need some ammunition."

"You'll have to wait and see. I do remember the day he first saw your mum. He was smitten at first sight, and she pretended to ignore him as if he wasn't there. He was like a puppy following her around, but he wore her down in the end."

"He says he never looked at anyone else. It's romantic really, don't you think, only ever loving one person? I envy them. I hope I can have a relationship like theirs, but so far I've only found a few frogs."

"And kissed a few?"

"Now, that would be telling. What about you? Any frogs in your background?" Had he pushed too far?

Riley didn't reply immediately but paused as if trying to find the words. "More like toads in my experience. Well, here we are again."

Dylan gazed out of the windscreen. How had they got there? He hadn't noticed. Now he wouldn't be able to ask more. Toads, huh? You didn't usually call women frogs or toads. Hope blossomed in his chest. He undid his seatbelt. "I'll see you here later then." He turned to wave on the top step before going in. This time Riley waved back.

* * * *

An hour or so later, now showered and dressed, Riley sat on his bed, fiddling with his hair and thinking about his conversation with Dylan. *Why the hell did I say that?* Somehow Dylan's chatter had loosened his tongue, and now he had to spend the rest of the evening with him and his parents.

He'd met Tony almost as soon as he'd been born. He supposed he could say they'd met even before that as their mothers had been friends in the way people who live in small places often are. It was primary school that had cemented their friendship. A tiny place, with pupils gathered from the surrounding villages, the school had been closed a few years back to save money. Now all the local children were bussed into Clitheroe for primary and secondary education and the old building had been converted into a private residence.

Tony and Dylan looked nothing alike. Tony had been dark compared with Dylan's ginger inherited from his mother's side of the family. Tony was also inches shorter than his only son and had been a solid rather than gangly youth. They'd roamed the village and surrounding countryside together, pinching apples, getting chased by local farmers for trespassing in their fields, swimming in the river or more likely falling in from the rope swing. There had been a gang of them all the same age, but he and Tony had been close despite the differences in their academic ability. Riley had loved school and loved learning, Tony not so much. His interest lay in making money. He bought sweets and pop cheaply and resold them until caught by the school. Every time, he'd come up with another way. He was a born salesman and usually managed to talk himself out of any awkward situation.

Although separated for secondary school, they'd remained friends. Tony had asked him once why he didn't have a girlfriend. They'd been fourteen at the time and Tony had met Lori. Riley had stammered something about concentrating on his future career and girls being a distraction. He'd often wondered if Tony had guessed the truth.

Riley parked his car across the road, picked up the rather fine bottle of red wine he'd bought in town and crossed the road, clicking the car closed behind him. The door opened before he reached the top step. Dylan stood in the space, dressed in jeans and jumper.

"Thought it would be you. Come in. Mum's in the kitchen and Dad's through here."

The house followed the usual plan. At the front there was a room most families kept for best. Straight ahead were stairs and the other door led to the middle room and kitchen. Tony rose from his armchair. Always a hugger, he wrapped his arms around Riley. "It's good to see you. We should have done this before. Can't think why we haven't."

Because I kept putting you off. "You know what it's been like with my father. I brought some wine. I hope it'll go with dinner."

Tony examined the bottle. "This'll do nicely. Lori has done her best steak and ale pie. Her pastry is to die for." He patted his stomach. "Sit down. I've some good news about your Clarice Cliff set." Riley sat on the sofa with Dylan positioned next to him.

"I suppose Riley's been telling you all about the things he and I got up to when we were young," Tony said to Dylan.

"Nooo." Dylan gazed at him with a questioning smile. "Pray do tell me more."

Riley searched his memory for something appropriate. "Well, there was the occasion with the bull. Your dad decided to take a short-cut across a field.

We tried to stop him, but he ignored us. When the bull started to charge toward him, he ran faster than I've ever seen him move and crashed through the fence ripping his shirt and back on the barbed wire. Ended up going to hospital for stitches."

"I still have the scar. But I got my own back. When the bull went to market, we had steaks from it. The local butcher liked to tell us the names of his sources."

Dylan pulled a face. "I'm glad they don't do that now. I can't imagine going in a supermarket and seeing pictures of the animals. Did Riley get up to anything interesting? He told me he played bass with your band."

"He did. He was good as well. God, do you remember the talent contest in Liverpool? We could have been the next great thing if Lee hadn't got pissed and played the drums so badly he passed out in the middle of the audition."

"I didn't know you'd entered anything. I asked Riley if he'd play for me."

Tony gazed pointedly at his son. "Riley again, is it?"

"It's fine, Tony. Mr. Ormerod was my dad. And it's no good playing bass on my own. Maybe your dad could get out his guitar as well sometime."

"Up to the table everyone," Lori called from the kitchen.

"I'll open the wine," Tony said, taking a corkscrew from the sideboard drawer.

Dylan patted a seat. "You're next to me," he said.

The pie turned out to be wonderful, and Riley groaned as he ate. "I'm sorry. I can't remember the last time I tasted something as delicious as this."

"So, Riley, you haven't said much about living in London. It must be a big culture shock coming back here." Lori's innocent question gave Riley the usual problems. It was one of the reasons he'd avoided such events. Did he lie again or not exactly lie but omit?

"I bet you had one of those beautiful flats in the city and got to go to shows and museums," Tony added.

He was safe talking about the apartment if he kept it to description. "I did have a flat near Regent's Park. With the windows open, you could hear the big cats roaring from the zoo."

"Worth a fortune, I expect," Tony said. "I hope you got a decent price for it if you intend to do up your dad's place."

"Tony, don't embarrass the man. It's none of our business. Your job must have been interesting."

"Not especially. I mostly worked with companies on corporate and tax law, checking deals — mergers and acquisitions. Everyone thinks of lawyers working with criminals, but that wasn't my thing."

Tony nodded. "Crime's not where the money is. With so much business going on in London, I bet you were busy doing all sorts helping people avoid tax. Never annoys me that, when they go on about it on the telly. Why wouldn't you want to avoid tax if you could? Laws need tightening. No use complaining about what's legal in my view. We have to deal with the taxman, don't we, Lori? Still, having this one to go through the books helps. He's a whizz with figures. I bet you're the same."

Tony's obvious pride in his son's ability shone through. "Not exactly. Others did the number crunching. I had the wording to deal with."

"Ah, all the party of the first, second and third part. Never understand those bloody things. May as well be in bloody Greek as far as I'm concerned. Should have them in English. Still, I suppose it gives you lot work."

"You mentioned the Clarice Cliff," Riley said in the hope of changing the subject.

"Yep, got a great price for you. We won't talk now. I've got some of the stuff to take to auction. You'll probably get a few hundred in the general sale."

"Could we not talk shop over dinner?" Lori said. "You were a long time in London, Riley. Must be over twenty years with university. We expected you to marry some rich heiress, or the daughter of a company director."

Riley shifted in his seat. He noticed Tony nudge Lori. "Not everyone is as lucky as we are, Lori. Places like London. People don't talk to each other there, not like round here when everyone knows your business. It's not always easy to meet someone."

Lori blushed. "I'm sorry, Riley. I didn't mean to pry."

Dylan had stopped eating next to him as if he was waiting. So much of Riley wanted to tell the truth. What would it matter now? It's not as if they were homophobic. And now Sue knew. Tony was his oldest friend and he hated the gap of omission between them. "It's fine, Lori. I know I've never said much about my personal life." He rubbed his now clammy hands up and down his thighs. "There was someone. We were together for nearly twenty years…" Dylan clutched his arm, sending heat running through him.

"Oh God, she died, didn't she? That's why you came back home, not just for your dad. I'm so sorry, Riley."

Dylan's leap caught him unawares. Lori stood as if she intended to come around the table and hug him. "Why didn't you tell anyone? We would have helped."

Riley needed to stop this. "Please, no, nobody died." His heart thumped so loudly, surely, they could all hear it. Dylan's hand remained on his arm.

He picked up the glass and took a couple of swallows. "A little while before I finished my degree, I met someone and we were together as I said." He coughed, picked up the glass and took another large mouthful of the pleasant-tasting wine. "Together that is until *he* had an affair, well, more than one. He decided to share with me how he'd found a new, younger man, so I left him and came back here to look after my father."

Dylan moved his hand and knocked his fork from his plate. It clattered to the ground. "Shit. Sorry." He scrabbled under the table to find it while Tony and Lori remained silent.

No one else said anything. "I'm sorry... I — "

"No, don't be," Tony interrupted. "I'm sure you had your reasons for not telling me when we were young, if you knew then. Did you know then?"

"I've always known. But if you don't mind, maybe now isn't the time to talk about it."

Dylan sat up and passed his now empty plate to his mother. "If you ask me, the bloke is obviously blind as a bat, not to mention a stupid bastard who doesn't recognize a good thing when it's right in front of him. Is it trifle for dessert, Mum?"

Lori found her voice. "Yes, love, lemon drizzle. I found the recipe online."

"Sounds yummy," Tony said, staring at his son.

Had they realized the implication of Dylan's words? *Oh hell, I should have kept quiet.*

Nothing more was said about his confession. Conversation centered on finding out about the others from their old gang and what had happened to them, who had married, who had children, what they did, where they were and that one of their number had died. All those things people catch up on. No one spoke again of the elephant in the room. Would Dylan say anything in the morning? Would Tony and Lori warn Dylan off or even stop him getting a lift just when Riley had begun to look forward to the time they spent together? They were probably being polite and once he'd gone, all hell would break loose. It shook him how concerned these thoughts made him. He'd wanted to mend fences, not build new ones. His stomach churned, and he swallowed down the newly formed lump in his throat.

Dylan handed him his coat. "You all right?" he whispered. "You've gone white as a sheet."

"Yeah, I'm fine." Dylan's hand caressed his back. He lurched forward and turned to Tony and Lori. "Thank you for a lovely evening. The food was wonderful. You both must come round to mine." *If you're still speaking to me, that is.*

They hugged him when he left. That had to mean something. As he lay in bed not sleeping, Riley argued with himself about whether honesty was always the best policy after all. And, talking of honesty, there was the minor matter of his growing attraction to Dylan to consider. Not for the first time, he desperately wished for someone who'd listen.

Chapter Eight

Woken by his alarm, Dylan yawned and stretched then scratched absentmindedly at his morning wood wondering if he had time to... Then he remembered. He sat up. It had taken some time for him to get to sleep after last night's bombshell. *Riley is gay. Riley likes men.* The man he'd dreamed about, created a million fantasies about, liked men.

Dylan stared at his reflection in the mirror, assessing. Should he shave his beard off? Would Riley prefer him without? His body looked as if it had never seen the sun. Maybe his ribs didn't quite show, but his chest and arms lacked defined muscles. Added to his appearance, he was a twenty-two-year-old man who still lived with his parents, and Riley had spent the last twenty years in London, no doubt with a sophisticated crowd of educated and erudite people. "Gay or not. Why the hell would he look at you?"

"Dylan, get a move on. You don't want to keep Mr. Ormerod waiting."

"I'll be ten minutes, Mum."

After washing and dressing, ten minutes became twenty and as usual he was running behind. "Sorry, needed a shower," he said, snatching a piece of toast from the rack.

"Your tea will be cold by now. Your lunch box is on the side. It'll save you some money and stop you eating rubbish at lunch."

"Yes, Mum."

"Well, you want a car of your own, don't you? Then you won't have to depend on someone else to get you to work." She paused. "Dylan..."

"Okay, Mum." He waited, wondering what was coming next. He knew the tone, but he couldn't think of anything in particular he'd done recently. He swallowed down the lukewarm contents of his mug in one go.

"Perhaps it would be better if you didn't mention last night's conversation to Mr. Ormerod."

"His name is Riley, Mum. He asked me to use his first name. He said his father was Mr. Ormerod. And I don't intend to say anything unless he does. I'm glad he told us, though. It must have been difficult keeping everything to himself. Imagine living a double life." He shivered.

"I'm sure he had his reasons. Times change, love. Clause twenty-eight still existed back then, and I doubt Riley's father would have been thrilled about having a gay son. He always seemed so old-fashioned, like he still lived in the fifties."

Dylan moved next to his mum and put an arm around her. "Thanks, Mum."

"What for?"

"Not batting an eyelid when I told you."

"Oh, love. You were never in. We always knew you were gay, but we waited for you to tell us in your own time. It's never made a damn bit of difference to us. Now, look at the clock. Riley will be waiting outside."

Dylan kissed his mother's cheek.

"Ah, be off with you, you soppy devil, and don't forget your lunchbox, and remember…"

"Yes, Mum," he called from the hall. Grabbing his coat, he opened the door to be greeted by a cold, biting wind and the sight of Riley tapping away on his steering wheel to some unknown tune. He ran down the steps and rushed round to the passenger door, opening it as soon as there was a gap in the traffic.

"Morning," he said. "It's bloody cold out there." He placed his box on the dashboard and snuggled into the leather. "Oh, I love this heated seat." It was the first time they'd been on when he jumped in. "My arse will be toasty in no time at all."

"And morning to you, too." Riley shifted the car into gear and set off into the traffic.

For a while, Riley said nothing as they both hummed along to the music. When he braked suddenly, the box flung itself, hitting Dylan in the chest before he could catch it.

"Fuck." He rubbed himself.

"You okay?"

"Yeah, I'll put it on the back seat. Mum decided I needed to save money so I can get my own car, and I won't need to bother you anymore."

"Oh, I see."

Even though he couldn't see Riley's face, his tone told Dylan enough. "It's not that I don't want to get a lift with you, because I do. I like spending time with you. I'd miss our journeys. Mum thinks I'm a burden for you, having to wait for me and listen to me prattle on in the mornings. I bet you're used to quiet being in that big house all by yourself. It must be lonely after London with all the noise and bustle."

Riley didn't answer immediately. Had Dylan said too much? Not for the first time, his mother would say. Riley checked his mirrors and eased the car into a gap in the motorway traffic.

"I find I like the quiet. I can wake up and hear the birds, and I enjoy cooking, even if it is only for myself. London can be a lonely place as well."

"I suppose it can. Everyone knows everyone here. You only have to sneeze, and people ask how you are. You can't keep anything hidden..." The words died. Plainly from the confession of the man next to him, you could. "I'm sorry. I didn't mean anything."

Riley glanced at him briefly. *Oh hell, those eyes, even when they're sad, maybe especially when they're sad.* Dylan pushed away the desire to reach out a hand and touch him.

"It's fine. And I'm sure lots of people manage to keep secrets, even in a small village like ours."

Sod it. "It can't have been easy, though, when you were young, not telling anyone about, you know."

"When I was fourteen, *Frankie Goes to Hollywood* hit the charts with *Relax.* I remember the first time I heard it on a TV show called *The Tube* on Channel Four. I couldn't believe they'd allowed a song with such obvious gay lyrics on the TV. My dad walked in and heard it. He watched for a few minutes while I squirmed in my seat. Once he'd listened to the words and watched, he got up and turned the channel over, calling it filth. Later, when the BBC banned the song, he agreed. I decided then not to tell him I was like them, well the lead singers. He didn't spout homophobia much, just enough for me to know how he felt. He was a small-town man, with small-town views, in his mid-fifties at the time. Then, it seemed easier to have my life down there and not mix the two. He'd have hated Nate."

"Do you want to talk about him?" Dylan felt he had to ask and he was curious about the sort of man Riley had been attracted to.

"No. I haven't seen or heard from him in over twelve months. A friend told me a few months back my replacement was still there. Anyway, thank you for offering, but no, that part of my life is over. I'm going to do up the house here and bring it into the twenty-first century. Then I'll decide what to do with it."

"I'm a dab hand with a paintbrush," Dylan said.

"I expect I'll get professional help. Sue's sister does decorating."

"I could help choose colors then." *Don't sound too fucking desperate.*

"I might take you up on your offer." The car slowed to a halt. "Shall I drop you here today as there's room?"

Dylan glanced out of the car surprised, once more, to find they were outside the town hall. "Thanks, I'll see you at the usual time." He opened the door.

"Don't forget your lunchbox," Riley said, handing him the plastic container.

Dylan waved as Riley moved off, turned and hurried up the steps.

* * * *

Riley put the document to one side. Time to admit he needed to get his eyes tested. He lifted his head and shouted, "Come in," at the knock on the door.

"I thought you might need a coffee." Katie, the practice trainee, placed a large mug in front of him.

"Thanks. You're a life saver, but there's no need. It's not in your job description. You're here to learn, not make us old fogies drinks."

"You're hardly old." She sat in one of the chairs on the other side of his desk.

"Hmm, not sure about that. I've decided to bite the bullet and get my eyes tested. I reckon reading glasses are next."

She smiled. Katie had been the outstanding candidate at the interviews. With her first-class degree and superb references, she could have done her two years training in any of the big London practices. He returned her smile.

"Can I be of any assistance?" he asked. "You can ask without the flattery. We're here to help you."

"I *would* like to pick your brain about something, but it'll wait until our usual training meeting." She hesitated, her hands gripping the arms of the chair. He feared what might be coming next. *Now you are flattering your own ego.*

"Um, I've seen you dropping off and picking up someone every day, and I thought he might be your son and wondered if he was seeing anyone." Her face had turned a stunning shade of puce.

Light dawned. "Oh." Relief swept over him. "You mean Dylan. He's not my son, not with that hair. I was in school with his father. He lives in the same village as me, and works at the town hall, but…" How did he say this? Dylan wouldn't care if he told the truth.

"It's all right. I guessed someone so cute wouldn't be single."

"No, it's not that. He's gay," he explained.

"Again? Why are all the good-looking ones gay? No chance he's even slightly bisexual?"

Riley shook his head. "No, sorry, totally and happily gay, but I'll tell him you think he's cute. He'll enjoy that."

"Well, don't you think he is?" She stopped abruptly. "Sorry, I didn't mean to imply anything. Take no notice of me. I'll shut up now. I need to get on with the house conveyance." She stood, brushed down her jacket then turned to leave.

"Katie? Are you all right?" A surprising urge to smile threatened to overwhelm him. He fixed his expression to one of concern, not amusement.

"I'm fine. Don't worry. Sometimes I open my mouth and nonsense comes out. It's none of my business..."

If he'd made a start last night, here was a chance to say more. Why should he hide who he was now? "I am gay, Katie, but Dylan and I aren't an item. He's way too young for me. And I'd rather you kept that information to yourself for now."

"Of course. Anyway, age is simply a state of mind, or so my gran tells me. My step-granddad is fifteen years younger than her, and she said she was too old for him, but he persisted, and they've been married five years now. They're always going to new places in the world and she's having the time of her life. *She's* the one who told me to ask you about Dylan—nothing ventured, nothing gained and all that. She worries about me being all work and no play."

There were occasions when Katie had looked tired, but she hadn't mentioned much about her personal life, and he hadn't asked. He waited for her to continue.

"You see, I didn't go out much at university. I wanted a first. I wanted the career I'd always dreamed of. Then Mum got diagnosed with MS when I was in my third year, and I've three younger siblings, so I came home after graduating. Don't get me wrong, I love working here, but most of my school friends haven't returned and—"

"It's all right, Katie." *Well, that explains a few things.*

"Sorry, I told you, my mouth can run away with itself when I'm nervous. Please take no notice of me."

Riley put his hands up. He wished she'd mentioned her circumstances before. "It's okay. I came back here to look after my father when he was ill. I understand. Tell you what, I'll speak to Dylan anyway. He knows lots of people your age. Even if he's not on the right team, he's friendly. He'll be here around five-thirty and I can introduce you. I can't have the best trainee I've ever had not having a work-life balance, now, can I?"

"I don't want to impose."

"Nonsense. I told you, he's a people pleaser and easy to talk to." He thought about how much Dylan had made him laugh on their journeys, even shaking him out of bad moods. How he'd worried about giving him a lift. How much he'd begun to look forward to discussing things with him, even if it was only TV shows they'd watched. If he got a car, Riley knew he'd miss him.

"Right, work to do, and thank you for the coffee. If you need any help, let me know, and we'll go through the document together."

Katie nodded and smiled before leaving the room, and Riley to his thoughts.

At the end of the working day, Riley walked out with Katie. Dylan had beaten them to the car park and was stood leaning against the car reading his Kindle. When he lifted his gaze and smiled, Riley's heart did a tiny flip. He admonished himself for taking in Dylan's lean figure with his head of bright red hair and his bright blue eyes and those long limbs which sometimes made him resemble a baby giraffe. He stood a good few inches taller than Riley and towered over Katie.

"Have you been waiting long?" he asked.

"Nah, about ten minutes, and the sun is shining, unlike earlier, so I thought I'd get some rays." He peered at Katie. "Do I get an introduction?"

"This is Katie. She's doing her two-year training course with us."

Dylan put out his hand, which she took. "Happy to meet you, Katie. Love the suit."

Funny, he always said the right thing. Katie straightened up and returned his smile.

"I'll see you tomorrow then, Mr. Ormerod. Good to meet you too, Dylan." She strolled across to her Mini and waved after she'd climbed in.

"She seems like a lovely girl," Dylan said, once they were both in Riley's car.

"She is, and bright as well, if rather lonely." He filled Dylan in on her situation. "And she thought you were cute."

"Well, I am cute. Don't you think so?" This time Riley knew Dylan was flirting with him, but he wasn't sure if he meant it only kindly, knowing what had happened.

"I wondered if you'd invite her out with your friends sometime," he continued. "She's finding it hard to adjust to being back home, and I know how that can feel."

"You say she's bright?"

"Yes, very." Riley glanced at Dylan with a puzzled expression on his face.

"Perfect. There's a quiz at the pub on Friday night. Each team needs six members and we need all the help we can get to stop the same team winning again. If she's as bright as you say, I'll invite her to join us, on one condition."

"O-kay." *What have I got myself into?*

"That you come out with us, too."

Chapter Nine

Dylan stared at his arse from every angle. *Maybe exercise would help? Could I work out to develop a bubble butt?* Still. These black jeans showed what he had to its best advantage. *Now, which T-shirt?*

He held two up, having finally narrowed his choice down this far. Should he go with a funny slogan or a rainbow flag? A knock at his bedroom door made him turn.

"Are you decent, love?"

"Yes, Mum, just trying to decide what to wear." He held up two shirts when his mother entered. "Which do you think?"

"The rainbow one. Not everyone likes a slogan."

He pulled the T-shirt over his head. "Good choice, Mum. Is everything all right?"

"Yes, love. Your dad is champing at the bit. He's determined to win tonight. You know what he's like, and you've never beaten Stan's team."

"Well, this time I've pulled in two extras. I persuaded Riley to come and he's bringing Katie, the trainee from his practice. So, it'll be me, Dad, Matt, Dan and them. I reckon we've a good chance this time. Dad would be made up to win, and this way he gets to spend the evening with Riley again. I know they were close once."

"Maybe as youngsters, but then Riley went to grammar school and, although they stayed friends, your dad says it wasn't the same. Then Riley went off to London."

"Maybe the gay thing didn't help. He obviously didn't want Dad to know. Is he okay with it now?"

"He's getting used to it. With you we always knew, but he says he had no idea about Riley, that no one did. There weren't even any rumors. It must have been hard for him. Dylan..."

Her tone made his Spidey sense tingle. "Yes, Mum."

"You will be careful around him, won't you?"

"I don't know what you mean."

"You've always worn your heart on your sleeve. We always knew when it was broken, when someone had upset you or when you were happy. I didn't miss the comment you made when he was here for dinner. He might be twice your age, but I get the feeling he's still getting over what happened to him. I don't want you to get carried away, or think you need to rescue him out of his despair. You've so much ahead of you, and...I don't want either of you to get hurt."

He'd rarely lied to his parents. He'd never needed to. His life was an open book, so he hesitated before replying. "He's a good man, Mum, and funny. He has this dry sense of humor. We talk about all sorts of things in the car and I like to listen to him, but sometimes he's just so sad. It would be good to get him and Dad back as friends like they once were."

His mum hugged him. "You're a good, caring boy with a kind heart and I'm proud of you, but sometimes too much time has passed. Don't push, that's all, and don't think you have to rescue Riley. He's a grown man. Now, you'd better get off. You wouldn't want to miss the quiz."

When Dylan walked into the pub with his father, Riley and Katie were already at a table in the corner. He waved over. "I'll get the drinks in, Dad. You sit down."

Matt and Dan were perched on stools at the bar, with its gleaming mahogany counter and polished brass footrail. The pub had once been a stopping place for travelers, and still offered bed and breakfast, though the stables had long been turned into a restaurant. Simply selling alcohol didn't keep pubs open, even if this was the only drinking place left in the village. In summer, hanging baskets covered the front and people sat outside to enjoy the view of the narrow river with its ancient packhorse bridge. Dylan clapped his oldest friends on their shoulders.

"You ready to win tonight, lads. I've got us a couple of ringers. My dad's old mate, Riley, who's a solicitor, and his trainee, Katie."

Matt turned around. "Wow, she's a bit of all right."

"Down, boy, give her a chance before you turn on the charm. Hopefully, she'll be as good as Maxine. How's she doing, Dan?"

"Could pop at any time, she says. I left her with her feet up and a box of chocs for company. She would have come, but she's not sleeping well with the baby bouncing on her bladder." Dylan caught the eye of the barmaid.

"Two pints please, Della."

"Usual, Dylan?"

"Yes, please. Busy tonight."

"Always is on quiz night. Fancy your chances then? Should be a fair old prize with the numbers in."

"We've a couple of new members tonight instead of Mum and Maxine, so we're hopeful." He picked up the pints. "Come on, you two, I'll introduce you. Just put your tongue in, though, Matt. You don't want to frighten the poor woman."

Introductions made, the team discussed their chances. Matt had taken the seat next to Katie and was busy chatting away with her. Dylan had known Matt and Dan all his life. They were good blokes, not exactly sophisticated, but without a bad bone in their bodies. They'd never cared about his sexuality and had punched anyone else who had an opinion they didn't agree with.

"Dad and Riley go way back, like us," he explained to Matt and Dan. "They were talking about all the things they got up to the other night, including escaping a charging bull."

Tony raised his eyebrows. "For some reason, Dylan was keen to hear about our exploits. I told him most of them were Riley's fault, like when you dared me to shoplift those sweets and I got caught, and now you're a representative of the law."

Riley blushed. "Well, you'd dared me to knock on old Mrs. Hendon's door and she came out waving her broom. I had to get my own back somehow."

"Hmm, nice to know you have some secrets," Dylan said. Then he realized the implication of his words as Riley's face flushed a deep shade of pink. He picked up his pint and swallowed several mouthfuls. Dylan watched Riley's Adam's apple move as the liquid flowed down his throat and brushed away the powerful desire to kiss his neck. Would he ever get the chance? He shifted in his seat. Dan nudged him, then whispered in his ear, "You're staring." Dylan picked up his own pint and elbowed Dan in the ribs.

"I'm sure I wasn't as bad as your dad might imply. It was his fault he got caught," Riley said. "And as for the bull, did he tell you he fell in the river afterward and got covered in mud? Your grandmother wasn't best pleased. Now, what can we expect from this quiz?"

A man with the stature of a prop forward stopped at the table. "I see you've got some new members tonight, Tony. No worries, we'll still hand you your arses on plates."

"You know they say pride comes before a fall, Stan. We'll see. I reckon you're going down this time. You remember Riley Ormerod from school?"

"Bloody hell. I thought you'd gone off to London to be a soft southerner. Back for a holiday, are you?"

Dylan felt Riley stiffen beside him. "I've been back a while. You haven't changed much, I see." He stuck out his chin. Obviously, these two had a history Dylan wasn't aware of. They glared at each other for a few seconds until the other man gave way and strode off.

"Whew," Dylan said, glancing between his dad and Riley. "What don't I know?"

"The man was a bully and still is," his father explained. "He tried to put my head through the school railings until Riley kicked him in the balls. Then his mates piled on us, and Riley ended up with a broken arm. We have to beat that bastard tonight."

"We most certainly do," Riley agreed.

A bell rang at the bar and Della announced the quiz was about to start. After ten rounds of questions, Dylan reckoned they had a chance of winning. Katie proved to be great at film and books, while Riley's knowledge of geography and art surprised him.

"I think we're going to take them this time," Dylan whispered to his father.

"I hope so, son. I'd love to wipe the smile off Stan's face. Look at him over there grinning away as he hands over their answers. Get us another round in."

Riley rose at the same time. "I'll give you a hand. I need to stretch my legs."

At the bar, Dylan ordered more drinks. "I'll just scoot to the loo. Need to make some room for more liquid. Perch on a stool, I won't be long."

Surprisingly, the toilets were empty when Dylan got there. He stood at the urinal thinking about Riley — again. Should he simply tell him he fancied him and didn't care about the age difference, or would Riley regard him as merely a kid? Every time he saw Riley, his desire grew stronger. And tonight, out of the suit and tie, wearing casual jeans and jumper, Riley looked just as good. The door opened behind him as he pulled up his zip.

"Might have guessed I'd find you in here."

Dylan turned to see his father's nemesis staring at him.

"Your lot are always trying to get a look at some bloke's dick. I'd be ashamed to be seen with you if you were mine."

"Believe me, the feeling is mutual. My dad is worth ten of you. And I bet your dick isn't worth looking at, anyway." Dylan waved his little finger.

The other man moved more swiftly than he expected and pinned him against the wall. "Keep your filthy mouth closed."

"Oh, you've no idea how filthy this mouth can be." Where was this bravado coming from? Yes, he had height over Stan Parr, but the man had weight behind his fists.

"Get your hands off him, Stan." Dylan glanced up to see Riley standing in the doorway.

"You gonna make me? You're nowt but a big girl's blouse, yoursen."

"If I have to. A lot has changed since we were young. Your muscles appear to have traveled south, whereas I work out three times a week, and have studied martial arts. London can be a rough place if you can't look after yourself. So, I repeat, put him down and get out before I have to do something we'll both regret."

Riley's tone, and the way he stared at the man holding him by the collar, sent shivers of a good kind down Dylan's spine.

"Maybe you'd better do as he says," Dylan whispered.

Stan pulled away and brushed past Riley at the door. "Faggots, the pair of you."

Riley closed the space between them. "Are you all right? You were a while, and I saw him heading this way, so I thought I'd better check."

"I'm fine but thank you." They stood for a few moments simply gazing at each other. The butterflies in Dylan's stomach had nothing to do with what the other man had done. Neither did the pounding of his heart, or the drying of his mouth. One step and he'd be near enough to kiss Riley. Would he let him? Would he wrap his arms around him and pull Dylan forward until their bodies were pressed together? Would Riley drag him into one of the cubicles and press him down to his knees?

"We'd better get back, or we'll miss the result of the quiz," Riley said, ending the silence.

"Yeah, of course." He wasn't sure his knees would hold him. "I need a drink." He followed Riley back to their table.

"We thought you'd fallen in," Dan said.

"Everything all right?" Tony asked. "I saw Stan come from the door with a scowl on his face."

"Words were exchanged, that's all," Riley said. "Now, have we had the results yet?"

As he finished speaking, the bell rang again, and Della stood with a piece of paper in her hand. "Quiet, everyone. We, the bar team, have checked all the answers. Mr. Johnson has added the scores, and as he's a math teacher there will be no arguments. I have to tell you it was a close result with only a couple of points separating the top two teams. So, without any more ado—"

"Get on with it. This isn't some bloody quiz show."

Della scowled at Stan. "Well then, I have immense pleasure in announcing that tonight's winning team is…." She still kept them waiting for at least a minute. "Tony's People, who win by two points! Well done. If you'd like to collect your check for one hundred pounds, Tony… The next quiz will be two weeks from today."

The beam on his father's face as he stood to go and collect their prize warmed the cockles of Dylan's heart, as did the scowl on the face of Stan Parr. He held up his pint and clinked glasses with the others.

"Someone's not pleased," Matt said. "You'll have to come again, Katie, and you, of course, Riley."

Tony waved the check at the pub as a whole. "We've decided to donate the whole amount to charity. Dylan, can you think of an LGBT organization that would benefit?"

"Lots," Dylan replied, smiling broadly, knowing it would put their opponents' nose seriously out of joint.

"Excellent. And we'll be sure to see you the next time." Tony strode back to their table and handed the check over to Dylan.

"I'm going to get off now," Tony said. "You stay if you want. I said to your mum I wouldn't drink too much."

"I need to go, too," Dan said. "Or there won't be a chocolate left for me in the house."

"And I've a drive back to Preston," Katie agreed.

Matt stood. "I'll see you to your car."

When all four had left, Dylan turned to Riley. "Only the two of us, then."

"Looks like it."

"I fancy some curry and chips. What about you?"

"I can't remember the last time I had such an exotic dish."

"There's a place on the edge of Clitheroe, a bit out of our way, but I could walk back from yours after we've eaten, if that's okay with you." Dylan had his fingers crossed under the table. If he could get Riley on his own, in his house, who knew what could happen.

"Sounds like a plan to me," Riley agreed. "We did win after all, so we should celebrate."

Chapter Ten

What the hell am I thinking bringing him back here?

Dylan unwrapped the newspaper parcels. "There's something about chip shop curry that's different to all other curry sauce. At the Chinese, it's more bitter. This is sweeter and gloopier."

Riley opened the fridge and pulled out the bottle of Pinot Noir he'd put there earlier. "I've beer as well," he said.

"Nah, white wine and chips go together like Tom and Jerry."

"But they hated each other," Riley replied.

"So, it works both ways then."

Dylan gave him one of those cute, lopsided grins. *Oh hell, I used the C-word. He is not cute. He is young and more than a little tipsy.* "I suppose there's some logic in that." Riley rummaged in the drawer and found a corkscrew.

"Sit down or this gourmet food will get cold and claggy," Dylan instructed.

Riley did as he'd been told, opened the bottle and poured some into each glass. Dylan picked his up.

"To victory! My dad will be dining out on that for ages. And to putting a homophobic bastard in his place. Thanks for rescuing me, by the way. Do you really do martial arts?"

"No, I said that for effect."

Dylan pouted, and Riley's stomach flipped. "So, no thrice-weekly workout either? And here was me wondering whether I should ask to see your six-pack."

Dylan's words sent heat rushing into Riley's face. He'd kept himself in shape for Nate, but he hadn't set foot in a gym for nearly two years. He willed the embarrassed blush away. Unable to meet Dylan's gaze, he stared at the food he'd never allowed himself to eat in his previous life. "I haven't worked out since I left London. Our apartment block had a gym in the basement, and a pool. We haven't even managed a run yet, either."

Dylan picked up a chip, dipped it in the curry, placed it between his lips and sucked it in, leaving curry sauce on his mouth which he licked up with deliberate slowness. "I'm lucky. I've never had to exercise and can eat anything. My sister hates me. Still, it'll probably catch up with me later when I'm old and gray, not that us gingers really go gray. We sort of go salt and pepper. There has to be some advantage to having this carrot top. There should be laws, you know, against discrimination against gingers."

Riley chuckled. Dylan pointed at him, his arm wavering. "Don't you laugh. It's a real thing. They have laws to protect everyone else, don't they? You're a lawyer. Why aren't gingers protected?"

"I don't have a problem with redheads," Riley said.

"Don't you? Good." Dylan slammed his hand on the table. "And I've got blue eyes as well. Did you know the combination is rare, I mean the rarest rare there is?"

Riley suppressed a grin. "I didn't."

"Well, it is." Dylan picked up another chip. "These are awesome. You can't beat a proper chip. I bet you ate all sorts of fancy stuff in London, didn't you? Expensive restaurants where they serve little blobs of things and call it food, then charge you the earth. At least up north we have real food, not that poncey nonsense. You wouldn't get cottage pie there unless it was deconstructed or some such nonsense."

"You all have very fixed views about London up here." Riley couldn't help being amused. "I'm sure there are gastropubs around here too."

"Did *he* take you out to posh places then, this ex of yours?"

Riley stiffened. "I'd rather not talk about him."

Dylan swallowed the glass of wine, poured another and drank most of it down before Riley could stop him. He held the glass up and waved it about rather unsteadily, spilling some on the table. "I bet he did. I bet he didn't have a hair out of place, used moisturizer and had manicures and pedicures. Didn't stop him being a cheating bastard, though."

All of that was true. "No, it didn't." He didn't explain how he'd always known, that there had been an unspoken agreement as long as Nate was careful and didn't parade his conquests.

Dylan leaned forward. "I'd never cheat. I hate cheating."

"I'm sure you wouldn't."

"No, I mean it. I can't understand why anyone would cheat on you."

Before he could stop him, Dylan had stood and closed the space between them. He swayed slightly. Riley rose and held each arm. "You've had too much to drink. I'm not sure you're in any fit state to walk."

"I'll be fine. Stop worrying."

"I think you'd better stay here. I have a spare bed. We'll prop you up properly with some pillows. I'll text your dad and let him know."

"You know you're really handsome." Dylan stared at him with his big blue eyes, then leaned forward and kissed him. For a few seconds, Riley let him, then stepped back. The pout returned.

"Why did you stop? You have such soft lips. I wanted to kiss you."

Riley needed an excuse, needed to get himself under control. "Dylan, you've had too much to drink. You don't know what you're doing."

"Nah, I know. Wanted to kiss you. Wanted you to kiss me. Wanted you since…" He lurched. "Think I'm going to be sick." Riley led him to the sink.

"Sorry."

As Dylan threw up, Riley thought maybe chips, curry and wine weren't a match made in heaven after all. He poured Dylan a glass of water. "Can you swallow some sips of this?"

Dylan shook his head. "Need to sleep. Tired."

"Let's get you upstairs and into bed then. At least we don't have to get up for work in the morning."

He held Dylan up as they climbed the stairs, and helped him out of his shirt and jeans then into bed, placing pillows along his back just in case. He didn't want him to fall over and be sick again. He sat on the edge of the bed and stroked Dylan's head.

"Mmm, that's lovely. Sorry I kissed you."

"It's okay, no harm done. Now try to get some sleep. I've left the glass of water next to you. If you wake up, try to drink some, or you'll feel awful in the morning."

"I don't get hangovers," Dylan mumbled. "You could get in with me if you want."

"I think we both know that's not a sensible idea. Now sleep. I'll see you in the morning."

In his own room, Riley got undressed and settled into bed. Despite cleaning his teeth, he could still taste Dylan's lips on his own. He shook his head. *Stop it. He's got a crush on you, that's all.* It had been over a year and a half since he'd had sex with anyone other than himself, and he hadn't had any interest in even that recently. He picked up his phone and found Tony's number.

"Tony, it's Riley. Dylan's had too much to drink so he's snoring away in the back bedroom as we speak."

"Bloody idiot. He's never been able to handle his booze." Riley was grateful not to hear the slightest hint of suspicion in Tony's voice. "Though beer doesn't usually affect him too much."

"We went for curry and chips and he had a couple of glasses of wine too quickly. I didn't realize. I've propped him up to make sure he's safe."

"Ah, that would explain it. Tell the idiot to get to the shop tomorrow if he's fit, but if he isn't, I don't want him breathing on the customers if he's got the hangover from hell. His mother will be working as well."

"Don't worry, I'll look after him."

"I know you will. And thanks for tonight. Maybe you should come out with the team again."

"I'd like that, Tony. It was fun. I'll bring him home in the morning. Night."

He snuggled down under the duvet. The nights were colder now. He smiled, hearing the snores coming from across the landing, closed his eyes, and slipped into sleep himself.

* * * *

Riley woke to singing coming from the bathroom. It turned out Dylan could be a morning person after all. Riley rubbed the sleep out of his eyes, threw back the duvet and positioned himself on the edge of the bed. The creak of a door and the padding of feet along the wooden flooring of the landing told him Dylan had finished. Before he could reach for his robe, there was a knock and a smiling face peered around the door.

"Oh, you are up then. I hope you don't mind, I had a shower." Dylan stepped fully into the room, wearing nothing more than a towel wrapped around his middle. Riley noted the freckles on his arms and shoulders along with his pale chest and tiny smattering of ginger hair linking pink nipples. Dylan stared back at him. Conscious of his own nakedness except for the shorts he usually slept in, he stopped himself, pulling the covers over like some shy teenager but couldn't decide what to do with his hands. Dylan licked his lips, lips he'd used to kiss Riley the night before. Did he even remember?

"No, no, of course not." Riley stuttered. "How's your head?"

"Nothing a full English won't cure. I need something to soak up what's left of the alcohol. Thanks for letting me stay, and..."

Would he mention the kiss?

"Sorry about the throwing up—wine and beer don't mix with curry and chips."

"Not a problem. Give me fifteen minutes for a quick shower and I'll be down to make breakfast." Riley needed Dylan out of the room and dressed. Had it been so long that he was reduced to speculating how Dylan's pale flesh would feel under his fingertips, or whether those nipples enjoyed being licked and sucked, or how those lips would feel in the cold light of day?

"I'll, um, leave you to it then if there's nothing more you want, nothing I can help with."

Riley's stomach squirmed. *I'm forty-two years old. Please don't let me blush.* He glanced up and caught Dylan's smirk. Clearly, this young man knew exactly what he was doing and which buttons to press. Did he really mean what his words implied? No. *Get a grip, man.*

"I'll see you in the kitchen then." Dylan closed the door and Riley breathed out. He held up his hand, noting the slight shake. He needed to nip this in the bud and tell Dylan he wasn't interested. But was he? Was this some middle-aged crisis? His bladder reminded him he needed the loo. Grabbing his robe, Riley hurried to the bathroom. Maybe the water would wash away these ridiculous feelings.

The smell of bacon hit him as soon as he reached the bottom of the stairs. His mouth watered. He hurried along the hallway to the kitchen and opened the door to see Dylan at the cooker, breaking a couple of eggs into the pan while strips of bacon lay on the plates alongside fried bread. Fried bread. He couldn't remember the last time he'd eaten such greasy crunchy goodness.

"There you are. I hope you don't mind me cooking. I found everything in the fridge and thought I might as well. I didn't do tomatoes. I don't like them fried, but I can do some for you if you want, or beans, I don't mind."

"No, eggs and bacon are great. I'll make the tea." He filled the kettle and plugged it in. Standing next to Dylan, creating breakfast together as if they did this every day — oh hell, so much for giving Dylan 'the talk' he'd planned in the shower. When the water boiled, he poured it into the mugs and stirred until the tea looked a decent color.

"I like it strong," Dylan said, placing the fried eggs on the plates. "Don't put too much milk in."

"Don't worry, I'm the same," Riley replied, putting the mugs on the small kitchen table and taking a seat. Dylan brought the plates and cutlery and sat in the seat adjacent to him.

"Any plans for today?" Dylan asked.

"No, not really. More sorting, I suppose, and I need to decide on a new kitchen. Sue knows someone who fits them. Your dad suggested you should go to the shop. I could take you."

Dylan sighed. "I think I might pull a sicky just between you and me. You won't rat on me, will you? It can be our little secret." He winked, making Riley's cock twitch.

"Your secret is safe with me and this is cooked to perfection, by the way."

Dylan smiled. Little crinkles appeared around his eyes, as well as the cutest dimples. *Damn. Stop this.* He crunched on the bread, letting the grease squeeze out onto his tongue.

"Sue cared for your father, didn't she? It must have been hard coming back here and watching him fade away, especially after what happened in London."

"In some ways, but in others, it was good to get to know him again. Dad always wanted me to follow him into the profession. I enjoyed learning, and I wanted him to be proud of me. I've never regretted choosing law."

"At least saying you're a lawyer sounds exciting. On TV they're always glamorous, standing in court, making speeches, and winning cases."

"I was never that sort of lawyer. Those are the barristers. They're the performers," Riley said.

Dylan shrugged. "Well, then. Try being an accountant. No one except other accountants, bookkeepers or mathematicians understands the joy of a row or column of figures. I even love spreadsheets."

"Okay, you win. I'll grant you, that *is* odd."

"Was your ex a bit of a performer?"

The question caught Riley by surprise. He opened his mouth and closed it again, dug his fork into the bacon and chewed on the salty piece dipped in the egg yolk. When Dylan leaned over and placed his fingers on Riley's arm, he stared at it, feeling the warmth spreading over his skin.

"Sorry, I shouldn't have asked. It's none of my business. Curiosity got the better of me. I wanted to know what sort of man could attract and keep you for so long."

Riley jerked back as if he'd been stung. Did he want to talk about Nate? He'd left without talking to anyone. At first people had called, people he considered friends, but they'd given up when he ignored their messages. Secondly, did he want to share his innermost secrets with this young man who he'd only known for weeks, but who he now considered, he realized, to be a friend?

"Nate's older than me. When I first saw him, he came to the university to give a guest lecture. He strode into the room wearing an Armani suit, highly polished black shoes and with a haircut which probably cost enough to keep me in food for weeks. He had jet-black hair, the sort of color that turns to blue in a certain light, and the greenest eyes. He stood over six feet tall and had shoulders more appropriate on a swimmer. I sat in the first row and stared transfixed. Every now and again, he looked in my direction and I swear I stopped breathing. After the lecture, I waited to talk to him like some groupie. He leaned forward and whispered he'd like to meet me again then slipped a card into my pocket. That first time, he took me out to dinner then back to his flat. I hadn't even graduated before I moved in."

"Wow, I don't know what else to say."

Riley shook his head. "Sometimes I find it hard to believe myself. He introduced me to his circle and helped get me a training position in one of the top practices in London. Don't get me wrong, I earned that place. Without a first, they wouldn't have taken me on. When I told my dad, it was one of the few times I ever felt he was proud of me."

"Some fathers," Dylan said, tutting.

"Not your dad, though. He's proud of you both."

"No, not my dad. He may have his faults, but Kayleigh and I have always felt loved by both of them."

"I'm glad. A child should feel loved. My father loved my mother, but I was a constant reminder of her absence. I never felt I could tell him the truth about me or about Nate, so I didn't ask him to visit, and my visits here got fewer and fewer. I read his diaries recently. Not all of them, just those from when he met my mum and from when I was born. I can't face the others yet."

"But you came home for him."

Did I? He sighed. "I came home for both of us. After what happened with Nate, I couldn't stay. I got out of there intending to find somewhere else to live, came home to visit and found how bad he really was so decided to stay. Dad rang his old partner and pulled a few strings to get me the job in Preston. I bought in as partner soon after. Dad and I rubbed along, but if I'd hoped for some seismic shift in our relationship, I was wrong."

"Well, I'm glad you came home. I remember you being here a few years back. I'd have been about fifteen. I'd always known I was gay but hadn't come out then. Seeing you confirmed everything. I only wanted you to notice me, but I was this scrawny, ginger kid with too many spots and an inconvenient erection."

How the hell did he reply to that? "Dylan, we all have crushes when we're teenagers. You grow out of them." Did he remember the kiss from the night before?

"Nate was an idiot to cheat on you. You deserve someone who loves you heart and soul." Dylan's grip on Riley's arm increased, and the way he gazed at Riley made the hairs stand up on the back of his neck. But he couldn't. He couldn't use this lovely, sweet, kind young man, or take advantage of Dylan's feelings. He picked up Dylan's arm and placed it on the table.

"Dylan, you're twenty-two years old with the whole of your future ahead of you. Given time, you'll find someone to love who'll love you back, and maybe you'll get married and even have kids."

"Why do people always say that? I'm old enough to know my own mind and what I want. Don't treat me like a child, Riley. When I kissed you last night, you kissed me back. I may have been slightly drunk, but I remember the taste of your lips on mine and how it felt having your body pressed against me." He stood, pushing the chair back.

"Dylan, I'm sorry, I shouldn't have... Maybe you should try to find someone else to give you a lift."

"Will you still give me a lift to work and back until I do?"

"Of course. I wouldn't leave you in the lurch." He hated the way the color leached out of Dylan's face.

"Right. Okay. I'll do that. Have a good weekend. I'll see you Monday morning."

Dylan stumbled, catching his foot on the leg of the table as he hurried out of the room. The slam of the front door shook the house. Riley placed his elbows on the table and his head into his hands. He'd wanted to let Dylan down lightly. He'd get over his crush. He stood and picked up the plates to wash up. Only as he stood over the sink did he realize a single tear had slipped down his face and dropped into the water.

Chapter Eleven

I should have told him I wouldn't give up.

"Are you okay, love?" Monday morning, his mother placed the rack of toast in front of him. He glanced up.

"Yeah, I'm fine." He picked up a piece and spread butter on, making sure it reached the edges, but instead of eating it, he stared at it watching the butter disappear.

"It's just you've been quiet all weekend since you came home from Riley's and you're up early today. Are you sure there's nothing bothering you, nothing you need to talk to me about? You know you can tell me anything."

Dylan crunched the toast, chewed then swallowed. "I told you, I'm fine. I had too much to drink on Friday, and Riley kindly let me stay. Talking of Riley, I'd better get going. He's probably waiting in the rain. The forecast is lousy today." Raindrops ran down the kitchen window. "Winter's coming. They even mentioned the possibility of snow for the first week in November."

He stuffed the rest of the toast in his mouth, stood, grabbed his coat and hurried to the front door. A gust of wind hit him as he opened it, halting him in his tracks. As expected, Riley was sitting in his car, staring out of the windscreen. *You can do this. Be a grown up. You made a play and got knocked back. You don't always get two sixes at the first throw of the dice. He may say he isn't interested...*

Taking a breath, Dylan hurried down the steps, pulled open the car door after checking for oncoming traffic and jumped in. "Filthy morning," he said in as cheerful a tone as he could manage.

"No toast this morning?" Riley said without looking at him.

"Nope, I was up early enough to eat in a civilized fashion in the kitchen." A knock on the window made them both turn. His mum stood there with a coat over her head waving his lunch box. So much for being efficient. Riley wound down the window.

"You forgot your lunch," she said, leaning in. Riley took the box and handed it over to him. He edged forward.

"Thanks, Mum." He expected her to hurry back in.

"Thanks for looking after him on Friday night, Riley. Young men can be irresponsible at times. It's good he had you to take care of him."

Dylan dug his hands into his pockets, certain she suspected something had happened and was digging.

"It was no problem, Lori, and we've all imbibed too much at some point. We need to get off. The weather's not going to help this morning." Riley wound up the window cutting his mother off, put the car into gear and set off.

Neither of them spoke. The tension was palpable. Dylan could stand it no longer and reached to turn on the radio. "Do you mind?" he asked.

"No, of course not. Did you have a good weekend?"

"I hung around at home. You?"

"Same, but I did decide on a kitchen and color scheme. I've got to give Sue's contact a ring today. Sooner it's done, the sooner they can get on with the bathroom. Everything needs updating. I've got an electrician coming around tonight to check the wiring, which might have to be done first, and that'll mean more redecoration."

"Sounds like you're putting your own stamp on the place. I wasn't sure if you intended to stay." *Please say you are.*

"I wasn't sure to begin with — lots of bad memories — but I'm enjoying choosing the units and the color schemes. I have to remind myself I had some good times here as well."

"You can always change your mind, I suppose."

Riley put his foot down and overtook a pair of huge lorries sending spray all over the car and temporarily obscuring the view. "I hate this weather," he grumbled. "But I'm not planning to go anywhere."

"I thought you'd considered moving nearer to work. That would cut out traveling on the motorway on days like this." Dylan didn't mention looking for someone else to give him a lift. Instead, he found a change of topic.

"While I think about it, would you ask Katie what she thought of Matt? He's rather smitten with her."

"Just like his dad was the first time he set eyes on Sandra. He always complained playing the drums meant he didn't get the girls because he was at the back of the group. Sandra was with a group of friends and came up to us after a gig. Such a pity what happened to him. I lost touch with everyone after I left."

Dad said you stopped taking calls and he gave up. Dylan kept his thoughts to himself. Maybe there'd been a reason.

"Matt junior's a good lad. He has a look of his dad."

"He's good as gold. Katie could do a lot worse than him. His mum had problems after his dad died in the accident. Matt held the family together, went out to work at sixteen so the twins could stay on in school and go to university, and he's a damn good plasterer. You could use him if you do up your house."

"Yeah, Sue mentioned him. Not sure exactly what I'm doing in other rooms yet, but I'll keep him in mind." Riley pulled up at the roundabout. "Thank goodness we're off the motorway."

Dylan guessed this was the end of the conversation. He stared out of the window at the others on their way to work. The traffic moved slowly as usual on a Monday morning until they finally turned off the outer road into the city center. Riley stopped outside the town hall.

"I'll drop you here again, and I'll be ready at five-fifteen as I've got to get back for the workmen."

"I'll be there. Riley?" *Don't be a fucking wimp. Say it.*

"Yes." Riley turned to face him.

"I know you think I'm too young for you, but I know my own mind. I meant that kiss."

Riley gripped the wheel tighter and shifted in his seat. A car horn sounded behind them. "You'd better hurry and get out. I'll see you later."

Dylan climbed out, then stood in the rain watching the BMW pull away. *At least I said something.*

* * * *

After the partners' meeting, Riley grabbed a coffee and settled down at his desk. He opened the document and stared at the words, words he'd read so many times over with only the names and numbers being different each time. Conveyancing could be like those fill-in-the-gap exercises he'd done at school. The buying and selling of property, large and small, had occupied his time for years. Of course, in Lancashire, he wasn't dealing with six-figure sums for buildings which would be developed and left empty at a price way beyond the purse of the average Londoner. Here, the company in question intended to turn the old mill building into affordable flats. Maybe he'd mention the development to Dylan, and he could get himself on the list.

He chewed on the end of his pencil, a habit he'd never managed to get rid of. Dylan? What the hell should he do? Dylan had made his feelings quite clear. And yes, having a man half his age show interest in him was flattering. But this wasn't any younger man. This was the son of his oldest friend. A fling was out of the question, and Riley had never done flings anyway. It was twenty years since he'd slept with someone new. And after what Nate had done, after what he'd said, how he'd deliberately made sure Riley had found him fucking a tattooed twink tied to their bed and continued fucking him while Riley watched, unable to tear himself away. When he finally had, his mind reeling, Nate had strolled naked into their kitchen five minutes later.

'You should have joined us. Did you see the size of his dick? Such a waste he doesn't get to use it on me, but we could have

taken you together, one at each end. Make us a mug of tea, would you?'

Finally, after those last words, Riley had found courage from somewhere. *'Get rid of him. I want to pack. My father's ill and needs me.'*

Of course, he'd still made the tea. The twink had gone when he returned to the bedroom. The room smelt of sex and, on automatic pilot, he'd stripped the bed and put the sheets into the laundry basket. He'd packed a suitcase, taking a few things — he didn't need much — then dragged the case into the living room where Nate lay on the sofa.

'If you leave now, don't expect me to take you back. You've become so old and boring. To think you were once as young as he is. Who could blame me for finding someone else? And he's so deliciously common. Go on then, run home to Daddy.'

Riley had picked up his car keys, gone down in the lift to the basement, climbed into the car and kept driving until he couldn't see for the tears. He'd slept in the car for a couple of hours then driven home. His father hadn't greeted him like the long-lost prodigal son, but eventually they'd learned to get along.

But Dylan, he looked up to him. Dylan thought Riley was some sophisticated city dweller. He didn't know the truth of what he'd become. Even choosing units for the kitchen had sent him into a panic until he'd told himself only his view mattered. He was a work in progress. He lifted his head at the knock on the door. He'd lost thirty minutes.

"Come in, Katie."

The door opened. "We have our weekly meeting," Katie said.

"So we have. Come in. You sit down, and I'll get us a coffee and biscuit each."

After the usual discussion of the clients and work in progress, Riley sat back in his chair. "You're doing well. Mrs. Ryan was impressed with your thorough approach dealing with the ins and outs of her husband's estate."

"Mr. Whewell wants me to deal with writing wills for another couple this afternoon. They're buying a house together and want to make sure, if one of them dies, the other gets the house."

"We get more of them now. With more people deciding not to get married, it can be difficult if one of them dies intestate. I'm here if anything gets complicated."

Katie smiled. "Friday night was fun, wasn't it? Dylan's, umm, friendly."

"He asked me to mention Matt to you. It appears he's somewhat smitten with you and wanted to know if you were interested."

"I could be," she replied. "Tell Dylan to get Matt to call me himself."

Riley grinned. "I will. Did you have a good weekend? How's your mum?"

They talked for a while until Katie glanced at her watch. "I'd better get on. I need to pop out for lunch to get a few things for home. You're okay with me arriving late tomorrow?"

"Of course, you need to go to the appointment with your mum. You'll make up the time. You always do."

"Not everyone would be so accommodating. I appreciate it."

"I know what it's like to have a parent with an illness."

She hovered at the door for longer than he expected.

"Is there something else?" he asked.

"I may be speaking out of turn, but you know Dylan has a thing for you, don't you? I didn't know if you knew. With you giving him a lift and things, it might be awkward for both of you."

Riley sighed. *I might be developing a thing for him myself.* Should he tell her off? She was only trying to help, so neither of them ended up being embarrassed. "Thank you for telling me." He didn't mention she wasn't the first person to notice.

"Um, yeah, all right, I'll get off then."

Would it do any harm if he and Dylan spent some time together? Relationships with age gaps didn't always end in disaster, did they? Maybe it was time to find out.

Chapter Twelve

The next day dawned bright and sunny for late October, and the forecast promised more of the same. Dylan had racked his brain, trying to think of reasons for him to need Riley's help. There was always that run, if Riley would still go with him. On the journey home the night before, he'd talked about work to avoid anything more awkward. After Dylan jumped in the car, Riley spoke first.

"I forgot to tell you yesterday that I spoke to Katie. She said to tell you to tell Matt to call her himself. He needs to know she doesn't get a lot of time to herself. Her mum's ill and she looks after her younger siblings. I'll give you her contact number for him."

"She and Matt have much in common, then, after what happened with his dad. The driver who hit him did six months for driving while over the limit. So much for the law. At least his firm paid some compensation and they kept the house." He needed to find something to talk about if they couldn't talk about how either of them felt. "Talking of houses, did you finally choose the kitchen units last night?"

"I did. I'm also thinking about getting a cat or a dog or even both. I couldn't have a pet in London, but it would do me good to get out and walk a dog, and it would keep me company."

Dylan wanted to scream, *if you wanted company, you could have me*, but instead he kept the conversation on a more even keel. "Sounds like a good plan. We had our dog for years. You can get some cute crossovers these days. I saw a Pomsky the other day, a cross between a Pomeranian and a husky, just made for cuddling. There's a rescue center on the outskirts of Burnley. I could go with you, if you want." *Yes, now I have an excuse to spend more time with him.*

"I'd like that. I'll need someone sensible with me, or I'll end up with half a dozen."

Warmth bloomed in Dylan's chest. "You think I'm sensible?"

Riley glanced across to him. "I think you've a good head on your shoulders. You work hard, and you've ambitions to improve yourself and have your own business. Not everyone your age is so focused."

Dylan thought about the kiss. "I can be as stupid as anyone else given the right circumstances, if I've read the situation the wrong way. And I'm terrible in the mornings."

"But you're hardly one for getting totally drunk or taking drugs, are you?"

"I got drunk once at university and woke up with some bloke I met at a party. I had no idea what we'd done. For the next few months, I panicked until I had more than one test. Don't get me wrong—if I know I'm in safe company, I'll have a few, like with you, but not otherwise. I've never fancied drugs. What about you?"

Riley stiffened next to him.

"Sorry, none of my business."

"No, I asked you. Your question is fair enough. The answer is a few times, cocaine usually. My ex had parties, and there was a lot of it about, along with other more dubious substances. Some of his friends had more money than sense."

Dylan noted Riley referred to these people as his ex's friends, not his own. Dylan wanted to know more but driving on the M65 at eight in the morning wasn't the best time or place for such conversations.

Time to put his plan into action. "Have you ever been to the Illuminations at Blackpool?" he asked.

Riley shook his head. "No. Why?"

"It's been a few years since I've been there, and I can't go without a car. I wondered if you fancied going on Saturday." He had thought to mention Halloween, but he didn't think dressing up would be Riley's thing. "We could go to the Pleasure Beach, even go on a few rides, get some fish and chips—there's a place that won prizes. Then when it gets dark, we can drive from the south shore through the lights. You said you could do with getting out. Maybe on Sunday morning, we could go to the rescue place to have a look. Then there's the bonfire and firework display."

"I forgot about Bonfire Night. I don't usually bother with Guy Fawkes or Halloween. I suppose All Hallow's Eve is a big deal around here. Do people still dress up as witches and prance around on Pendle Hill?"

"They banned them from going up there because of the fire risk, but you'll get a few trick or treaters, and every village around here has someone who claims to be related to the most famous of the Pendle witches, Alice Nutter. We're all off to a spooky evening at the pub. You could come, too, if you fancied it."

Riley shook his head. "Nah, not my thing at all. But are you sure you want to spend so much time with me? I wouldn't want to take up all your weekend."

"Don't be silly. I enjoy spending time with you." It was weird. When he'd first met him, Dylan had expected Riley to be a sophisticated city dweller who'd look down on him, but instead, he sometimes appeared tentative and unsure of himself, not wanting to impose, but at least he hadn't cast him out of his life. After what had happened, he wasn't sure. If he could just keep them talking.

"So, what d'you think?"

"If you're sure, I'd love to go to Blackpool with you."

Dylan smiled to himself. If he played his cards right maybe he could try for another kiss in the dark. He had no doubt he'd need to take the lead. Riley's ex had certainly done a number on him. Suddenly the age gap between them didn't seem like such a mountain to climb.

* * * *

He and Riley discussed art, drama, favorite films, TV shows and even politics on the drive for the rest of the week, anything but Riley's past, or even his own.

"I totally ship them," Dylan said discussing one of the soaps.

"Ship?" Riley questioned.

"You know, when you think two people should be together when they aren't in the actual show or film and give them a joined-up name."

Riley shook his head. "Is that a thing now?"

"Has been for a while. It started with Spock and Kirk. People used to write stories with them being in a relationship."

"But Kirk had a different woman every week," Riley protested.

"That doesn't matter. It's all about representation for many. People write fanfiction about their favorites. Some of it is pretty good, too. You can read loads online. Some shows are full of subtext. Don't you ever think what it would be like if Worf and Riker had been at it?"

Riley shook his head. "I can't say I ever thought about it."

Dylan rubbed his hands together. "Hmm, I think I need to show you a few examples. You're never too late to learn something new." *And give me an excuse to spend time with you.*

By Saturday afternoon, Dylan was like a cat on hot bricks, unable to stay still for a moment. He'd even tidied his room. At two-forty-five, his mother knocked his bedroom door.

"Bloody hell. I'd forgotten the carpet was this shade of blue. Did you find any new lifeforms under the bed?" She pressed her hand to his forehead. "Funny — you don't have a fever."

"Ha bloody ha, Mum."

She glanced at the clothes on his bed. "Are you sorting out some stuff for the charity bag as well?"

Dylan stuck out his chin. "No, don't you dare. Some of this is new. I treated myself. If you must know, I'm trying to decide what to wear. It'll get cold tonight, but I'll be in the car, and Riley's BMW has heated seats.

We're only having fish and chips so I'm going to wear my jeans, but I can't decide on T-shirt, jumper or shirt."

"Why not wear the shirt under the jumper? They match, and you can take the jumper off if you're too warm. Layers can be useful."

"Good idea. I'd better get on. Riley said he'd pick me up at three, so we can get in a few rides before it's too dark."

His mother sat on the newly cleared bed. "I can't remember the last time we saw the lights. You know me and your dad had our first date there. I got all dressed up to go to a dance in the Tower ballroom. We caught the train from Burnley and were early enough for the football. The Clarets were playing Blackpool, so your dad dragged me onto the terraces and made me stand there for two hours in the wind in my four-inch heels. I nearly finished with him there and then. Ruined my hairdo. But I'd never met a lad who could ballroom dance, so I forgave him."

Dylan smiled. He'd heard the story before. His dad had taken some stick for the dancing, but, as he said, it was the best magnate for pulling. He and Dylan's mum were still big fans of *Strictly*. They'd suggested he take lessons, but all he'd done was fall over his own feet.

"Will you be staying over at Riley's tonight?"

Dylan noted how she'd kept her voice light and gentle rather than inquisitional. "I don't know. It might be late when we get back, and I wouldn't want to disturb you."

"You will text us, though. And you will be careful. You know you can tell me anything, don't you?"

He recalled their previous conversation. "There's nothing to tell, Mum." *Well not much, not yet, maybe after tonight.* "I enjoy his company, and the age difference doesn't matter. We're both grown-ups regardless of what you think. We talk about all sorts. There are lots of places around here he's never been to, and he did help us win the quiz."

"Just remember what I said. None of us really know what happened in London."

"Mum, if Riley wants to talk to me, I'll be there to listen. You know I worked on the gay switchboard at Durham."

She stood and picked a thread from her sleeve. "I know you're a grown-up, but you're still my little boy. And don't bring us home a stick of rock — never liked the stuff. I'll leave you to get changed." She glanced at the window. "At least the forecast is good for today and Bonfire Night tomorrow. The whole village will be at the hall as usual for the food and fireworks."

"I'll be there. Riley's coming too. The last time he came to the display, he was seventeen." He stood and kissed her cheek. "Stop fretting, Mum."

"Only when I'm dead, love. Only when I'm dead."

Dylan dressed, grabbed his backpack and put in his camera, a bottle of water, a couple of CDs and a hoodie for if they spent any time out of the car. At five on the dot, he checked the window and saw Riley's car pull up across the road. He took the stairs two at a time and opened the door.

"Bye, Mum. Have a good evening watching the dancing with Dad, and don't do anything I wouldn't do."

He skipped down the steps and crossed the road, getting in the passenger side. "As punctual as always," he said.

Riley grinned at him. "I'm looking forward to this. I thought we'd take the motorway, but you'll have to navigate us off the M55 to get to South Shore."

"I can read a map. I'm surprised you don't have a sat-nav."

"Can't stand them, and they're not much help in London. Not that I had a car in town—the Tube was quicker. Average speed around the city is about twelve miles an hour. Hopefully, we'll be a lot quicker tonight, but it is the final weekend so there may be more visitors."

Dylan reached into the bottom of his bag. "I brought us some music for the journey." He held up the cover.

"Really, driving rock tunes?"

"I'll have you know there are some classics on here. I defy you not to join in singing." Of course, by halfway through *All Right Now* they were both singing at the tops of their voices.

* * * *

Ninety minutes later, after an enjoyable journey, the first thing they'd done at the funfair was ride on the Big One. Riley couldn't remember the last time he'd had such fun, raising his hands high as they swooped up, down and around the track. He'd failed to notice Dylan hanging on for dear life, white as a sheet next to him until he'd practically crawled out of the carriage and bent over clasping his knees.

"I'm never ever going on one of those things again."

"You're not going to be sick, are you?" Riley asked. The warmth of his hand spread across Dylan's back. It was almost worth experiencing the Big One to feel Riley touch him—almost.

"No, at least I don't think so." He stood up, but the world still spun around him. He swayed. Riley slipped an arm through his.

"Here, come on, let's sit you down. If I'd known you'd hate rollercoasters so much, I'd never have insisted on us taking a ride. I hadn't been on before. *You* suggested coming here."

Riley guided Dylan to the giant's bench. Dylan sat down then reached into his backpack for the bottle of water and chugged most of it down in one go. "When you said you hadn't been since you were young and had never been on the Big One, I thought we had time before we saw the lights, and that I'd give it a try. I couldn't chicken out and admit I've never been on it before, now, could I? It must have been the G-force strength. It felt like I was going to fall out. You must think I'm such a wimp. You had your arms up and everything while I held on for grim death."

Riley rubbed Dylan's back. "I've always loved rollercoasters. Dad brought Mum and me here a few times. I wasn't big enough for a lot of the rides, but Mum took me on the old wooden rollercoaster and the Grand National. She adored them. I suppose I got my love from her." He paused as if trying to decide whether to continue. Dylan waited rather than fill the silence.

"When she was diagnosed with cancer, she didn't tell me at first. She didn't want to worry me. I remember she did a parachute jump. I watched, terrified, as she seemingly fell out of the sky attached to someone else. After she'd landed and taken off all the equipment, she hugged me so hard. I assumed it was because she'd survived, but later I found out she'd been told it was terminal the day before and this was her last chance to do something she'd always wanted to do. She never did manage the bungee jump. By then the cancer had got into her bones. They told me the day after my ninth birthday. She only lasted a few months."

"I'm so sorry. It must have been a lonely way to grow up." Dylan couldn't imagine not having his family yelling at him. "Dad said it hit you hard." His father had said a lot more, but this wasn't the time.

"I pushed your dad and the others away. My father wanted me to meet a better class of boy, as he put it. I didn't want to go to the grammar, but it pleased him, and I was desperate to do that."

Dylan wanted to wrap his arms around Riley. This was supposed to be a fun day out, yet here they were sitting on this huge bench with their feet swinging over the edge pouring out confessions. "Did reading your father's diaries help?"

"Reading them was hard. I look like her, you see. He wrote that every time he saw me, he saw her, the woman he'd loved and lost. He railed against the universe about how unfair it was someone so young and beautiful inside and out should be taken away from those who loved and needed her. He lost his faith then as well." He wiped away a tear. "I'm sorry. We were supposed to have fun and here's me getting all maudlin. How are you feeling now?"

Dylan took a deep breath. The frigid air hit his lungs and he coughed. "I was going to say I'm all right. Shall we get a coffee and get warmed up? We've time to get one to go and do a few more rides if you want."

"Sounds good to me."

They both dug their hands into their pockets and strolled along to the nearest café. Fueled up with coffee, Dylan opened the map of the rides. "Maybe we should try the *Wallace and Gromit* ride. I might be able to cope with that."

"Or we could sit in teacups for *Alice in Wonderland*, but it might look a bit odd, two grown men on a children's ride."

"*Wallace and Gromit* it is then. You know it's amazing how he managed to get such expressions out of a dog with so few facial features."

On the way, they passed the dodgems and couldn't resist a go. With it being the final weekend of the season, the park wasn't too busy, but the darkness had come on fast. It appeared different in the dark with the rides still lit up. Dylan spent his time crashing into the sides and into Riley who did the same. He couldn't remember laughing so much. When the ride stopped, Riley strode toward him and offered a hand to help him out.

"I have to say, if you drive like that in real life, remind me never to be on the same road as you."

Dylan rubbed his neck. "I think I may have whiplash. Who do I sue?" Riley still held his hand.

"Come on, let's have one more ride and find somewhere for fish and chips. Shame we haven't got time for *Ripley's Believe It or Not*. They have this two-headed calf there and shrunken heads. It must be thirty years since I went. I have to admit it frightened me as a kid."

Dylan grinned. "We went to the wax museum once. Who knew some people were such a funny color? Come on then. One more ride and you're buying us a gourmet meal. We may have to find somewhere inside as it's bloody freezing now. Still, at least it isn't raining."

In the end, Dylan suggested taking the food back to the car parked near the start of the lights at the southern end of Blackpool. The Illuminations sparkled and flickered while a steady stream of cars drove through. Some of the passing trams were also covered with colored bulbs turning them into trains or even rockets, and in the distance, the lights of the Tower could be seen stretching up into the night sky.

"So, what sort of a pet do you fancy getting?" Dylan asked as they hurried back to the car.

"A cat or two would be more sensible as I'm out all day and they'll be able to fend for themselves."

"You know there's someone in the village who does dog walking for people who aren't able to during the day. Her name's Isabel Parkinson. She has a card in the window of Mum's shop, and I've seen her walking them in groups. You could give her a ring. Then you could have a dog if you wanted, or a cat and a dog. Some animals get along with each other."

"I would like a small one. Pugs and French bulldogs seem to be all the rage right now, but I doubt a rescue center would have one of them. Dad never let me have a pet. He thought they were a nuisance. And our apartment in London didn't allow animals. It would be good not to rattle around on my own."

At the wistful tone in Riley's voice, Dylan wanted nothing more than to hug him as they walked along side by side. Suspicions of the nature of Riley's relationship with his ex had begun to form in his mind and he couldn't shift them. He'd always been lucky and had the freedom to choose his own path and make his own decisions. His parents had always told him a person only learnt from mistakes, and he'd made many of those. Many people would say lusting after a man twice his age was yet another pie-in-the sky desire, but Riley had a vulnerable side that brought out the alpha male in him, something Dylan didn't even know lanky lads with ginger hair who liked math could have. He seriously wanted to punch this man Riley had wasted so much of his life with.

Back at the car, Riley opened the door and turned on the heat.

"Are you sure we're all right to eat in here?" Dylan asked before opening his food.

"Eating in the car is fine. I can wind the window down if I need to, and I like to hear the waves anyway. We should come back here in daytime. I like the coast in winter, even if it's cold." They opened the wrappers and began to eat from the paper.

Dylan glanced over as Riley squeezed a sachet. "I can't believe you have mayo with your chips, and you a northerner too — soft southern habit."

Riley shrugged. "I like mayo. Hmm, this fish is good. It's always better by the seaside. Thanks for suggesting we come. It's been great to get out to somewhere other than work."

"There are lots of places we could go along the coast, and there's the Lake District. Even in winter it can be lovely, if it doesn't snow. I don't know how much of a walker you are. Knowsley Safari Park is better in the spring. Then there's Chester Zoo as well, down the motorway. We could go to the theater in Manchester if you wanted, or the cinema in Preston. There's all sorts."

"I wouldn't want to monopolize you. I'm sure you'd like to spend time with Matt and Dan, and I've the house renovations."

Dylan turned slightly so he faced Riley. "It may have escaped your notice, but I like spending time with you. I like you — a lot. Dan's about to become a father and Matt hasn't stopped talking about Katie since they were introduced. My uni friends live far away, and I find I like making you smile. I like making you laugh even more."

Taking his courage in both hands, Dylan leaned forward, put a palm around the back of Riley's neck and pulled him close enough to kiss him. Riley wasn't responsive at first, but Dylan pushed at his lips with his tongue until Riley kissed him open-mouthed with purpose. The small groan he emitted went straight to Dylan's cock. He held the back of Riley's head more firmly and eased closer, wishing the gear stick wasn't such an obstacle, and that they didn't each have a chip supper in their laps. He could taste the salt and grease and wanted more, needed more. Somehow, he had to persuade Riley to take him seriously. Finally, Riley pulled away as the contents of his Polystyrene tray threatened to spill.

Dylan sat back and grinned like the Cheshire cat. "I'm going to enjoy kissing you," he said, as Riley fumbled to capture a stray chip from the floor. Riley closed the container and returned Dylan's gaze. He opened his mouth to speak but hesitated.

"Don't you dare say I'm too young," Dylan began. "I don't care if you're twice my age. There are lots of couples with bigger age gaps than us. I fancy you. I've fancied you for years since I first saw you and I was old enough to realize I was gay. I remember that day so well. You were dressed in a dark suit with a white shirt and blue tie. Your hair was slicked back with gel and your shoes so shiny. I wasn't so tall back then. My growth spurt kicked in later, but I was this gawky ginger-haired freckle-faced kid, and you were a god. I wanted to climb you like a tree. Instead I hid behind

Dad, terrified you'd notice my red face and tented jeans. I was so hard that as soon as I got home, I had to disappear upstairs."

"I had no idea," Riley said, his lips curling slightly. "I'm not sure I know how to reply to such a declaration, especially sitting in a car eating chips."

"Okay, I'll admit my timing is a bit off. I'd planned to be nearer a bedroom, but I mean every word. Shall we get going?"

"I think that would be wise."

Shit. Shit. Shit! I must have sounded like such a pillock. Now he'll make an excuse when we get home and any chance of spending the night has gone. Damn my stupid mouth.

Dylan pulled on his seatbelt and stared out of the window at the twinkling lights in the distance. The drive, though, took less than an hour as there wasn't bumper-to-bumper traffic. Dylan desperately wanted to know what was going on in Riley's mind, but he said nothing except to comment on the Illuminations as they passed. When they got to the end, they made their way to the motorway and so to home. Dylan switched on the CD player, choosing a collection of rock ballads this time. They both hummed along to the music but said little. Strangely, Dylan didn't feel uncomfortable as they drove along in the dark. There wasn't an atmosphere at all.

Back at the village, Dylan expected Riley to turn to his home to drop him off but instead, he turned right along the narrow lane that led to his own house. Once they'd parked in the drive, Dylan waited.

"I've been thinking about what you said all the way home," Riley said, still staring out of the windscreen. "You mentioned somewhere with a bed. There's more than one in there. So, would you like to come in?"

Chapter Thirteen

What the fuck was I thinking? Riley sat on the edge of his bed, fully dressed, shaking hands gripping his knees while Dylan abluted in the bathroom. Before he could say anything, Dylan had dragged him upstairs, into his bedroom, and told him to sit and wait. So here he was — sitting and waiting.

"You made this decision." He spoke out loud to himself. "You can still change your mind. If you say no even now, Dylan will respect your choice. Dylan isn't Nate. You aren't the man you were. You left him — finally. You have a fantastic job, the respect of colleagues, and if you want to have sex with a man half your age, then that's no one's business but yours and his, and he wants you, has always wanted you, as shocking as that might be."

His bedroom door opened, letting in light from the landing. Dylan leaned against the doorjamb with his shirt hanging open and jumper slung over his arm. His chest had only a brief smattering of hair. Although he was on the thin side, no ribs were visible, but the low-slung jeans revealed pelvic bones which hinted at the perfect V-shape. Dylan had the sort of figure which wouldn't look out of place on a catwalk. Riley's mouth watered at the thought of licking that pale skin so common on those with bright red hair.

Without speaking, Dylan crossed the floor in a couple of strides and knelt on the carpet in front of him. "Are you all right?" he asked, staring up at Riley with those pale blue eyes. "You look like a rabbit caught in headlights. If you've changed your mind, I'll understand, but I hope you haven't."

"I haven't." Riley said, his voice hardly a whisper.

Dylan lifted himself. Still on his knees, he began to undo the buttons on Riley's shirt one by one, then pushed the cotton fabric from his shoulders back onto the bed.

"Oh goody, I was hoping you'd have some chest hair with you being so dark." Dylan ran his fingers through the small curls. "It's so soft."

Riley jerked as Dylan brushed a fingertip over one nipple. Seeing his reaction, Dylan squeezed the dusky pink nub. Riley groaned. Without warning, Dylan moved closer, stuck out his tongue and licked then sucked. Riley's cock sprang to attention in his jeans, straining at his zip. He let his head fall back as Dylan continued to lick and suck and squeeze and tease. Finally, Riley lifted a hand and threaded his fingers through Dylan's hair.

"Oh God, so good." He couldn't remember the last time he'd been treated to such attention. While still caressing Riley's chest with tongue, lips and teeth, Dylan had his hands on his belt, undoing the buckle, then the zip. He had to be leaking already. Dylan lifted his head, stared at him for a few seconds then kissed him on the lips pressing in his tongue. Riley opened his mouth letting his tongue meet the welcome intrusion.

The kiss lasted minutes with several changes of direction. Dylan's lips were surprisingly soft, and Riley couldn't get enough. He kept his hand in Dylan's hair, wanting him closer just to lose himself in the taste and feel of the man before him. Dylan removed the palm that had been pressing on Riley's growing bulge and he moved back breathing heavily.

"Wow," he said, grinning. "You can kiss. I might become addicted to the sensation." He glanced down to where his hand hovered over Riley's cock as if waiting for permission to proceed.

"Please," Riley begged. If Dylan didn't continue touching him, he might die of frustration.

"Lift yourself up."

Riley did as instructed while Dylan grabbed his jeans and briefs and dragged them down to his feet then off to be tossed away, leaving him naked. Well, except for his socks. For someone who'd never felt entirely comfortable with having his body on show, Riley was surprised to discover he didn't care. He was in reasonable shape. Yes, he didn't have a six-pack or muscles to die for, but the look in Dylan's eyes as he sat back on his haunches and stared suggested he liked what he saw, his expression like that of a small child contemplating an ice cream. Riley would have sworn his cock filled simply from the way Dylan ran his tongue across his lips.

"I want to suck you."

"Sorry?" Riley replied automatically. So much of this experience was new to him. In the past, he'd always been the one on his knees. Thoughts of Nate threatened to kill the moment along with intrusive questions. How did Dylan see him? What did he want? He wasn't a top. He'd always followed rather than led. Panic assailed him.

"You know I'm not any sort of daddy figure, don't you?" he said, unscrambling his thoughts. "If that's what you want…"

Dylan pressed a finger to his lips. "I don't need a daddy, or a dom, or anything like that. I'm not some twink experiencing his first crush. I've always gone after what I want, and what I want right now is you."

"But…"

"Enough," Dylan said softly. He took Riley's cock into his large hand and wrapped his fingers around the base. "I'm going to suck your cock until you come down my throat screaming my name. Or you can come on my face. I don't care. I just want to hear you and feel the weight of this gorgeous dick on my tongue. I've imagined the sounds you'd make so many times, lying in my bed. Now I want to find out for real, if it's okay with you."

A host of giant butterflies released in Riley's stomach and he swallowed hard then nodded, unable to find the words. Without further conversation, Dylan enclosed the tip of Riley's cock and sucked in his cheeks. Unused to such attention, Riley found he wanted to thrust but held back. With his free hand, Dylan grabbed Riley's hand and placed it on his head. Getting the message, Riley clutched at Dylan's hair, threading his fingers through the ginger strands, pulling slightly. He glanced down to check, but Dylan's moan told him he'd done right.

He pressed on Dylan's head. Reacting, Dylan eased forward, taking in nearly all of Riley's erection while his fist moved up and down. When he took Riley's balls in his other hand and gave them a gentle squeeze, Riley squirmed, but Dylan continued. Telltale tingles began to run down his spine as his climax gathered force. With this dual stimulation, Riley knew he wouldn't be able to hold off coming for too long. He closed his eyes, letting the feelings wash over him,

"More," he growled. "Faster, harder." Immediately, Dylan sped up rubbing and sucking.

"I'm so close," Riley warned, opening his eyes and meeting Dylan's gaze. Dylan didn't stop sucking and licking, obviously trusting him, but instead stared up, then winked.

"Oh, hell, yeah, don't stop, please," Riley begged as he came in pulses down Dylan's throat. Dylan milked every drop, then licked every inch of his cock before licking his own lips and sitting back with a smirk on his face.

Riley hadn't come so hard in a long time. In the past, sex had never been about his needs, yet Dylan hadn't cared about himself or his satisfaction at all. Tears pricked at Riley's eyes. With Dylan, he'd simply let go and loved the feeling. Now, he needed to pull himself together. He wasn't ready to show Dylan how raw he felt, how exposed or how much that simple act of love had meant to him.

"Bloody hell. If they gave away Olympic medals for blow jobs, you'd be a gold contender. That's some suction power you have there." He had to say something to stop the overwhelming need to break down and cry.

"Come here. I need to hold you." Dylan moved closer while still on his knees, putting his cheek to Riley's chest as Riley wrapped his arms around him. They stayed in the same position for a couple of minutes.

"Um, I could do with getting off my knees now," Dylan said. "These floorboards are a bit hard."

"Oh, hell. Sorry. Get undressed and let's get under the duvet." He stood and pulled back the cover while Dylan stripped. Riley had been right about those pelvic bones. Dylan's erection stood clear of neatly trimmed bright red pubic hair. His balls hung low and full. Riley found himself longing to bury his face in those curls. He shifted over, but instead of lying next to him, Dylan sat astride his chest with his cock almost hitting Riley's chin, his intention clear. Riley opened his mouth and caught the drip of clear liquid on his tongue. This he could do.

"Nice cock and balls," he said.

Dylan edged forward. "Thank you, and your chest hair is tickling my thighs, in an enjoyable way."

He held his cock and bopped it on Riley's chin before positioning himself over Riley so the tip of his erection fitted into Riley's welcoming mouth. Then he leaned over, placing both hands on the headboard. Riley made an O-shape and Dylan thrust. A little at first then more until he touched the back of Riley's throat. He opened to accept him, his gag reflex long gone after years of practice. Riley sucked hard, providing a warm damp tunnel and using his tongue to stimulate the ridge underneath. Dylan didn't need to be as careful as he was, but in this position, he could hardly tell him.

"You have an amazing mouth," Dylan said.

Riley wrapped his arms around Dylan's back and grabbed his arse to pull him deeper.

"Oh hell, how aren't you gagging? I don't know about me winning gold. You've more suction than a Hoover. Oh yeah, just like that. Nearly there."

Riley let his fingers wander toward Dylan's entrance, brushing over the puckered skin.

Dylan lurched at his touch. "So bloody good. Close now. Oh hell, yeah, there. Suck me, please. Make me come."

Riley pressed a finger inside Dylan, who jerked. His cock hit the back of Riley's throat. Riley hardly paused as Dylan tensed. He braced himself to swallow, but at the last moment, Dylan reared away and grabbed his cock, taking hurried strokes before finally squeezing out his orgasm and covering Riley's chest and chin in white streaks. He reached out his tongue to lick off a stray bit of liquid, loving the bitter taste, while Dylan sat back on his heels, resting on Riley's stomach his deflating cock still in hand, breathing heavily.

"Bugger me. That was every bit as brilliant as I dreamed it would be." He glanced down. "Sorry, I've got cum in your chest hair. I'll need to get a towel or something, or it'll be nasty in the morning." He made to move.

"Stay a minute," Riley said, not sure of why.

"Are you okay?" Dylan asked. "That was truly awesome. Can I sleep with you? I told the parents if I was late, I wouldn't disturb them, with them getting up early to work in the shops. Mum does the papers so she's up at five and it's now after one."

Talk of his friends brought Riley back to reality. He'd had sex with his childhood friend's son. What would Tony do if he found out? Would he punch him, accuse him of cradle-snatching? Doubt wrapped itself around his heart. Despite his misgivings, he didn't feel as if he'd just made the biggest mistake of his life. He'd wanted Dylan and Dylan had wanted him. The man lying next to him was just that—a man—a gorgeous, generous, wonderful man who'd brought fun back into Riley's life for the first time in forever. *Fuck it. I want to wake up not on my own in the morning.*

"I'd love you to stay. We can have breakfast, then go off to the animal shelter and maybe have lunch somewhere. Then it's the bonfire and fireworks display on the village green. I can't remember the last time I went to such an event."

Dylan leaned forward and kissed him. "I'll go and get that towel." He hurried out of the door, giving Riley a magnificent view of his arse, then returned a minute later with a flannel ready to wash off the remnants of his orgasm. Riley grabbed his hand as he cleaned. "Thank you for tonight, for Blackpool, not just this, though this was incredible."

Dylan finished his task and threw the flannel onto the chest of drawers. "I told you. This was a dream come true for me, and I don't want the dream to be over any time soon. I want you, Riley Ormerod. I want to be a part of your life for as long as you'll have me. I want to sleep in your arms and wake up with you. I may be relatively young, but I've always had an old head on these shoulders, and, as I said, I've always known what I wanted and gone for it."

Riley had no idea how to answer, so he opened his arms, and Dylan settled down against him with his cheek pressed to Riley's chest. In the dark, his emotions threatened to get the better of him. This experience was so different from what he'd known for nearly twenty years. For some reason this man wanted him and, despite his panic and reservations about the age difference, Riley couldn't deny wanting Dylan too. For now, it was just them in the dark. He hoped Dylan wouldn't mind keeping it that way. The rest of the world didn't have to exist yet. He kissed the top of Dylan's head.

"Stop thinking, Riley, and get some sleep. I want you bright-eyed and bushy-tailed in the morning, ready for round two."

"You'll be the death of me," he murmured.

"Yeah, but what a wonderful way to go." Dylan snuggled against him. Riley pushed away all his doubts and fears, then closed his eyes and let sleep take him away, smiling to himself about what the next day might bring.

Chapter Fourteen

Dylan bumped the door open with his elbow and carried the tray into the room. Riley lay, still asleep, his head on the pillow. In the light coming from the gap above the curtain, Dylan could see hints of silver among the dark strands of hair on Riley's chest and head. Riley sniffed then opened his eyes.

"I thought I was dreaming, but it appears I'm not. You didn't need to make breakfast." He sat up, rubbing his face.

"I wanted to," Dylan said, placing the tray on the bedside cabinet. "It's only scrambled egg on toast, and tea."

"It smells wonderful. The kitchen will be out of bounds from tomorrow while I'm having the new one fitted."

"You didn't show me what you'd decided to have done." Dylan passed a plate and cutlery to Riley who took a big bite of the toast and crunched before swallowing.

"They're taking everything out. I'm having wooden units painted jade green with beech worktops and handles. There'll be a fitted oven, microwave and dishwasher as well as a gas hob and a Belfast sink. I did think about getting a range but decided against. The floor will have stone tiles. It needs to be leveled, which is a pain. There will be matching green splashbacks and the walls will be painted cream. The table and chairs will stay. When that's finished, I'm having the bathroom done and I'll get the decorators in to spruce up the rooms. I might even invest in a new bed."

"Wow, you're serious, aren't you? The wallpaper in my bedroom's been there for years. I'm glad you've not chosen gray. Everyone seems to have gray kitchens or bedrooms." Dylan crunched into the toast and glanced around the room. "You get the morning sun in here such as it is." He settled down next to Riley, still eating and hoping not too many crumbs escaped.

"About last night," Riley said.

Dylan finished the toast and put down the plate so he could concentrate on Riley. "I enjoyed every moment of it, so I don't want to hear any regrets."

"I don't have any regrets. A few worries, yes, but no regrets. We need to make a few decisions."

Dylan sighed. "Do we? Can't we simply enjoy each other for a little while? I've got a list of activities I'm keen to explore."

"Oh, really?"

Dylan loved the way Riley couldn't stop himself smiling.

"And what would this list consist of?"

"Hmm, let me think. More sex obviously, in a variety of ways and positions. When your new kitchen is finished, we could christen it, and I hope you're getting a big shower enclosure as well as a bath?"

"You want to have sex in a bath?" Riley asked.

"Why not? I want to have sex everywhere with you." He rolled on top of Riley and kissed him. "I want you inside me and me inside you. I want us to rub together like we are now until we explode. I've always fancied being bent over a desk covered in spreadsheets of accounts having my arse fucked or rimmed. Do you rim?" He felt Riley's erection press into his and wriggled then saw the redness in his cheeks.

"Sorry, I didn't mean to embarrass you. Only I don't think there's any point in pussyfooting around. You should say what you like, what you need. For example, last night I discovered you like this if the noises you made were anything to go by." He licked one of Riley's nipples, then sucked while pressing down with his groin, enjoying the friction. Deciding to up the stakes, he used his teeth to nip at the hardened nub and the skin around it. Riley moved underneath him, meeting his thrusts.

"So," he said, grinning, "do you rim? Because my arse loves a good tongue fuck."

Riley nodded. But there was something else. Riley had stopped moving. Dylan brushed back the hair from Riley's face. There was panic in his eyes.

"Riley? Are you okay? I know I can be full-on. Have I gone too far?"

"No, it's just..."

"What?" He sat up, still astride Riley's hips. "Tell me. I like to talk. It's a fault of mine. I promise I won't be shocked." *What the hell's going on behind those worried eyes?*

"I'm not sure this is the time or the place."

"If something is bothering you, then I want to know, whatever it is. I'm not just here for the sex, Riley. Tell me." Riley's Adam's apple bobbed as he swallowed, and he looked anywhere but at him.

"I was with Nate a long time —"

"I know, and I don't care."

"Please let me say this. It's not easy. It'll change the way you see me."

Dylan wanted to assure him nothing he said could do that, but he remained silent and waited while Riley clutched the sheet either side of him and stared at the ceiling.

"Nate liked to have sex his way. He topped — always. He'd dress me how he wanted me dressed, and always fucked me from behind, pressing my head down into the mattress or the floor. Oh God, this is so…"

Dylan reached out and squeezed Riley's hand as he breathed in and out, lifting his shoulders to calm himself.

"Sometimes he'd fuck one of his university groupies. He made no secret of it. Said they meant nothing. We didn't exactly have an open relationship, but I gave him his freedom as long as he didn't rub my nose in it."

Shit! Dylan swallowed back the lump forming in his throat. "Okay, I'm listening."

"There was always a student or three willing to offer his arse to the great barrister. I'd been one of them, after all. Usually he'd fuck them somewhere else, but then he brought one home, knowing I'd find them. He wanted me to join in, to spice things up. He kept fucking this bloke he'd picked up somewhere. This one wasn't even a student, just some gym bunny. I didn't move. I stood there and watched, exactly like he wanted me to. Don't get me wrong, he didn't ever hit me, or force me, or tie me up, but I didn't say no to whatever he wanted either. In the end, I think he did it to provoke me. He wanted me to argue, to fight back so he could force me. He said I'd got staid and boring like some country bumpkin wife."

Dylan wasn't sure what to say. He'd guessed there was something, but that Riley had given away so much control, even down to how he dressed, when he was a highly qualified professional who could surely have afforded to leave at any time he wanted, confused him. He needed to be positive.

"But you managed to leave him in the end. *You* decided, and *you* got out of there."

"The day before this happened, I'd had a new client whose partner had done the same to her. I didn't usually work such cases, but this was a pro bono at a place I did some voluntary work. The more she explained, the more I saw myself in her. She made me question my whole existence. When I found them in our bed, when he taunted me, it was too much on top of finding out about my dad. Sue, his carer, had phoned me that afternoon as I drove home. I'd just signed a multi-million-pound deal on a development of apartments. I'd bought champagne to celebrate and Sue told me my father had terminal cancer. I didn't know. He hadn't wanted to bother me. Then I found Nate and something in me snapped. I packed a bag, got in my car and drove."

"Have you spoken to him since?"

"No need. I didn't want anything from him. He'd chosen all my clothes, so I left them and bought some myself. I'd managed to fill one backpack after twenty years. I nearly went back a few times, but Dad needed me. He didn't talk to me much, except about Mum. We didn't have any sort of amazing father and son reunion. I didn't tell him I was gay. But I've no regrets. I'm glad I was here for him. So, do you still want to do all those things with me now you know the truth? I'll understand if you've changed your mind."

Had he? Despite his doubts, to him, Riley was still a confident, professional, older man. This information had turned all he'd ever thought on its head. Riley obviously had issues to work through. *Am I up for that? I have to be. This has never been simply a need for a little fun.* It wasn't love, not quite, not yet, but he had no doubt it could be.

"Dylan?"

"No, I haven't changed my mind, but maybe we should slow up and get to know each other more. Give ourselves more than the time we've had in the car."

"You mean go out on a few dates?" Finally, Riley lowered his head and met Dylan's gaze.

"Yeah, perhaps we need to explore each other first before we announce ourselves to the world, to my parents. I tend to go at things like a bull in a china shop. Dad always keeps me away from the breakables. Let's get up and dressed then go out to the rescue center and find you the perfect pet. They always listen even when you talk nonsense. Then we can find somewhere for Sunday lunch and have our first official date. I've one condition."

"Okay…"

"You never refer to our age difference as an obstacle to us being together. I don't care about your age. I never have. Everything else we work through. Deal?"

"Deal."

Riley couldn't quite believe he'd managed to tell Dylan so much, but it had felt so good to unburden himself. Dylan hadn't judged him, at least not out loud. Making himself so vulnerable had taken all his courage, but he needed Dylan to understand he wasn't the cool, calm, collected professional man Dylan might have thought him to be. He was a work in progress, still figuring out his own likes and dislikes, needs and wants. Even choosing color schemes had thrown him.

The apartment had been white. Now he could have walls with bookcases full of books and colorful spines rather than having them behind doors so they wouldn't spoil the look. He could have wood and not stainless steel in the kitchen. He could have a conservatory and, today, he could choose a pet. He grinned. He wanted the hairiest cat or dog he could find, or one of each. Size and breed didn't matter. He pulled on his jeans and a pale blue jumper and ran a comb through his hair. He liked it longer.

Dylan was sitting at the kitchen table when he arrived downstairs. "I made us another coffee. It's chilly out there, with some freezing fog by the look of it. I've checked on the directions for the rescue place. It's this side of Burnley, so it won't take us long to get there. Have you decided what you want?"

"Not really," Riley said, taking a seat, grateful Dylan had changed the topic of conversation. "I just want something furry. A cat or a dog or both—nothing too big. And we won't simply be able to take one away today. They check you out first, so I'll need to make sure I can get someone to walk a dog as they don't approve of leaving them all day. I don't want a puppy, too much work, but a slightly older dog or cat would be good."

"Shall we go as soon as we've finished these, then?" Dylan said chuckling.

"They are open at ten." He caught Dylan smiling at him. "What? Okay, I might be a smidgen excited."

Dylan got up, came around behind him and hugged him. "I love how excited you are. Come on, let's go. The sooner we get there, the sooner you can choose."

* * * *

An hour or so later, at the animal shelter, the volunteer showed them the occupants of another pen. A photograph showed two dogs and a cat. "These three were brought in after their owner died. We'd like to keep them together if we can, especially the dogs, but if you fancy a cat as well, this would be the perfect solution. As I said, we'd need to do a house check, but a detached house set away from main roads with an enclosed garden sounds perfect for them, and you say there's a local dog walker."

Riley knelt to pet the dogs, a seven-year-old pug and an eight-year-old terrier type. The terrier rolled over onto her back and wriggled as he rubbed her belly. He had to admit these two sweeties would be perfect. He glanced at Dylan, who stood smiling at the door. "Can we see the cat?"

"Of course. We did have someone interested in her, but we've held out to see if anyone would take all three. She's a real beauty. Will there be any younger children in the house or just you and your son?"

Before Riley could reply, Dylan spoke. "Oh, I'm not his son. I'm here to make sure he doesn't take all the animals home with him." He winked, and Riley's face filled with heat.

The woman laughed. "I get that. You don't want to know how many I have at home. Just as well my partner is as soft as me." She put the dogs back into the pen and led them toward the cat section.

"Stop it," Dylan whispered in his ear as they followed. "It doesn't matter what she said."

Riley nodded but said nothing. They passed through a couple of doors into another long corridor with cat pens on either side. Some meowed loudly, while others cowered at the back of the cages or in their beds or boxes.

"Here we are. This is Queenie."

"Great name," Dylan said.

Riley's heart melted. She was beautiful with long black hair and a smidgen of white on her chest. Her gaze, through beautiful green eyes, appeared to be assessing him. "Can we open the door?"

"Of course. She's friendly, loves to cuddle and bosses the dogs. I've never seen her run anywhere. She parades up and down here with her tail in the air as if she owns the place. That's why the lady who owned her named her Queenie."

With the glass door open, Queenie stood. Riley reached toward her and, with one graceful jump, she landed on him and he gathered her in. She head-butted his chin and purred like an engine as he ran his hand over her fur. "You are gorgeous, aren't you? So, would you like to come live with me? I have a big house where you can hide from the dogs if you want to, and a garden. Does she go out?"

"She did in her previous home. She can be fussy about food and loves biscuits more. You'll need to feed her away from the dogs, but she will bat them away. So, what do you think?"

Riley turned to Dylan. "Will three be too many?"

"The dogs are small, and Isabel will walk them for you. You could easily dog-proof the garden and use a flap big enough to let them out. Come on, can't you imagine us all cuddled up on the sofa of an evening?"

Riley glanced at the assistant. If she'd thought anything about Dylan's remark, her face didn't show it. "When could I have them? I'm having a new kitchen put in this week, so it would be better if they aren't there then. Could I have them next weekend?"

"I don't see why not. Queenie has voted with her paws. We'll get someone around to do a quick visit in the next couple of days. We have a leaflet explaining what to buy for them and lots of advice. If you have any problems, you can contact us, but I can't see any difficulties with these three. All they need is love, food and somewhere to sleep. If you'd like to fill in the paperwork, we'll get the ball rolling. They are all spayed and vaccinated so are ready to go. I'm just happy they can go together."

Back outside a while later, Riley sat in his car, gripping the wheel. "Oh my God. I'm adopting three of them. Am I mad? I can't wait to get them now. They won't turn me down, will they?"

"Don't be daft. You can give all of them a great life. They were practically grabbing your hands off. Will you keep their names?"

"They're used to them now — Bonnie, Millie and Queenie."

"And they're the perfect size for little outfits. Can you imagine them at Christmas?" Dylan clapped his hands. "Oh, how much gayer could I get?" He leaned over and kissed Riley. "Let's celebrate. Take me to lunch."

Christmas was now only seven weeks away. Riley didn't want to let himself imagine what it might be like this year after he'd spent the day with his father the year before. He'd been so ill at that stage, they'd been discussing him going into a hospice. In the end, he'd died in his own bed. This year, Riley would have the girls to wake up with and spoil. He grinned. He was already imagining them together.

"What?" Dylan said. "You've got a secret smile. What contorted little thoughts have broken loose?"

"Nothing really, just about all the stuff I'll have to buy." He didn't want to think about the day itself, about the possibility of them being together, about telling others and coming out. He couldn't allow himself, not yet. He put the car into gear. The pub wasn't far, and he found he felt surprisingly hungry.

Chapter Fifteen

"I can't believe you've never played a computer game."

"I don't have a Facebook page or Twitter, either," Riley replied. "I've never felt the need to share the minutiae of my life with others. Why do people take photos of their food? It's beyond me. And selfies? I take photos of places and people. In my defense, I do have a Kindle."

Dylan swallowed the last of his main course and moaned with pleasure. "We must come back here. The food is wonderful, but I don't think I've room for pudding. I fancy a coffee, though. And *I* don't have a Kindle. I must admit, I don't read enough. Math was always my thing at school, not English. What should I read?"

Riley pushed away his plate, let out a small burp, went red and apologized while glancing around to see if anyone had noticed. "Sorry, it's been a while since I had such rich food. Eating out in London means lots of fancy stuff that doesn't fill you up but looks pretty. I had to do a lot of business lunches then spend time in the gym. At least having the dogs will get me out again. And as for reading, I'm no expert. I used to read to Dad when he couldn't. He loved crime books, particularly Agatha Christie. I used to say it must spoil it if you knew who did it, but he still insisted on hearing the same ones mixed in with the odd John Le Carré or Raymond Chandler."

"You've a great voice. I bet you read well. You've lost most of your accent, living in London."

The waiter cleared their plates, and they ordered coffee.

"I suppose what you should read depends on what you're into. There are the classics, of course, Dickens, Austen, the Brontës, but you might like science fiction or fantasy. What about *The Hobbit* or *The Lord of the Rings*? You might like Douglas Adams, too."

"I've seen the films and watched *The Hitchhikers' Guide to the Galaxy* with Dad. I do love films, especially old black and white ones. I bet I've seen every one of the Marx Brothers'."

"That'll be your dad's influence. He loved all those, Laurel and Hardy, Abbott and Costello, The Three Stooges. Your granddad loved them too. What about gay lit?"

"Don't they all end in someone dying? I saw *Brokeback Mountain* and a few others, but they were always so sad."

"There's always gay romance. Lots of them have happy endings and interesting sex."

"What, like chick lit for men? I can't imagine reading that," Dylan said.

"It's mostly read and written by women. I have some on my Kindle. I read all sorts. And as for gay films, what about *Pride* or *Maurice* or *My Beautiful Laundrette*? There's *God's Own Country*, set in Yorkshire. We could see if it's on in Preston and go if you want to."

"I'd love it. We could get a burger." He noticed Riley pull a face. "You're going to tell me you've never had a Big Mac, aren't you?"

Riley raised his eyebrows. "Guilty as charged. I've always been a bit wary. I do eat pizza and Chinese."

"It's a date, then. Fast food and the pictures. Now, what shall we do this afternoon? The bonfire is lit at seven and the fireworks at eight as well as the barbecue and drinks. We could go back to yours..." He left Riley to fill in the gaps.

"Oh, I see what you mean." Riley's face burned red again. Dylan winked at him. "Drink up, then, and all this could be yours."

* * * *

"I need to shower before we go out." Dylan flicked at his chest. "I've your jizz all over me." He loved teasing Riley, whose face and neck had reddened immediately.

"I'm not sure I can stand," Riley replied. "You go ahead. I'll lie here for a while and follow you in later."

"Shame you can't join me. When you have the bathroom updated, don't forget to get a shower big enough for two." Dylan shivered at the thought of pressing Riley against the tiles, fucking him as water flowed over their joined bodies. His cock twitched. *Bloody hell. If I keep this up, I'll have to slap another one out.* He stood, totally naked without any care at all, then turned to see Riley lying back with his hands over his head and chest exposed.

He stepped closer to the bed, smirking broadly. "Are you absolutely certain you couldn't go again? We've time before the food arrives."

"Get going and leave this old man alone." Riley's smile did something to Dylan's heart. Nearly every fantasy he'd had about the man in front of him had come true, but instead of feeling sated, he wanted more. He pushed away a worry.

"I won't be long. Don't fall asleep."

"Cheeky bastard. I'm wide awake."

In the shower, Dylan let his mind drift to thoughts of doing this every day. Sleeping together at night, waking in the morning, drinking, eating, going places. When they were together, it sounded so simple, but how would others react? The woman in the rescue center had assumed they were father and son and others would undoubtedly do the same. Dylan didn't care, but he'd seen how awkward Riley felt. Then there was his father. How would he react to his friend fucking his son—not that he had. He suspected his mother had some idea. Mothers often knew their children enough to guess these things, but his father?

As he washed, he recalled the day he'd told his dad about being gay. He'd said nothing for a while then his first words had been, '*I suppose I sort of hoped you weren't.*' Dylan had nearly bitten his lip in an effort not to ask why. His father had continued after a few minutes of silence.

'*I worry, that's all. I want you to be happy, to find someone to love who'll love you, to get married and have children. There are so many dangers out there. I've read the papers.*'

'*Dad, I can get married now. I can settle down if I find someone. I can have children. I'm not planning on attending* sex parties or behaving stupidly and putting myself in danger.'

'But there are men, older men who could –'

'The same might happen to Kayleigh. I'll make mistakes, Dad, but I've got to make them for myself. I've known I was gay since before I can remember. That's not going to change. I'm not bisexual. I've never looked at a girl and felt anything. Are we okay?'

His father had stood and hugged him. 'Of course we're okay. You're my son. I love you, and I worry about you in the same way as your sister. I want you to feel you can come to your mum and me if you need to. It's a tough world out there, and you're not making it any easier for yourself. There's still prejudice no matter what the law says, and it breaks my heart people might hurt you simply because of who you love.'

Dylan washed the suds off, grabbed a towel and wrapped it around his waist. Maybe his dad would be all right with him and Riley because he hated lying and tonight would be the beginning of doing exactly that, until Riley was ready.

"We'll see you tomorrow morning around ten then." Dylan watched Riley shake hands with the kitchen fitters. He'd helped Riley move the last of the kitchen's contents into the dining room. For a week he'd be living on microwave meals or eating out. They'd already arranged a couple of nights out together.

"You look happy," Dylan said as they walked through the village to the community center.

"I can't wait for next weekend. A new kitchen with all the mod cons and everything built in, with a new floor and splashbacks. All that lovely wood and those drawers that close themselves with a place for everything, all before the three amigos arrive next weekend. You are coming with me to collect them, aren't you?"

"Of course. I wouldn't miss helping them settle in. Let's get some food. Mum and Dad must be around here somewhere."

They strolled across to the community center. Luckily the night had stayed fine. No one liked a bonfire in the rain.

"There you are." His dad put out a hand for Riley to shake. *Old people are strange. Except Riley isn't old.* "Your mum is helping with the food. There's a good spread this year."

"I'll get us something, shall I?" Riley said. "You talk to your dad."

"Great. If they've quiche, get me some. Real men do eat it." Riley made his way across the room while Dylan sat with his father.

"I hope you weren't annoying and on your phone all the time," Tony said. "How were the lights?"

"They were amazing. You should have gone. Maybe next year. You and Mum should have more time together—maybe a weekend away. I could look after the shop if you want. I'm sure Riley would help. You hardly ever get holidays. You could go to London, take Mum to a show."

"Sounds like you're trying to get rid of us. And I'm sure Riley has better things to do with his weekend. Don't become a nuisance, lad. You don't want him getting fed up with you and not giving you a lift. He's had a lot to put up with by the sound of it."

"That's why he needs taking out of himself. I think he's forgotten how to have fun."

"You have other friends, Dylan. Friends your age. Riley needs to find his own way. You do understand, don't you? He's a kind man and he wouldn't tell you..."

"Here we are." Riley put two plates on the table. "Did he tell you about the pet rescue center this morning?"

"No," Tony said, glancing at both of them.

"I'm adopting two dogs and a cat. They had an elderly owner who died, and they wanted them kept together, so I'm picking them up next Saturday if the house visit goes okay. I need to speak to Isabel Parkinson about walking the dogs when I'm at work. Dylan thought she'd be here."

"Three? All at once? Wow, you don't do anything by halves, do you?"

"I always wanted a pet, but Dad would never have them. Now the house is mine, I can do what I want. The new kitchen will be fitted, then I'm going to do the bathroom and get rid of the old dark furniture. I'm looking forward to it. The dogs will get me out of the house as well. I need the exercise and fresh air. I've been treading water. Dylan's showed me that. He has a mature head on his young shoulders. Not everyone his age has ambition like he does."

Someone tapped a microphone. "Hello, everyone, we're about to light the bonfire. Bring your food if you want but remember to put the rubbish in the bags provided. We don't want to litter the green."

"Come on," Dylan said. "The fireworks will be set off soon as well." He wanted to hold out his hand to Riley, but he didn't. Some of his father's words had increased his wariness. Riley had been right. They needed to go slow.

They milled with the crowd on the green while they lit the bonfire. Someone threw the guy on the fire and the flames shot up from the bottom creating light and warmth.

"It's quite gruesome really, celebrating the torture and execution of someone every year by throwing his effigy on a huge great pile of burning wood."

"Well, Guy Fawkes did try to blow up the King and Parliament," Riley pointed out.

Dylan shivered then tucked his hands into his pockets, wishing he'd brought some gloves. Children ran around, making patterns in the air with sparklers.

"We never came to these," Riley said. "I begged for fireworks and Mum got us some a couple of times, but Dad said they were a waste of money, literally going up in smoke. I can't remember the last time I went to a display."

"Not even to New Year's in London? They are spectacular. I'd love to see them for real. You must have seen them."

"Odd flashes in the sky. We usually had a party at the apartment. I watched it on the TV with Dad last year. He mumbled about the waste then. This is nice, though, getting the village together."

"Found you." Lori Hargreaves appeared out of the crowd and threaded her arm through those of her husband and son. "Did you have a fun time in Blackpool?"

"Wonderful," Riley said. "I'd forgotten how good the fish and chips taste out of paper. And today we went to the rescue center, and I'm going to adopt a couple of dogs and a cat. Have you seen Isabel? I need to ask if she can walk them in the daytime when I'm at work."

"That'll be nice. They'll be company for you."

A red flash lit the sky as the first rocket flew up. Another followed another, with assorted colors sending all faces staring upward. Dylan gazed at Riley's face. His eyes shone with flecks of light and his smile sent butterflies fluttering in Dylan's chest. Hell, he wanted to kiss him. He leaned closer. "Come with me. We'll say we're taking the rubbish back."

Dylan collected the plates and carried everything with Riley to the side of the hall. With everyone staring at the fireworks, he pressed Riley against the wall and kissed him. "Sorry, I just had to. Your face watching those colors lighting up the sky. I wanted to hug you there and then."

Light from the fireworks reflected in Riley's blue eyes. He wrapped his arms around Dylan pulling him closer, pressing their bodies together. "Thank you for making this weekend special. I can't remember the last time I had so much fun."

Dylan grinned. He liked this bolder version. "Fun is my middle name." He leaned in and kissed Riley again, placing his hands in Riley's pockets while grinding against him lost in the taste and smell of the man, totally oblivious to the rest of the world.

"What the fuck!"

Riley jerked his head hitting the wall behind him while Dylan stepped back. "Dad."

His father stood there, his face contorted into a grimace. He raised his arm. "You, go back to your mother, now. What the hell were you thinking? Anyone could have seen you."

Dylan stood his ground. Against the wall, Riley stood completely white. All color had leached from his face. He stared at the ground, saying nothing.

"I don't care. I'm not a kid for you to send to my room, Dad. I'm a grown-up. I'm not going anywhere.

We weren't doing anything wrong. This has nothing to do with you."

Tony took one step forward. "I don't care how old you are, Dylan. This man is twice your age."

"Dylan, you should go." Riley finally found his voice. Dylan grabbed his hand, but Riley pulled away. "I can't. I shouldn't have. You need to go." A single tear dropping from Riley's cheek threatened to break Dylan's heart. "Please, don't make this worse. Listen to your father. You and I were a moment of madness."

"No, Riley, you don't believe that. I know you don't. He'll tell you I'm too young to know my own mind, and I'm not. I pinned you against the wall, not the other way around. I made all the running here. Everything we've done, I wanted. I won't be told to go to my room like some naughty child." *Please don't do this. Fight for us.*

Instead, Riley grabbed Dylan's arms and shook him. "Don't you see, he's right? We never had a future, no matter what you say. I let myself be persuaded otherwise. I wanted it to be true, but we're both living in cloud-cuckoo land. In a few years' time, you'd tire of me. Better to end this now before either of us is in too deep."

A vast hollow opened in his chest. He wanted to throw up. His knees threatened to buckle. This couldn't be happening. Everything had been perfect and now… "Riley, please…"

Lori appeared behind her husband. "Tony, what's going on? You're missing the display." Then she saw them. "Dylan? Riley?"

"I caught them snogging," Tony said. "God knows what else they've been up to. My so-called best friend and my son. I don't want to even think about it."

Dylan gazed at his mother. He saw the lack of surprise in her eyes. If only he could get her on his side, their side. "This is stupid. I'm going nowhere. I'm not leaving Riley here with you so you can persuade him not to see me anymore."

Riley sagged against him. "Dylan, please don't make this harder than it is. Your dad's right. I'm too old for you. Go with them. I told you, this was a stupid moment. That's all it is, a passing phase. You got me at a weak time. You're going to get fed up of me, and I couldn't bear going through all the heartache of losing someone again, or seeing them leave me for someone else, someone their own age. Please understand."

Anger welled up in him. Dylan spat out his words. "Don't tell me what I want. You'll miss me, Riley. You'll miss the person who loves you because others might disapprove, or because you feel embarrassed at the age difference between us, or you don't trust me to know what I want. You're just like him." Dylan turned to face his parents.

"I'm not a teenager anymore. I know my own mind. I've always known what I wanted." His father shrugged. He turned his attention back to Riley.

"Don't you see, Dylan? I don't trust myself, either, and I'm not prepared to tear your family apart. Your dad loves you."

Dylan attempted to take Riley's hand but he pulled away. "Dad will get over us. He's just shocked, that's all. And I won't walk away from you when you get older. Don't you see? I've loved you for so long. My dream has become a reality, and it's so much better than I ever imagined it could be. We fit, and not just in bed, and there we fit spectacularly." Fuck his parents being there. "I *know* you're older. Duh. That's hardly a shock. I don't have a thing about older men. I have a thing about you. So, run and hide if you want, Riley. Lock yourself away and tell yourself you aren't worth it, but I won't give up and I'll be here waiting until you come to your senses."

He didn't want to say he wouldn't wait forever, that would give Riley a chance to say *I told you so*. He couldn't believe their beginning was about to be snatched away from him so soon.

"Okay, so be it, but you know where to find me." He started to stride away, but Riley grabbed his arm and he stopped, letting hope slip in between the anger.

"Don't go like this, Dylan. Don't be angry at your parents. They're only thinking what's best for you. I'll go." Riley stumbled away, finally running toward the main road.

Dylan's father stepped forward and wrapped his arms around him. Dylan wriggled free and stared into the distance. "No, let me go. Don't you understand? I thought you were his friend. He needs me. I made him laugh. I don't think he's laughed for so long. He's not strong like me. Fucking hell. I can't believe you've done this."

"It's for your own good, son. If Riley has problems, he needs to work them out for himself. Like he said, you're far too young to get involved with a man twice your age with his own demons."

Dylan stepped back. Riley had disappeared into the darkness. "I don't care. I love him, Dad. I've loved him for years."

"Now you do sound like a child. It's a crush, like you'd have on a teacher. You'll get over it. I'll take you to Clitheroe in the morning. You can get a bus from there. I can open the shop later until we can find someone else to give you a lift. There must be someone where you work who lives out this way. Or I can drop you at the railway station every day. We'll work it out."

Dylan thought his heart might break. Riley hadn't fought for him. And now he sounded like some Disney princess. He'd give it time, but this wasn't over. If Riley wouldn't fight for him, he'd have to do the fighting himself.

Chapter Sixteen

He hadn't slept. His mobile remained switched off. As Riley stepped out of his door, he half expected to find Dylan waiting by the car. The dull, overcast weather matched his mood. A hint of wood smoke filled the air from the bonfire of the night before.

He climbed in the car, turned on the radio and turned it off again when they played a certain track. At the end of his short road, he almost turned left but instead he turned right out of the village toward the motorway. This morning there would be no one with him, no one making him laugh, no one singing along with the radio, no one telling him stories, no one making his heart flutter, or his body desire. All he had to do was convince himself he'd made the right decision.

At his office, Riley grabbed his post without engaging in conversation, followed by a much-needed large black coffee, then he settled himself at his desk. Outside, rain pattered against the window. The next thing he heard was a knock at his office door. He glanced up to see Katie put her head around his door.

"It's gone ten," she said. "We're gathered in the conference room for the weekly briefing."

Riley swallowed the cold coffee. "Sorry, slipped my mind. I'll be there now."

She stepped into the room. "Is everything all right? It's just you look terrible. Are you ill?"

"No, it's nothing, just a touch of insomnia. I'm having a new kitchen fitted this week and everything is upside down at the house."

"Well, there's hot coffee and cake if the others haven't eaten it all. It's my birthday."

Riley sighed. "I'm sorry, I forgot with everything. Happy birthday, Katie. Do you have any plans?" He stood and gathered together the documents he needed for the meeting.

"Matt's taking me out for dinner tonight. I had a party with the family yesterday."

"Good, that sounds like fun. We'd better get going."

Riley sat through the meeting, saying little except when he needed to. Fortunately, today didn't have anything too demanding on the agenda. He drank the coffee this time and took a slice of cake back to his office. Would Dylan tell Matt? Would Matt tell Katie? Why had he let things get out of hand? He should have known better—a man his age. What the hell had he been thinking? It could never work. He slammed his hand down on the table and immediately regretted it as pain shot through his wrist.

For the rest of the morning, Riley worked his way through his emails, arranged some meetings and made phone calls to a few clients about various property sales. That afternoon he was seeing a couple about making their wills. He couldn't say he was looking forward to the meeting. The man was a long-standing client who had recently remarried. He owned a considerable number of assets even after the divorce, which Riley's partner had handled. His new wife was thirty years his junior. *And Dylan is twenty years younger than you. Everyone can be foolish and turned by a pretty face. Enough.*

He extracted his mobile from his briefcase and turned it on — twenty messages. The first was a reply to the one he'd sent to Tony as soon as he'd arrived home. The one in which he'd told him he would end the relationship. Tony's reply was brief and to the point — *Good.*

The other messages came from Dylan. He deleted each of them without reading. The last text had come from the rescue center, giving him a time for their visit. Should he go ahead? He couldn't cancel now. They needed a home and he needed them. He couldn't bear the thought of being there on his own, rattling around in that place — lonely again. And after hoping he and Tony had cleared the air, now he didn't have him to talk to either. *Everything's such a fucking mess.* Putting down his pen, Riley placed his elbows on the table and his head in his hands. He had no one. A single tear ran down one cheek. This time yesterday the future had been full of promise, of love and a life, and now twenty-four hours later... *Happiness is so fleeting.*

The next five days passed in a blur. The kitchen fitting went surprisingly well with no problems. Riley had to admit they'd done a superb job. The home check had gone equally well, and he'd arranged to pick up the three amigos as he called them on Saturday morning. Every night, bang on ten-thirty, he'd received a text from Dylan. Every time he deleted the text without reading its contents. He kept telling himself he'd done the right thing. Dylan would meet someone of his own age and be happy.

But what about me?

He jumped at a knock on the back door. The person didn't wait. "Only me."

Sue. To be honest, he was surprised she hadn't popped in earlier. He was sure the grapevine would have been vibrating with the news. He could imagine what people were saying about him.

"In the kitchen," he called back.

"I thought I'd come and see how it looked." Sue glanced around the room. "No, don't get up. I'll make us a pot of tea, shall I?" He knew from experience saying no to Sue would be a waste of time.

"They've done a grand job, and I like the wood." She made the tea and placed the mug in front of him. "So, are you going to tell me what's going on with you? The village wire says you aren't giving a certain young man a lift to work anymore."

Riley couldn't help himself. He didn't care if men didn't cry. He'd cried once over Nate, and not at all when his father died, but now tears flowed, and he couldn't stop them. Sue jumped up and put her arms around him. For several minutes, his body shook as the floodgates opened.

"It's all right. You let it all out, lovey." Sue's voice soothed him. "Sometimes you need to let go of everything."

He muttered a "Thank you" between sobs until he pulled away. Sue passed him some paper towel and he wiped his eyes. "I'm sorry—not very manly."

"Who gets to say how a man should behave? Not me, that's for certain. Do you want to talk about it?"

"I don't know."

"It could help."

Sue might only be ten years older than him, but she often acted like the mother he'd lost when far too young. "Oh, Sue, I've made such a mess of my life. I wasted nearly twenty years on a man who didn't really love me, doing a job I didn't like, helping wealthy men make even more money at the expense of others. Then I came home to watch my father die and ended up alone in this place. I should have sold up and gone somewhere else, but no, I stayed, hoping to recover my past and find the friends I once had. Finally, a young man showed interest in me, and, flattered, I told myself it was okay. He made me feel things, woke up bits of me I thought were long dead, so much so I began looking forward to his dopey smile."

"Ah."

"Yes, ah."

"So, he dumped you?" She placed a hand on his arm.

"Oh no. I finished it. Tony saw us kissing on Bonfire Night and lost it. I finished it. Dylan needs someone his own age. He's just too young to realize. When I'm sixty, he'll be forty. I have no right to tie him down to an old man."

"You've made the decision for him, then, you and Tony. Pardon my French, but for fuck's sake, he's twenty-two, not twelve. At his age, I'd been married for three years and was a mother. I'm still married, and Neil is eight years older than me."

"Eight isn't twenty. You've got to see I've done the right thing."

"Are you trying to persuade me, or yourself? Sounds to me like you're not sure. Maybe you should have given him a chance, or both of you a chance. Love doesn't come around so often you can ignore when it does."

Riley shrugged. "I couldn't come between him and his father, and he'll get over me. It's best for him."

Sue growled. "When you were his age, would you have listened to anyone who tried to tell you how to feel?"

All his friends had told him to stay away from Nate whose reputation preceded him, but he'd thought he knew better, that *he* was different, that Nate wouldn't be the same with him. "But don't you see? It turns out I should have listened to everyone else. If I had way back then, I might have found someone better for me, someone who didn't control my life and, in the end, treat me like dirt on his shoe. At twenty-two, I was a blind, lovestruck idiot. I don't want Dylan to regret everything like I do."

"But Dylan isn't you, and you're not Nate. What does Dylan have to say?"

"I don't know. I deleted all his texts and emails. He hasn't been here, though, so I guess he's moved on."

"He could be giving you space, and if he's still texting you..."

"Look, Sue, I'm grateful, but—"

"Riley Whittaker Ormerod, you need to shut up and listen. I think you're completely wrong and cutting off your nose to spite your face. Chances at love don't come along often. Dylan's a great young man with a sensible head on his shoulders. He's never been an idiot like lots of others I could mention, including his father. I remember what Tony was like until Lori got hold of him. I listened to your dad's regrets, how he wished you two had been closer, and how much he missed your mother. It broke his heart when she died, but he once told me he'd have married her again given a second chance, even though he was much older than her. Think about that when you lie alone at night. You only get one life." She hesitated. "Wow, listen to me, but I'm right this time, and I'd better get off. Neil's bringing home pizza."

If she'd slapped him, he wouldn't have felt worse. "Thanks, Sue. I think."

She paused at the open door. "Don't thank me. Do something before it's too late."

* * * *

Matt took his shot. They watched the black ball drop into a pocket. Dylan sighed. "I can't concentrate enough for snooker," he said while Matt replaced the ball on its spot.

He moved around the table to line up the final red. "Look, I have no idea what you should do, Dylan, but you told me you intended to fight for him."

Dylan picked up his pint and took several deep swallows. "Sometimes you need to be crafty and take a more indirect approach. This way my dad stays off my back, while I work on Mum, and I keep letting Riley know how much I love him."

Beer splashed off the table as Matt knocked his glass with his cue. "Whoa, it's a bit early for the L-word, isn't it?" He glanced at his phone when it beeped.

Dylan grinned. "My, look at you, worrying whether you should answer Katie's call or not. You can, by the way. I won't think you're at her beck and call. Ouch! What was that for?" He rubbed his arm.

"Shut the fuck up. Without me, you wouldn't know Riley's been like a bear with a sore head all week. Katie says she hasn't seen him smile once, and he's had huge dark circles under his eyes. Looks like he hasn't been sleeping, and he's been eating fast food, which he never does, according to her."

"She hasn't said anything, has she? You know, about me and Riley?"

"Of course not. I doubt she would if she knew."

"Good, it's just I've no idea whether Riley is out at work or not."

Matt took his next shot. "That must be difficult, always having to take care with every word."

"He was out in London but not with his father. I haven't told him my boss knows him. She passed a comment about me getting a lift from Harry in the housing department when I met her coming from the carpark, and she asked if Riley was all right because he wasn't giving me a lift. Seems her husband plays golf with Riley's partner at work."

"And I thought living in a village was bad," Matt said. "What did you say to her?"

"Only that Riley was a friend of my dad's. I wasn't sure what else to say. What if she suspects? I kissed him once. What if she saw? What if his partner knows?"

"Stop it. You can't do anything now and Katie will keep quiet. She likes Riley." He sighed. "She's so awesome. I think she's the one, Dyl." Matt cleared the last red easily, followed swiftly by the black.

Dylan tapped his fingers on the edge of his glass. "And you tell me it's too soon when you've known her all of two weeks. I've fancied Riley since I was fifteen. I know what films he likes, what music, how to make him laugh and what a bastard his ex-boyfriend was to him."

Matt raised his eyebrows. "I'm betting you know more about him than that."

"Shut up and clear the table." Dylan plonked himself down on a seat and watched as Matt did exactly that then joined him on the bench seat.

"You've slept with him, haven't you? Don't try to deny it. I know you, Dylan Hargreaves. You're a pathetic liar and you've never been backward about getting what you want from when you were little."

"Can I help my charming personality?"

"You were the same at school—had every teacher eating out of your hand. Mr. Brown thought he'd died and gone to heaven, having you for math."

"Those grades got me to university. In a few years, hopefully, I'll have my own business—accountancy and financial advice. I've already dabbled in the stock market, but that's between you and me."

Matt stared at him open-mouthed. "But I thought you only got a lift because you had no money for a car." He paused. "You sneaky bastard. You planned all this, didn't you? All along you dropped hints to your dad and got him to ask Riley to give you a lift so you could get close to him."

"Well, it worked, didn't it? Until Dad went batshit, and Riley backed off. I miscalculated on that one. I thought he'd be okay. Mum's on my side, though. She'd already guessed about Riley. Mums must have this inner radar or something. She said she'd work on him, but I don't know. I've given Dad time to calm down, but now I need to move up a gear. Riley should be getting his pets tomorrow and the dogs will need walking. I may coincidentally be around when he takes them out, even if I do have to hang about. Now, fancy a game of darts?" Dylan stood. "I'll get us another round and the arrows from behind the bar."

Matt put a hand out and pulled his shirt. "I hope the weather's fine if you're planning a little stalking, and I hope you know what you're doing."

The expression on Matt's face made Dylan pause. "One way or the other, I need to show Riley and my dad I'm serious, and I miss him, Matt. I didn't realize how much I would until I didn't get to see him every morning. I love making him smile and laugh and, well, yes, other things. Maybe I'm old-fashioned, wanting to settle down with a husband and pets, and even children eventually. I've never wanted the bright lights, or a different man every night. I liked waking up and seeing his face. If it makes me a lovesick fool then, hey, I'll embrace that." He glanced over to the other bar. "Come on, the dartboard's free now. Winner buys the next round."

Chapter Seventeen

Queenie had already gone off to explore, or to cower under a bed, Riley wasn't sure. The dogs had wagged their tails and accepted a few treats, run around chasing each other and sniffing everything, then settled down in front of the fire. Riley made himself a coffee then sat on the sofa to read the paper and eat a bacon sandwich. Immediately, two heads lifted and sniffed. Seconds later both had taken position, sitting in front of him staring up expectantly.

"No, we're not starting that already. You've had your dinners. I'm head of this pack, not you." As he spoke, Queenie appeared and jumped on the arm of the sofa. She too stared at him.

"So, it's going to be like this, is it? You will not persuade me. This is my bacon."

Queenie nudged his elbow, opened her mouth and let out a yowl. The dogs joined in. Riley refused to be provoked and ate his sandwich slowly. The cat, already bored, jumped off the furniture and lay on the mat. Riley thought how much Dylan would have been laughing by now as Bonnie and Millie wagged their tails in hope — well, Bonnie the pug sort of wagged her bottom.

"Dylan should be here now. He'd have sneaked you some bacon. We'd planned to collect you, have lunch then take you for a long walk. Now you'll have to put up with me." He swallowed the last mouthful.

"Right," Riley said, standing. "I think we'll have a long walk to tire you out before our first night together." With most of the trees now bare, the ground was covered with piles of leaves, perfect for small dogs to play about in.

The dogs followed him into the kitchen, and he put on their halters. He'd been advised these were better for small dogs. He was almost out of the door when he remembered the other items every responsible dog owner took out — plastic bags.

After stuffing the bags in his pocket, he stood quietly as the volunteer at the center had suggested, rather than getting them excited and jumping about. Instinctively, the dogs sat in front of him. Riley patted their heads, gave them a treat then led them outside.

The afternoon was cold, but not windy. The trees stayed silent and still, and the air felt heavy, even though the mist had cleared. He strolled to the back of the house toward the footpath. The dogs skipped ahead, and he let the leads extend so they could sniff in the leaves and run through the muddy puddles. At least they *were* both small. He'd need to wash both in the sink when they got home.

"You got them then."

Riley turned to see Dylan behind him. His heart skipped a few beats while the dogs attempted to run toward the new person. He halted them before they reached their target. "Yes, we're having a walk to tire them out and help them settle."

Dylan moved closer. "Like the person at the rescue center said." He reached a couple of strides away but didn't come nearer. Riley took a deep breath, hoping to still his racing pulse, and coughed.

"It's cold out here," Dylan said, glancing around. "Are you okay?"

Riley wanted to scream he wasn't, but he didn't. "I'm fine. Lots to do, and these two will keep me busy. Isabel has agreed to walk them every day to get them into a routine. How are things at home?" *Why the hell did I ask him?*

"We should keep walking," Dylan said.

"Yes, you're right." And somehow, he found himself walking next to Dylan as they'd originally planned.

"Things at home are...okay." Dylan didn't exactly sound convincing. "Dad took me to work for a couple of days, and it turns out Harry in the housing department lives in Clitheroe, so he's dropping me off at Dad's shop and picking me up there in the morning. Dad can hardly whinge about having to get up earlier to get me there, now, can he? You know he didn't mean those words he said. He was shocked, that's all."

Riley had no idea if Dylan was telling the truth. He wanted to ask about Harry. Who was he? Was he Dylan's age? Was he handsome? Was he gay? The name sounded old, but many parents had named their children after the prince, so he could be younger. He clutched the leads, digging his nails into his palm, hoping he looked calmer than he felt. "When I texted Tony to say I wouldn't be giving you a lift again, his only reply was 'good'. Has the situation moved on from there?"

"Not exactly, but Mum will work on him."

Riley stopped. "Please tell her not to. I don't want them to argue. I can't cope with all this angst, and I told you I won't get in between you and your family. I'm not even sure I'm ready for a relationship yet, after all that's happened."

This time Dylan completely closed the distance between them while the dogs milled around their ankles. He moved straight into Riley's personal space.

"You seemed fine in bed with me, and that was only a week ago. You don't have to be alone, Riley. And I wasn't lying when I said I don't care how old you are. I've always been old, or so my mum says. Teachers told me I had an old head on young shoulders because I always knew I wanted to be an accountant while most other lads dreamed of being rock stars or footballers. Don't get me wrong. I can be stupid and drink too much, but I'm relentless in pursuing what I want, and what I want is you."

A massive shiver ran up Riley's spine, raising every hair on his body. He looked away, unable to cope with the scrutiny of Dylan's gaze.

"You're lying to yourself, Riley. You want me as much as I want you. You want me touching you." Fingers stroked his cheek and eased his head around to face their owner. "Dad will get over his qualms. And if he doesn't then that's up to him."

"Please, Dylan, don't do this. I'm begging you. With what we've done already I've lost my oldest friend, and my newest." Leaves rustled behind him and the dogs yapped. He pulled them closer as a couple strolled past with a Labrador.

"Stay, girls. Sit." Astonishingly, the dogs obeyed. "I need to walk these two. Please go home, Dylan. I can't do this, and I don't want to move away. Please don't make me or make this awkward. We had an enjoyable time, but that's all it was." *Please believe me.*

"You don't believe those words any more than I do, but yes, I'll go. But know this. I've wanted you for years and I don't intend to give up so easily. I'll make you see I'm the right man for you. I'll persuade my father I know what I'm doing. I want to go to sleep with you every night and wake with you every morning and take these two on long, long walks. I'll even make an honest man of you, given half a chance."

Riley grabbed hold of the leads, having nearly dropped them. His brain wanted to explode. Did he *want* Dylan to fight for him? No one had ever fought for him before. "I have to go," he whispered.

Turning, he gathered the dogs and set off. Dylan didn't follow him. Instead, he called out, "Do I have to tell you how stupid you're being?"

His walk turned into a trot, then a run. By the time he got home, all three of them were breathing heavily. That night, his plan to keep the girls downstairs failed straight away. Having them next to him gave him comfort. Sleep eluded him. Instead, he stared at the ceiling contemplating Dylan's words while the dogs happily snored at his side.

Another week passed. Every night Dylan sent him a text. Sometimes he told him about his day, and other times he reminded him of places they'd talked about going to, and what they could be doing if he was there with him. Work had been busy, but in every unoccupied moment, his mind strayed to thoughts of what had been and what might be.

Every night the dogs slept at his feet, sometimes joined by Queenie. Being greeted by the three of them when he arrived home helped lift his mood. They were a distraction and accepted cuddles and fuss as often as he was prepared to hand them out.

Friday night, he arrived home to find Sue waiting on his doorstep. "You should have gone in out of the cold," he said. "You still have your key."

"It didn't seem right. Anyway, I haven't been here long, and I didn't want to disturb the dogs."

Riley opened the door to excited yaps. The dogs slid across the tiles in the hall to land at their feet, panting, with lolling tongues. He knelt and patted them both. "Why don't you go in the living room and I'll feed these three and make us a drink. Tea?"

"That would be lovely. I'll put the fire on and warm the place up."

As he stirred the tea, his heart rate increased. He had no doubt Sue knew nothing on his side had changed. Had she heard something from Lori? He entered the living room carrying the mugs while the dogs followed him in as always, to find Sue on the sofa scowling at him despite the cat now sat contentedly in her lap.

"What?" he snapped, sitting in the armchair. *How much more petulant could I sound?*

"You know very well. How long are you going to let this go on? You know Lori and I go way back. Well, she needed someone to talk to. She's worried about him, Riley. Apparently, he sits in his room every night and, even though his dad gives him a lift to Clitheroe every day, they aren't speaking more than necessary. She's tried talking to both. She's been close to coming here a few times."

Millie pawed his leg and he picked her up. He stared at the fire, unable to meet Sue's questioning gaze, while stroking Millie's head. "I don't know what to do. Tony won't talk to me. I tried to ring him again, but he put the phone down. Dylan's his son. I can understand how he feels about me, and that I might be taking advantage of him."

"But you aren't, are you? I've known you for a while now and, somehow, I doubt you made the running here. Dylan is a determined young man, always has been. Tony's floated through life. He inherited the shop from his father, and, despite claiming he hated working there, took over the reins when he died. Did you know Lori proposed to him during a leap year? He couldn't even manage that despite being smitten with her from the moment they met."

Riley shook his head and chuckled. "Sounds like Tony."

"She says she'd still be waiting now if it was up to him. Dylan is like her, and for some reason, he's set his sights on you."

"Don't ask me. I've no idea why. I'm nothing special. I've made a complete mess of my life — "

Sue leaned forward, spilling the cat from her lap. "Stop right there. You've been a successful solicitor for twenty years. You're partner in a respected practice. So what, you fell for a bastard. We've all done that."

"But I let Nate — "

"It doesn't matter now. What matters is that you have a wonderful man who quite possibly loves the bones of you. And you love him too, don't you?"

Riley grabbed the arm of the chair. Did he love Dylan? "Of course I have feelings for him. But I thought I was in love with Nate for twenty years and now I can't think of him without the horror of knowing how I allowed myself to be taken in by him. Don't you see? It makes me doubt I even understand what love is."

"You think Dylan's too young to understand his own mind?"

"I don't know. What if I was simply flattered by his attention? He's fun and sexy and makes me laugh. He makes anything seem possible. He talks about his plans, and I've no doubt he'll achieve them all. I don't understand why he wants me in his life."

"You are rather handsome, even if you refuse to see it." She paused. "And I assume you two are compatible in, um…other areas."

Heat rushed into his face. Images appeared in his mind and his cock twitched. Oh yeah, they were compatible, and they had so much more to experience together. Could they make this relationship work? Would Tony come around? He buried his head in his hands, not wanting to meet Sue's gaze.

"Your dad worried so much about you being lonely, and he *knew* about loneliness. He always wished you'd been closer, and he blamed himself for pushing you away after your mother died. He was so glad to have you back at the end, but he always hoped you'd find someone like he did. He said those years with you and your mother were the best of his life. He couldn't believe she loved and wanted him either, just like you and Dylan. Your mother was young, bright and beautiful too."

"I read his diaries from when he met her and the early part of their lives together. I haven't been able to face reading any more. I remember bits of those early times before Mum became ill and he got angry. Glimpses of holidays at the beach and the way they looked at each other." Tears pricked at his eyes. He let his shoulders fall and sighed. "What do I do, Sue?"

"Well, funnily, that's why I'm here. Lori said to tell you Tony will be on his own at home tonight. She's coming round to mine again to down a glass of wine or two and eat chocolate. Dylan will be out with Dan and Matt. She said to get there about seven-thirty, and she's made chicken casserole and dumplings. Talk to him, Riley."

"He might not let me in."

"You won't know if you don't try. If there's a chance at love, you shouldn't let it pass you by. Who cares about age? Let yourself be loved. There's so much crap happening in the world."

"Anyone ever tell you how wise you are?"

Sue grinned. "I don't need to be told. I know. Maybe some wisdom has rubbed off from all the older people I've worked for. Now, I need to get home and sort something other than chocolate to eat. Grab a bottle of malt and get yourself over there." She stood. "I'll see myself out."

Riley remained seated.

The kitchen door slammed, caught on the breeze. Was Sue right? Whatever happened with Dylan, Tony was still his oldest friend. He picked up his mobile and stared at the selfie he'd taken with Dylan at Blackpool. His father had been brave enough to grab at happiness for however long it lasted. Perhaps he should at least try to do the same. He picked up a surprised Bonnie.

"We promised you two daddies, didn't we? So maybe it's time I did something about that."

Chapter Eighteen

Dylan ran his fingers through his hair, spreading gel to hold it in place. Perhaps it was time he had it cut. He pulled a hoodie over his T-shirt. It was cold, and he planned on walking to the pub.

It had been nearly a week since he'd seen Riley. Over the last few days, doubt had set in. He'd sent one text every night reminding Riley he wasn't alone, but Riley hadn't replied. Most nights he'd gone up to his room, unable to deal with his father. As far as Dylan was concerned, everything that had happened so far had only proved Riley had feelings for him. He had no doubt that his father was solely responsible for keeping them apart because Riley didn't want to cause a breach between father and son. Even though his father gave him a lift every morning and night, a vast chasm separated them. His mother had thrown her hands up and declared she'd had enough and was going out. Not wanting to be left with his father, he'd called Matt and Dan and arranged to play darts and pool. It was the first time Dan would be out after the birth of his daughter.

His father was sitting in his usual armchair in the living room when Dylan arrived downstairs. He glanced up at him, without speaking, then returned to his paper.

"This is ridiculous, Dad. I haven't seen Riley in two weeks." All right, that wasn't the truth but... "I don't understand why you're being like this."

His father folded his paper. "You're twenty-two."

"For heaven's sake." Dylan suppressed the urge to bang his head against the wall. "And by the time you were my age, you had two-year-old me. I mean, I know I wasn't exactly planned, and you and Mum brought forward the wedding, but you intended to get married anyway, so what did your age matter? You're still together after all these years, and not everyone can say that."

His father folded his arms. "I don't regret having you so early or marrying your mother. I had to grow up fast, but Riley is twice your age, and he's recently split up with a long-time partner. I don't want you to get hurt because he's on the rebound. And, what if it did work? He's twenty years older than you, son. He might get ill and need you to nurse him. He'll die before you. And do you know anything about his sexual history? This bloke he was with cheated on him. Heaven knows what he might have brought back to Riley. I'm not blaming him, but I've got to be concerned."

Dylan's mind spun, and he sank down on the arm of the sofa. "I never expected to hear *you* utter such nonsense. Shit, Dad. Have you heard yourself? If Riley and I ever took our relationship further, we would be safe. Do you think we've just plunged into this relationship willy-nilly? You know both of us better than that. Anyway, *I've* had more partners than him, or

I suspect I have. And for your information, I get tested regularly and have done since I was seventeen." His father's mouth fell open.

He made himself meet his father's gaze. "Yeah. Believe me, Dad, this is not a conversation I wanted to have with you, either."

His father raised his hands. "Me neither. Okay, son. I'm glad you're being sensible, and I'm not saying Riley would be reckless. But it sounds as if this ex of his wasn't too particular. I've been reading up online about issues in the gay community."

Oh God, what the hell has he found? Dylan braced himself.

"It seems there are some people who say this new drug PrEP makes people more careless. Then there are these chemsex parties in London."

The urge to bang his head against a wall threatened to overwhelm him again. "Can you *really* see Riley going to a chemsex party? Fucking hell, Dad, how many times do I have to say it? I'm in no danger. And as for having to look after Riley because he's older than me—who knows? Life doesn't give any guarantees. You know that. Riley's father was twenty years older than his mum and she died way before him. I intend to make sure we have as long as possible together. I knew he was the one the moment I saw him."

His father opened his mouth to speak. Dylan got in first.

"And don't tell me that's nonsense. At fifteen, I was old enough to see him and understand how my body reacted. This is not a crush and I'm not going to just get over it. You know me well enough to know I'm neither of those things. I never imagined having this chance with him." He gazed at his father, hoping his words might work.

"This is hard for me, son. I want you to be happy, that's all. Riley and I used to be close…"

Dylan sat up. Was that it? Was his dad jealous? He tilted his head to one side and raised his eyebrows, questioning his father's words.

His father shook his head. "Don't even go there. I can see what you're thinking. I won't deny it's good to have him back. And I don't think he'd put you in any real danger — not knowingly. It's just so hard to get my head around the thought of you and him and when I do…" He left the sentence hanging. Dylan didn't need any explanation.

"Your mum's been giving me earache too, not to mention your sister, who rang yesterday. Maybe I need some time — you know."

At last, there was the slightest chink of light in the long, dark tunnel. Dylan chuckled. "If I can live with the knowledge you and Mum…you know, I'm sure you could…"

His father put his fingers in his ears. "TMI."

Dylan pressed on. "So, if I spoke to Riley, you'd be okay, Dad?"

"I can see that he matters to you and you matter to me. Maybe I've been too hasty. I'd try to be okay."

Dylan stood, crossed the floor and kissed his dad on the head. "Thank you. Thank you so much."

As he walked through the misty dark to the pub with his hands in his jacket pocket, Dylan allowed himself a small smile and hummed *Happy* to himself.

* * * *

Riley waited until Dylan was far enough away not to see him get out of his car. Even at a distance, he'd seen the smile on his face as he hurried down the steps from the house. All his insecurities crashed back into his head. Perhaps Dylan wasn't bothered about him anymore—but he'd kept texting, so he must care. Whatever? It didn't matter. He still needed to clear the air with Tony.

He picked up the bottle of twenty-five-year-old malt whiskey and strolled to the house, taking each step slowly, before ringing the doorbell. Most of him wanted to turn and run as he and Tony had done as children playing rat-a-tat ginger.

A light came on in the hall—too late now. Tony opened the door and stood in the open space. Riley held up the bottle. "I bring a peace offering," he said. "I'm told there's a casserole available."

Tony raised his eyebrows then stood back. "You'd better come in. I was about to get the food out of the slow cooker." Riley followed Tony to the kitchen and watched as he ladled the stew into bowls and placed them on the breakfast bar.

"This is wonderful," Riley said, taking another mouthful. "I can't remember the last time I had dumplings."

"Lori is a great cook."

"I must ask her for the recipe. I've been thinking of getting a slow cooker, so I have something ready when I get home." The conversation might not be profound, but at least they were talking.

"I hear you've had your kitchen done," Tony said. "Lori wants us to update this place, but it's pricey. I wouldn't imagine it would be a problem for you."

Riley decided to ignore his tone. "I've been lucky, and Dad left a reasonable sum. He didn't like spending money, after all. I'm hoping to get the bathroom done next. As you saw, the place is full of old, dark furniture that needs replacing. Does anyone even want mahogany these days? You should come and have another look. I haven't checked the contents of the attic yet, so who knows what's in there."

"I might well do that. People still buy all sorts of stuff you'd never imagine, and there's always auctions or charity." He stood. "Do you want any more? There's lemon trifle for afters. Then we can have a few drams of this stuff."

Tony's conciliatory attitude had him puzzled. He hadn't expected polite conversation. He hadn't expected to get over the doorstep, even with the whiskey. "Trifle would be good. I'm not much of a stodgy pudding man."

"No, I bet it was all that nouvelle cuisine stuff in London—little bits of food, not enough to feed a gerbil."

Riley smiled. "Yeah, so I keep being told. It's becoming a bit of a theme." He watched while Tony spooned trifle into bowls.

"Let's take this into the living room, shall we?" Tony set off without hesitation. Riley followed him and sat on the sofa in the cozy room, while Tony took the armchair. They ate the trifle in silence. When he'd finished, Tony took two tumblers from the sideboard and poured them each a large measure of malt. Tony swallowed the contents down in one and poured himself another then sat down facing him.

"You and my son?"

Ah, Riley knew the rapprochement had been too good to last. "I know you're not happy about it – "

Tony raised his palm. "Stop. Before he went out tonight, Dylan gave me an earful. Lori's been doing the same all week. But I need to have my say. First of all, you should know I love my son and I'm proud of him. I don't care that he's gay. It hardly came as a shock when he told us. But the thought of you and him – I couldn't deal with it."

Riley noted the change of tense but didn't interrupt.

"He's never introduced us to anyone in his life, and whatever he got up to at university, I didn't know about. But this, it's here and it's you. If you were with Kayleigh, I'd feel the same."

"I can understand that. She'd still be a lot younger than me."

"No parent wants to think of their children as sexual beings, believe me. But Dylan reminded me he doesn't like thinking of me and Lori having sex, either."

Riley chuckled. "No, I imagine he wouldn't." He poured himself another glass. It had been a while since he'd drunk whiskey and the warmth as it slipped down his throat made him shiver. "But it's not all about sex, is it?"

"No, it isn't. Look, there's only one way to say this. I need to know if you have feelings for my son. He's always been level-headed despite his inability to get up in the morning. I don't want him hurt because you're on the rebound or you might decide you need to leave and go back to London."

"I can assure you I have no intention of returning to London. And, as to my feelings, I've spent a lot of time with Dylan driving to and fro to Preston. We've talked about all sorts of things. No one was more surprised than me to find out he had feelings for me, despite the age difference. Being with him has shown me new possibilities for happiness—a happiness I thought I'd never experience. I can't promise anything. No one can. All I'm sure of is that over the last couple of weeks, I've missed him more than I thought possible. I love how passionate he is...about everything. Believe me, I've had my doubts as well."

"But you don't now?"

"He has this habit of persuading me not to. He's texted me every night since the bonfire party. Last night he upped the game and emailed me a link showing pictures of couples with big age differences—gay and straight."

Tony snorted. "Sounds like him." He hesitated and took another drink. "I need to ask one other thing."

"Okay," Riley replied slowly, wondering what was coming next.

"You get tested, don't you? With what you said about your ex playing away..."

"I would never put Dylan in danger, and yes, I get tested. I'm fine. Would you like to see the paperwork? I can get it if you want."

Tony's face flushed red and not just from the whiskey. "No, I believe you. You understand I had to ask. He's my son. I want him safe." He leaned forward. "Look, Riley, I can't say I'm entirely happy with the age difference, or that it's you, because, frankly, I've seen you naked—"

"Not since we were sixteen and went skinny-dipping in the lake and the farmer nearly caught us. As I remember you decided we should hide in a bush. We both got scratched by the brambles. I've put on a few pounds since then."

Tony patted his stomach. "Not as much as I have."

"Look, we're going to take things step by step," Riley said. "We always intended to. I know you'll find it difficult, us being a couple, but I never wanted to fall out with you. I'd rather have your blessing." He giggled. "I think the whiskey is getting to me. I'm not much of a drinker. We're sounding like some Victorian melodrama."

Tony leaned over and picked up his guitar then plugged it into the amp. "Do you play much these days?" he asked, strumming.

"I haven't played in years," Riley admitted.

"There's a bass behind the sofa. Plug it in and let's see what you remember."

Riley grinned. Maybe everything would be all right, after all.

Chapter Nineteen

Dylan stopped on the top step to listen to the music. It sounded live — voices and guitars blending perfectly, and was that Living in a Box being sung? Curiosity overwhelmed him. He pushed open the door and stepped quietly along the hallway. A glance into the living room revealed his father and Riley, strumming away and somewhat unsteady on their feet as they swayed, almost in time, with the music. He watched, unable to stop a grin spreading across his face and a tear running down his cheek. The front door opened behind him and he gestured to his mother to be silent. She tiptoed toward him but was unable to stop a gasp escaping her lips. Tony lifted his head.

"Hello, love. Look who's here."

Riley stopped playing, swayed and collapsed giggling onto the sofa. "Sorry," he muttered. Lori entered the room only to be embraced by her husband.

"You look bloody gorgeous." He glanced over to Dylan still stood in the doorway. "You know your mother is the most beautiful woman in the world.

Always has been and always will be. I've never understood what she sees in me."

Lori pushed him away. "Bloody hell. You stink of whiskey."

Dylan noted an almost empty bottle on the table next to two similarly empty tumblers. On the sofa, Riley struggled to take off the guitar. Dylan moved toward him.

"Come on, let me help you. You don't want to break it or do yourself a mischief." Riley let him pull the strap over his head and place the guitar against the wall. He turned off the amp, foiling his father's attempt to serenade his reluctant mother.

"Sit down, you silly old fool, before you fall down. Take off the guitar first. I'm surprised the neighbors haven't been round here complaining about the noise." She too placed the guitar somewhere safe then pushed her husband down into his chair. "Stay there. Coffee all round, I think. Keep an eye on them, Dylan. I assume you're still capable."

"Of course I am."

His father leaned forward and waved his finger toward Riley. "You and him, you and him is okay with me. We talked. Just don't want to think about—you know."

Dylan's heart skipped a beat. Had he heard correctly? He gazed at Riley who nodded then beamed from ear to ear.

"We talked," he echoed. "Told him...feelings—you know...us. Told him I care—safe—not rebound. Missed you. Sorry. Stupid."

Warmth spread through Dylan's chest as Riley gazed at him, turning his head from side to side like a puzzled puppy. He sat next to him. "I missed you too. I've no idea how this reconciliation came about, and I don't care, as long as you and I…" God, he wanted to take Riley's face in his hands and kiss him senseless, but maybe not with his parents in the room. His mother entered, carrying a tray of mugs.

"Her." Riley pointed at his mother.

"Mum?" Dylan questioned.

"I might have mentioned to Sue that you and I would be out tonight. What she did with the information, I've no idea." She sat in the other armchair.

Riley nodded. "Told me, she did." Riley gave him the most shit-faced grin and Dylan's heart ached. "Told me to come. I brought whiskey. We ate stew and dumplings then got the guitars out."

"He's still got it," Tony said. "Have to get the band together again."

"Here." Dylan lifted the mug of coffee to Riley's lips. "Drink this. I hope you can walk."

"Can stay here," Tony said.

Riley shook his head. "Can't. Dogs and cat."

"I'll take him home and stay with him. Don't want him being sick in his sleep. That's quite an amount you've drunk between you. I'm surprised you could still stand."

"Be fine, after coffee."

"Still coming home with you. Don't worry I won't take advantage."

His father stuck his fingers in his ears. "La, la, la, don't want to hear."

"Shut up, Tony. You'll be wrecked in the morning. Not sure I want to sleep with you in this state."

"She loves me, really. Can't resist my charms. Never could." He stared at Dylan, his eyes steely. "He's my friend and you're my son. You'd both better treat each other properly. S'important." He yawned. Riley echoed him.

"We'd better get you home," Dylan said. "It's cold out there so that'll help sober you up. Let's see if you can stand."

Riley reeled but didn't fall. Dylan helped him into his coat. "I'll text to say we're there, Mum. Will you manage with Dad?"

"I have for over thirty years. Take care of him, too."

"I will, Mum. And thanks. This means the world to me."

"Love works in mysterious ways. I was eleven when I saw your dad fall off the fence, showing off on the first day of secondary school. I've never wanted anyone else. I've never regretted marrying him." A snore spoilt the moment. "I mean, what's not to love?"

Riley swayed again. "Come on, Riley. Let's get you home to the terrible trio."

Frost had begun to form on the pavements and Dylan had to take care. Riley garbled, mostly incoherently, about the conversation he'd had with Dylan's father. Dylan heard the word love a few times as he held him up for the half-mile between the houses. As soon as he'd managed to extricate the key from Riley's pocket, achieved with a certain amount of innuendo, the dogs barked in greeting and jumped up at them both, excited to see someone. Queenie strolled in and jumped on the kitchen table. Dylan deposited Riley onto a chair. He put some food out to settle the pair, placing Queenie's on the table, so the dogs wouldn't pinch it.

"Time for bed, you."

"You just want to see me naked and have your wicked way with me." Riley held his arms up.

"Not tonight, lover boy. Come on, let's get you up to bed."

Dylan manhandled Riley up the stairs and, after checking he could manage the bathroom, helped him to undress and put him under the duvet. He used the bathroom himself and returned to find Riley already snoring facing away from him. He stripped then spooned behind Riley, finally where he belonged and hoped to belong for as long as possible.

When he woke many hours later, Riley still lay snoring against him. Dylan slipped out of the bed, shushing the dogs who followed him, eager for food. He popped in the bathroom then crept down the stairs, microwaved bacon, eggs and beans, plated them with slices of toast, a couple of mugs of strong tea, and a bottle of orange juice before he returned to the bedroom. Riley opened his eyes and groaned.

"Did we?"

Dylan placed the breakfast tray on the chest of drawers. "No, I can assure you I was the perfect gentleman."

Riley's eyes twinkled. "Good. I'd hate to think I couldn't remember." He sat up, groaned again and rubbed his temples. "Remind me never to drink whiskey with your dad ever again."

"You remember that much then?" Dylan asked.

Riley nodded. "Oh God, that hurts. I'm not sure I could eat a full English." He breathed into his hands. "Eek, morning breath. I need to clean my teeth."

Dylan handed over the bottle of juice. "Here, get some vitamin C down you. Could you manage some toast?"

The smile Riley gave him made his heart skip a beat. "I can try," he said. Scratching at the door interrupted them. Dylan opened it and the dogs barreled in. Millie launched herself at the bed, landing right on Riley, who yelped loudly. An excited Bonnie leapt up and down at the side, unable to manage the height. Dylan lifted her and sat at the end to eat his plate of bacon, eggs and beans. "You don't know what you're missing and don't get crumbs in the bed."

Riley glanced up. "And whose bed is this again?"

"Judging by the way these two have settled in, I'd say it's theirs." Both dogs lay panting in the space next to Riley.

"You do realize we may never get to have sex again with these two around," Dylan said, stabbing the bacon with his fork.

"We could always put them in the kitchen and turn the radio up or take them for a long walk to wear them out," Riley suggested.

"As long as the long walk didn't wear us out, too."

Riley snorted. "I hope you aren't suggesting because I'm older than you I might fall asleep. I'll have you know, I can keep up."

"Really?" Dylan said, winking. "Care to prove that now? We've nothing else to do." He picked up a dog in each hand and put them outside the door with the leftovers to entertain them. Dylan leaned back against the door. "Now, you were saying." He stripped off his briefs and slid under the duvet.

"But I haven't finished my toast or tea yet," Riley protested.

"Tough. I've more interesting things you could do with your sexy mouth."

Riley put the plate to one side and slid down to face him. "Oh yeah?"

"Yeah, starting with kissing me." Dylan leaned forward until they met open-mouthed. As they kissed, Dylan moved his hands down Riley's chest and cupped his now erect and interested cock. He pulled back. "Maybe I'll go first."

Dylan dived under the bedding, revealed Riley's cock and encased it whole.

"Oh, yeah." Riley pushed the duvet down to reveal Dylan's head and threaded his fingers through Dylan's hair while Dylan continued licking and sucking. Riley thrust up, catching Dylan unawares, and he fought with his gag reflex, pulling back and taking the base of the shaft in his hand. He loved the way Riley's cock stretched his mouth, how it tasted all bitter and salty, and yeah, he loved being in control, knowing he could stop. His thoughts went to edging, getting Riley so close...but not today.

"You're torturing me here," Riley said.

Dylan glanced up to meet Riley's blue eyes gazing at him. He deliberately let Riley's cock drop out of his mouth with a popping sound while speeding up the movement of his hand. "Next time I might do that. Get you so close and leave you hanging, over and over until you beg me." Dylan stretched out his tongue and brushed it across the tip, tasting again.

"Please, Dylan. I'm begging you now. So close. Need you. Need this."

Riley writhed under him. Dylan plunged back, covering his cock, sucking hard and humming, creating the vibration he knew would result in waves of pleasure.

"Oh God, yes, this is so fucking incredible..." Riley's words turned to groans as he came shooting down Dylan's throat. Dylan swallowed, taking it all, feeling a sense of pride and wonder that the man shuddering under him was the same man he'd lusted after and fantasized about for so many years. All those nights he'd imagined them together, cock in hand, and now here he was doing it for real. He sat back on his knees and fisted himself. This wouldn't take long, especially with Riley watching him.

Riley propped himself up on his elbows. "Go on, come all over me. That is so hot. I love you don't shave down there."

"Some people don't like ginger," Dylan managed between breaths.

"Well, not me. I love your ginger hair and your freckles. See if you can reach my mouth."

A few pumps more and he'd be there. "Oh God, Riley." Dylan's orgasm exploded out of him, sending streaks of sticky liquid over Riley's abdomen and chest, not quite reaching any further. Riley's ran a finger through the mess and sucked on it.

"The next time you come, I want it to be inside me," Riley said, after letting his finger emerge from between those lips with a pop.

A shiver ran down Dylan's spine. "If you're sure. We don't have to. I don't always. You don't have to let me fuck you if it's not your thing."

Riley sat up. "It is my thing, but thank you for giving me the option. We need to talk about sex—what we like, what we don't like."

Dylan moved to lie facing Riley. "I will never expect you to do anything you don't want to or that makes you uncomfortable. And if you want something, we talk. For example, I have no problem riding you dressed as a cowboy."

Riley rolled them over until he lay on top of him, laughed then kissed him hard. "Are we talking your fantasies or mine?" he asked.

"Hmm, that would be telling."

A whining sound pierced the moment, followed by scrabbling at the door. Dylan caressed Riley's cheek. "We may have made a mistake getting those two. Still, it's great practice for having kids." Riley's eyes widened. Had Dylan dropped the idea too soon? He believed in being upfront.

"You want children," Riley said, sitting up.

"It's not a deal breaker, but I always thought I would, if I could, if I found someone I'd like to have kids with. I'll understand if you don't."

"I've never really thought about it. Nate didn't want to."

Dylan shifted, not wanting to react to the name. "I'd better let them in before they wreck the door. Then we need to take them for a long walk." He stood. *You bloody idiot. Way to go.* Had he scuppered this relationship already before they'd even got a chance to begin? *Damn my stupid mouth.*

The dogs rushed in once more, bouncing around and yapping with excitement. Dylan returned to the bed, not sure what to say. Riley took his hand.

"Stop it. You caught me unawares, that's all. I have so many more choices with you than I ever expected to have. Being with you changes everything. I'm dizzy with all the possibilities, but I need you to be honest. If this turns out not to be what you need, tell me. I feel like I'm falling too deep too quickly, but I've no desire to slow this rollercoaster down."

Dylan's heart thumped in his chest so loudly he imagined Riley could hear it. "Come on, let's get washed and dressed and take these two out. We can take things as slowly as you need. I've wanted you for years, but I get this is all new for you. Let's get the Sunday papers, have lunch somewhere, and slump on the sofa with some Netflix."

"And chill?" Riley asked.

Dylan grinned. "You never know, if you can get it up twice in a day, old man."

He leapt off the bed but not quickly enough to dodge the slap on his arse. He wriggled it in Riley's smiling face. "Last one in the shower buys lunch." Riley didn't even attempt to follow him.

Chapter Twenty

Riley woke up with a smile in his heart and surrounded by furry creatures. Bonnie the pug waddled up the bed and licked his face. He held her up and she wriggled in his hands.

"Time to get up, girls. You two need a walk and I have things to do and people to see." Today, he was back to picking Dylan up and taking him to work. They'd have forty-five minutes of talking and joking. Yesterday, they'd spent all afternoon fooling around on the sofa, not wanting to separate, but agreed in the end to take things gradually and not rush into — dare he even think about it — living together.

"Come on. I need to shower and dress, so you three try to be good." Of course, they'd waited for him and followed his every move until he got downstairs and fed them. He swallowed a couple of slices of toast while they ate, then poured tea into his Thermos mug and attached leads to their harnesses so they could get a quick walk.

Outside, frost covered the ground. The dogs ran into the frozen piles of leaves and sniffed everything, deciding where they'd pee. Isabel would be there at lunchtime to walk them both again and they'd get another walk when he came home. Perhaps Dylan would come with them. These morning walks certainly woke him up every day.

Thirty minutes later, Riley was sitting in his car, glad of the heated seats, waiting, as usual, for Dylan to appear and hurry down the steps. The front door swung open. Dylan appeared wearing his hooded jacket, clutching his Thermos. Riley's chest expanded, taking in the view, and he reached over to push open the passenger door.

"Bloody hell, it's brass monkeys out here this morning," Dylan said as he got into the car and wriggled in the seats. "Oh God, that feels good on my arse."

"No toast again this morning? You're slacking."

Dylan frowned then leaned over and kissed Riley who automatically glanced around to see if anyone was watching.

"Stop it," Dylan admonished. "I don't care who sees us and neither should you. It'll get out soon, anyway. You know what villages are like."

Riley's thoughts strayed to what other people would think, how they'd judge him, maybe even call him a cradle-snatcher.

Dylan play-punched his arm. "And you can stop those thoughts, too. What we do is no one else's business." He pulled out his phone and plugged it into the dash. "I downloaded us some tunes. I need to expand your musical knowledge."

Riley set off with gritted teeth, expecting some sort of rap or garage tune to blast out. What the hell was garage anyway? Just a lot of noise as far as he was concerned. He glanced down at the player only to hear opening bars from *The Rocky Horror Show*.

"What the hell?"

"It's on in Manchester starting on Saturday and I managed to get four tickets so Matt and Katie can go with us. Matt loves dressing up, and you said you hadn't even seen it at the pictures. So we're going."

"Please tell me I don't have to dress up, too." Riley desperately tried to think of a safe role while keeping his eyes on the road. The low November sun was fortunately behind them.

"Shame. I'd give a lot to see you in skimpy gold briefs. You could always dress as the narrator and keep your stockings and suspender belt hidden. I usually go as Riff-Raff. Matt likes to do the full Dr. Frank N. Furter, outfit and, believe me, he can rock a corset and heels despite being straight. Could you warn Katie she might need a French maid's outfit? Do they have a costume shop in Preston? I'll have to check."

They spent the rest of the journey singing along with Dylan teaching him all the correct responses.

As a result, Riley whistled *The Time Warp* as he strolled to his office. Having passed the time of day with Ruth, he bumped into Katie as he turned a corner in the corridor, sending her paperwork crashing to the floor.

"Sorry, I wasn't looking." He bent to pick up the folder.

"You sound happier. Please tell me you and Dylan sorted things out. Matt said he'd been moping around like a sad puppy."

"We have, as you say, sorted things out, thank you. And Dylan told me to tell you he's got us tickets for *The Rocky Horror Show* on Saturday night, so you'll need a French maid's outfit."

Katie clapped her hands. "I've only seen it at the cinema. There's an old picture house in Leeds and we saw it there once late at night, but I've never seen it live. And I'll be dressing as Janet. I have the perfect twinset and skirt. Matt can be Brad."

Riley grinned. "Umm, from what Dylan said you'd better be prepared for something else. How do you feel about Matt in a corset and feathers?"

Her eyes gleamed, and she grinned from ear to ear. "Well, he's got the legs for it. I wonder if he has his own shoes? I need to call him. I'll see you at ten for our weekly review." She strolled off singing. What had he let himself in for?

Ten minutes after he'd sat down and begun to check the morning's post, his phone rang.

"Riley Ormerod."

"Riley, do you have anyone with you at the moment?" His partner, Patrick Whewell, was an easygoing bloke in his early sixties. He'd been the younger partner to Riley's father and had practically bitten Riley's hand off in eagerness when approached by Riley to buy into the practice.

"No, I'm checking the post and emails before my mentoring meeting with Katie. Do you need anything?"

"Could you pop along to my office? I'd rather speak to you in person."

"Sure." Riley shuffled his papers into a neat pile in an attempt to ignore the lurch in his stomach. He racked his brain. Had something gone wrong with a client? A deal fallen through? He couldn't think of anything. "Okay, I'll be with you in a few minutes."

"Good. Good." The line went silent and Riley placed the phone in its cradle.

Subconsciously, he ran his fingers through his hair and brushed down his suit before hurrying through the corridor to the back of the building. His partner had the largest office overlooking the car park. He disliked the street noise. Riley knocked on the door and entered when told. The man behind the desk looked like he'd aged ten years over the weekend. His eyes had dark circles, his hair more gray strands, and his face more lines.

"Ah, Riley. Sit down."

"Is everything all right, Patrick?"

Patrick folded his arms and leaned forward. "No. Mary had a heart attack on Saturday. She needs a quadruple bypass. They're going to operate tomorrow."

"I'm so sorry, Patrick. But what are you doing here? You should be with her."

"I will be, but I needed to get some things done today. These are my current cases. I need you to take over the ones I've marked and distribute the others."

"Of course, whatever you want." Riley had a good idea of Patrick's workload. It would mean more hours and taking more home.

"Okay, Riley, I need you to listen. Since you've been here, we've brought in new business. The practice has gone from strength to strength, and I've no doubt it will continue to do so. But what's happened to Mary has made me consider my future, too. I want to sell up, Riley. My blood pressure isn't what it should be, and the doctor has advised I'm pre-diabetic. Mary and I need to live a little while we can. I'm sure you'll have no problem finding someone who wants to buy into this place. New blood would be good. Maybe you could get a criminal specialist as another string to our bow with you as senior partner. I have nothing but admiration for your work, as you know. The clients appreciate all you do, and the other members of the practice look up to you. So, what do you think?"

Did he want this? His surname would be first over the door. He could take the practice in any direction he wanted. "I won't deny this is a shock, but if you think the time is right for you and Mary, then you know I'll do the best job I can for this place."

"I certainly do. I've worked here forty years. I trained here. The job has changed and yet stayed the same. When I first started here, we didn't even have a computer. It'll be hard leaving but for the best, and I know I'll be leaving it in safe hands. I'll be back in again to clear this office, which will be yours, and I'd appreciate you telling everyone else about my decision. Now, I'm going to get to the hospital. Mary is terrified, even though the doctors say the operation is routine but serious." He stood and stretched out his hand.

Riley followed suit. They shook for a time. "We'll miss you around here," he said.

Patrick let go and glanced around. "And I'll miss this place, too. But, as you know, sometimes we have to make tough decisions for the best."

His partner crossed to the door and removed his coat from the hook. "Take care of the old place for me."

"I will," Riley said.

Riley followed Patrick as he hurried outside. They exchanged a wave and Patrick was gone. Back in his own room, Riley slumped into his chair. He picked up his phone and called Dylan.

"It's not even midday yet." Riley heard the laughter in Dylan's voice. "Can't get enough of me, ay?"

"I've news," he said. "Are you doing anything tonight?"

"Well, I was hoping to get an offer from this handsome solicitor I know, but I'm sure I can put him off."

"Dinner at my place then?" He'd phone Patrick later to check on Mary. He didn't want to appear callous, but he couldn't help being excited at the changes being senior partner would bring. Patrick would understand. "And no, I won't tell you until we each have champagne in our hands so don't give me twenty questions on the way home." He hoped Dylan would stay. Maybe it wasn't too soon to ask Dylan to move in with him. After all, Christmas was only a few weeks away.

Dylan chuckled. Riley loved the sound. "What's on that wicked mind of yours?" he asked.

"You were the one who mentioned champagne. Ever watched *My Beautiful Launderette*?"

Riley wondered where this was going. "Of course I have."

"Good, what say you and I re-enact the champagne scene tonight?"

A vision of the two main characters, naked, swigging champagne and kissing the faces off each other flashed into Riley's mind. His cock woke up. He beamed at the phone. "You, me and a bottle of bubbly. Who could ask for more?"

All the way home, Dylan didn't ask him anything. Riley rustled them up a quick pasta Bolognese while

Dylan walked the dogs. They sat at the kitchen table to eat.

"Well, are you going to keep me in suspense any longer?" Dylan asked.

"No. Patrick called me into his office this morning and told me he's decided to retire and sell his share of the practice. I'm going to buy some of his stake, giving me overall control, so I'll be the senior partner and have my name first. It'll mean more work, but I'll also be able to take the practice in any direction I want to and choose who buys in." He explained exactly what had been said. "Mary's operation was a complete success so for them it's full steam ahead for a new life in the sun."

Dylan put his fork down, reached over and wrapped his arms around Riley. He kissed him hard. "I'm sorry about your partner's wife but that's amazing. I'm so proud of you. We definitely need to celebrate." He sat back in his chair and popped open the champagne. Their food disappeared in record-breaking time, then Dylan dragged him straight upstairs to bed after snatching the remains of the bottle of champagne. They stripped without ceremony and jumped under the covers still laughing.

Riley lay back waiting, his cock already hard and leaking. Dylan leaned down to kiss him. He tasted of garlic and champagne. "You're leading me into bad ways," he said, slurring his words. Dylan kissed him again.

"Then my work here is done, but I could think of a few other bad ways I could lead you." He moved, nestling his cock against Riley's erection, then wriggled. Riley thrust up.

"Nah, nah, not yet," Dylan said, waggling a finger at him. His eyes shone in the lamplight. "We haven't role-played yet." Dylan dribbled champagne on Riley's chest, edged himself back and bent over to run his tongue across Riley's skin, taking each nipple and nipping then sucking. Riley lurched again as Dylan's stubbly beard created a delightful friction against his skin.

"Open your mouth," Dylan said before taking another swig and placing the bottle on the bedside cabinet. He brushed Riley's forehead then let the champagne dribble from his mouth, sending most of it streaming down Riley's cheeks to the pillow.

"You didn't stay still," Dylan protested.

"I did. You're just rubbish."

"I want to fuck you." Dylan grabbed his cock and moved up close enough to hold it against Riley's chin. "I want this inside you. I'm not too drunk."

A moment of panic hit as butterflies filled Riley's stomach and the hair stood up on the back of his neck, creating an odd mixture of excitement and fear. His memories of sex... No, this would be different. This was Dylan.

"Are you okay? We don't have to. Or you could fuck me. I don't care."

Riley swallowed hard, attempting to dampen down his disquiet. "No, I want you to, just go easy."

Dylan winked at him. "Oh, I love to go easy. All that slow movement in and out, brushing your sweet spot over and over, making it last until you can't stand it anymore and you begging me to go faster, grabbing yourself, throwing your head back and letting loose, contracting around my cock, dragging my orgasm out. Oh yeah, I can go as slow as you want."

"Shit!" Every hair on his body stood to attention and his cock and balls filled. Dylan grabbed a pillow.

"Lift your hips."

Riley did as instructed and Dylan placed the pillow under his arse.

"Pull your legs apart. That's it. Let me see you." Dylan opened the drawer, took out a tube and condom and laid them on the bed. He shuffled down until he lay between Riley's thighs. Shoulders pushed him back just as the tip of Dylan's tongue brushed over his balls, down his taint toward his hole. Riley shivered then groaned as Dylan lapped at him.

"Oh yeah, so good," he murmured, laying his head back and letting sensation take over. His breathing quickened, and he had to force himself not to stroke his cock. The feel of Dylan's tongue pushing into him sent him reaching to grab the sheet on either side. He wanted to move, to beg for more, to press down so Dylan would go deeper. A sudden need to be filled sent his senses reeling.

"Fuck me, please." He managed nothing more than a whisper. A finger breached him, followed by another while Dylan kept up his attention by sucking each ball in turn, spreading his fingers, stretching him. He couldn't remember ever feeling so good, so needy.

"Please, you're killing me."

Dylan lifted his head. "You taste so good. Are you sure you're ready?"

Riley had managed to find enough time to prepare himself as soon as he'd arrived home, hoping this might happen. "Yeah, can't wait anymore. So empty. Need to be full of you."

Dylan sheathed his cock and dribbled more lube on Riley's entrance while he spread as wide as he could, glad they'd be doing this face-to-face.

"Ready?" Dylan asked, pressing himself against Riley's hole.

"Yes." Riley prayed the dogs would stay occupied with the bones he had brought home. He braced himself. Dylan leaned forward then kissed down his chest.

"Relax," he said. "There's no hurry."

"Do it," Riley said. Dylan pushed forward, opening him up, stretching him. It burned, but not for long.

"That's it. Let me in. Let me fill you up. Nearly there. You feel amazing. Oh, so good."

Dylan had the perfect cock for Riley's needs, long, slightly curved, not too wide. He hit Riley's prostate. "Oh God, yeah, just there. More, I'm fine. Fuck me. Need you."

Dylan leaned forward, placing a hand either side of Riley's head, then pulled back and pushed in again, hitting his prostate with every thrust.

"Harder, I can take it. I want to feel this in the morning. That's if I ever let you go. It's like you were made for me. We fit together so well."

Dylan let loose, fucking him, hitting the spot with every thrust until Riley couldn't resist grabbing his cock. His body tingled with need as it barreled toward completion.

"That's it. Stroke yourself," Dylan urged. "Come around me. I want to feel you, see you, hear you. Don't hold back."

Riley couldn't have held back if he'd tried. He moaned with each stroke, not sure how he hadn't exploded already. His world centered on the sensations, his skin so sensitive. His orgasm exploded out of him, sending streams of liquid over both of them.

His arse contracted around Dylan. Seconds later, Dylan reared up, and warmth filled him.

"Oh fuck, Riley," he yelled.

Aftershocks kept his arse muscles holding Dylan in, not wanting him to pull away and leave him empty until his lover collapsed on his chest, breathing heavily. Dylan peppered his face with kisses, then laid his head on Riley's shoulder. Riley wrapped his arms around Dylan, not wanting to let him go. Never in his life had he felt like this after sex. Tears appeared out of nowhere as his emotions spiraled out of control. This man...

"I'm sorry," he said. Dylan lifted his head.

"Oh God, did I hurt you?" He stroked Riley's cheek to brush away the tears.

"No, I don't think you could ever hurt me. It's just, I've never. You made this about me, what I needed."

Dylan finally shifted, taking the condom and dropping it in the bin before sitting up next to Riley. "You're all that matters," he said. "And, believe me, I didn't exactly get nothing out of it. Your arse is the gift that keeps on giving. Such a grip. I want us to get tested again so we can fuck without the condom."

"Oh hell." His arse contracted again at the thought. Even his cock reacted, despite being totally drained. "Yes, let's do that." He yawned.

"Sorry, tired, and it is a work night. I'll never get up in the morning." He ran a finger over his stomach. "Ugh, I need to clean off or I'm going to be crusty. There are wipes in the drawer."

Dylan reached over and cleaned them both up. "Can I stay?" he asked.

Riley wanted to say forever as far as he was concerned, but it was too soon. Then again, life could be too short. "Yes, please do. Let me tuck in behind you."

The door burst open and Millie leapt up onto the bed.

"Good timing, you two. I hope Daddy didn't frighten you with his strange noises."

Riley tapped his fingers on Dylan's arm. "Umm, whose noises?"

Dylan groaned then leaned over and lifted Bonnie to join them. They settled down at the end of the bed. Small snuffles and snoring cut through the silence. Riley edged closer to Dylan and wrapped his arm around him before drifting off himself.

Chapter Twenty-One

"I wasn't sure you'd make it," Dan said when Dylan plonked three pints onto their table a few days later. "You've bigger bags under your eyes than me. Something keeping you awake then?"

Dylan gave him his best shit-faced grin and sat on the stool between his two friends. "What? Jealous, are you?"

Dan shoved his fingers into his ears. "La, la, la."

Dylan pulled his arm. "If you can't take it, don't give it."

Next to him, Matt sniggered. Dylan joined him until all three of them guffawed enough for people to glance in their direction. "Baby keeping you awake, then?"

"She's certainly got a voice. In fact, she's the reason I called you both. We want you two to be her godfathers. Well, not actually godfathers. Maxine wants to have a naming ceremony to welcome her into the world."

"And who doesn't love a party?" Dylan said, knowing his friends too well. "And I'd be honored. I assume I can bring Riley." This would be their first official occasion out together in the village.

"You most certainly can." Dan swallowed at least a third of his pint and licked his lips. He leaned forward. "So, you and him are an item now, then?"

Dylan noted a slight edge to his friend's voice. "We are. Dad was a bit of a dick about it, but we've sorted it now."

Dan coughed and glanced at Matt. "He *is* nearly twice your age."

Dylan stiffened and put his hand to his mouth. "No, you don't say. Thank you for bringing this to my attention. It's not as if I haven't examined every inch of him in detail, is it? Bloody hell, not you two as well. Listen carefully. I don't care how old he is. He's great company, we like the same things and he's sexy as fuck." A woman sitting a few feet away glared at him.

Dan lifted his hands. "Okay, okay. Don't get so defensive. We wouldn't be your friends if we didn't worry. He's your dad's age, Dylan. He's lived in London for years, which is a world away from Pendleside."

"Riley's settled here. He won't be going back to London if you're worried. He's having the house done up and he's recently adopted a couple of dogs and a cat. He's also been offered the senior partnership in his firm. I'm planning to do a few years at the town hall then go into business for myself."

"You're serious about him, then?" Dan asked.

"Yeah, I reckon I am. We just fit." Dylan paused. "Anyway, I've fancied him for years. Why d'you think I got my dad to ask him for a lift and didn't get a car straight away? I thought I might have a chance if I spent some time with him. You can learn a lot about someone in ninety minutes a day. I've even persuaded him to dress up on Saturday. Are you still getting the old corset and stockings out and going as Frank N. Furter, Matt?"

"I most certainly am."

Dan shook his head. "I don't know which of you is worse. I hope this woman knows what she's letting herself in for. And you'll have to let the corset out. You've put on a few pounds since you last wore it." Dan chuckled into his pint.

Matt stretched and patted his stomach. "You're just jealous. Katie's coming as Janet. She has this great outfit. She sent me a pic last night."

"It's forecast to be chilly out there on Saturday night if you're getting your nipples out," Dan continued.

"I'm wearing it under my clothes, all right? And I'll take a long coat, especially if we're eating out beforehand. I've got some rice as well. Katie's really excited as she's never been to a live show before."

"Riley neither. I tried to get him to go as Rocky, but he wasn't keen on the gold shorts." Dylan hoped to be able to persuade him to model the pair in private. "He's dressing as Eddie instead, with jeans, a leather coat and wig."

"I read it's sold out," Matt said. "Should be a good crowd. It's a pity you and Maxine couldn't go this time. When's this naming party, then? Christmas is coming, and a lot of places get booked up."

"First Saturday in December. It's proper suits and everything. Max wants it done right. We've hired the village hall and a DJ. There'll be food and drink—a right good family do."

Dylan glanced over their heads. "The pool table is free. Fancy a game?"

* * * *

The following Saturday, Riley slicked back his hair, ignoring the flecks of gray at each temple. He turned from side to side, admiring the cut of his new jeans teamed with a plain white T-shirt. He hadn't allowed Dylan to see his other purchases. He grinned at the tattoo sleeves adorning each arm. Dylan would love those. From the wardrobe, he removed the large box containing black leather boots with crisscrossed buckles and a rubber tread like crenulations on the walls of a castle. Finally, he added the leather jacket, a total indulgence on his part, but so soft. He should have had some sort of image placed on the back, but he hadn't wanted to spoil it. A wolf whistle told him he wasn't alone anymore. He turned.

"Will I do?"

"You'll more than do. I had no idea I had a thing for leather until now. You look awesome." He whipped out his phone and the camera flashed before Riley could protest.

"You don't look so bad yourself," Riley replied.

Dylan leaned against the door jamb dressed in a black tailed suit with a white shirt.

"Are those spats?" Riley asked.

Dylan held up one foot. "Yep. Dad found them in a house clearance years ago. I need to scruff it all up and add some dark circles under my eyes and the wig. I see you decided against yours." He glanced at his watch. "We'd better get moving. I said we'd pick up Matt and Katie in five minutes. I've no idea how long it'll take us to get into Manchester, but we can park nearby and there's a pizzeria around the corner from the theater.

I'm so looking forward to this. I've got the rice and water pistol."

Riley closed the distance between them, kissed Dylan briefly and led the way downstairs. He popped his head into the living room to find the dogs fast asleep and snoring on the sofa with Queenie stretched on her bed hung over the radiator. He closed the door slowly, hoping not to wake them. The long run earlier would mean they'd sleep, with any luck.

As he pulled up outside Matt's place, the curtain twitched. The door opened, and two figures rushed down the path.

"Fucking hell, it's fucking freezing out here tonight," Matt said as he jumped into the car wearing a long raincoat. Katie snuggled up next to him.

"I'm glad I went for the thick tights," she said.

"Are we ready?" Riley asked. He pressed a button on the dash. "This should help." From the back seat, Matt groaned and wriggled.

"Heated seats," he said. "I think I'm in love." Katie nudged him hard.

They returned to the car after dinner full of pasta, pizza and scrumptious waffles. Matt moaned about the constriction of his corset throughout. "Is the coast clear?" he asked.

Everyone glanced around. "Yes, be quick. We're cutting this fine and we want to see what everyone else is wearing." By now, Dylan had donned his wig and rubbed his clothes with dirt.

"Close your eyes," Matt said before appearing from behind the car. Everyone did.

"You can open them now."

Riley whistled. "You look like a strange dirty old man in a mac, though I can't say I've ever seen one in such an outfit before. You must be freezing. Can you walk in those heels?"

"He most certainly can," Dylan said.

Matt wore a black corset with black knickers and suspender belt decorated with red ribbons along with stockings and the highest of heels. The whole outfit was topped off with a curly black wig. Katie quickly added more makeup to finish his look.

"We'd better get going," Dylan said, chuckling.

The foyer of the theater was packed with all sorts of people sporting costumes for every one of the characters. Riley noted a few older men dressed as Eddie whose jackets had stunning embroidery.

"I'm too clean," he said to Dylan as they made their way to their seats in the fourth row of the stalls.

Dylan leaned into him. "Don't worry. We can be much dirtier later if you want." The wink sent blood rushing straight to his cock and his jeans gave him no room for expansion. He pushed up the sleeves of his jacket.

"Oh my, those are brilliant. We could get tattoos. Not like that, of course. Now you really look the part."

Once seated, Matt removed his coat, showing off his outfit in its full glory. The man sitting beside him stared, his tongue practically hanging out.

"Great outfit."

Matt muttered thanks and leaned into Katie. They swapped seats. The lights dimmed and the music began as the curtains opened.

Riley couldn't remember the last time he'd had so much fun. They'd chanted all the replies, squirted the water pistols for the rain, chucked the rice everywhere and held up their phones for a light in the darkness. He'd even joined in dancing *The Time Warp* and kissed

Dylan more than once, not caring who saw, brushing aside his concerns about Katie being there to see them. On the drive home, they sang every song at the tops of their voices. At Matt's house, they pulled up just after eleven. Katie's phone beeped, and she frowned.

"Is everything all right?" Riley asked, knowing her situation.

"Yes. Just Mum letting me know she's fine and off to bed and hoping I had a good night. She's been doing well lately. Thank you for taking us. I had a wonderful time."

Matt lived in a converted garage next to his family home, which allowed him some independence and privacy. The cost of buying a home for himself in the village meant it would take ages to save for a deposit or he'd have to leave.

Riley watched as Matt walked unsteadily up the small path with Katie holding them up. "Those two are getting along well," he said to Dylan who had laid his head on Riley's shoulder. "She needs something good in her life."

Dylan nodded and yawned.

"We'd better get you to bed."

"Promises, promises," Dylan replied.

Back in the house, they were greeted by two excited dogs and a somewhat indifferent cat. Upstairs, clothing simply dropped to the floor, and Dylan fell into bed wearing only his briefs and started snoring in minutes. Riley climbed in behind him and wrapped an arm around Dylan's waist, pulling him close enough to kiss the back of his neck and breathe in the remains of his aftershave. He yawned and rubbed his eyes then smiled to himself, moving so their bodies touched in as many places as possible.

This time last year he'd spent Christmas watching his father fade away. Now, he had this wonderful man, plans for updating his house, a new job. In fact, everything he'd ever wanted. This Christmas, he'd hopefully wake up just like this. He pinched himself. *Yep, not dreaming.* He kissed the back of Dylan's neck again. Was it too soon to ask Dylan to move in? He didn't want to waste any more time. He might have fought it to begin with, but he had no doubt of his feelings. He loved Dylan and couldn't see a future without him in it.

Several hours later, Riley awoke with a moan. He opened his eyes, lifted the duvet and glanced down to see Dylan's shining eyes. Dylan let Riley's cock drop from his mouth with a pop.

"Morning," he said, beaming. "What can I say? I had a longing."

Riley watched, entranced, as Dylan stuck out his tongue and swiped the tip of his cock. His whole body trembled with desire.

"Just in case you're wondering, the dogs have been fed and are shut in the living room. So, if you have no objections, I intend to continue." Dylan eased his hand up and down the base of Riley's erection then enclosed the tip of Riley's cock.

Riley stared. He wanted to reach down and press his hand on Dylan's head to encourage him to take in more of himself. Instead, he grabbed the sheet with one hand and dropped the duvet, arching his back and pushing his head back into the pillow. Under the bedding, Dylan hummed, sending vibrations through him. He clenched, his whole body tightening, waiting for climax, while Dylan sucked and fisted him

"Too good," he shouted. He opened his eyes when everything stopped. *What the hell?* His gaze immediately discovered the problem. Sitting, no doubt on Dylan's back, was Queenie. Giggles sounded underneath.

Riley glared at his cat. "Queenie, you are not helping Daddy. Please get off, there's a good girl."

Queenie mewed. Dylan returned to his task, sending the cat up and down.

"Shoo, silly cat." Queenie hopped off gracefully and settled on the corner of the bed. Riley closed his eyes again and concentrated. Under the duvet, Dylan moaned and moved his hand faster.

"Nearly," Riley cried, lifting his arse, wanting Dylan to take more. "Hell, Dylan, the way you..." He shuddered as his orgasm hit. Dylan took it all. When Riley was spent, he crawled up, emerging from under the duvet to kiss Riley, letting him taste himself on those gorgeous swollen lips. He settled astride Riley's chest, took hold of his own cock, letting pre-cum drip on Riley's chest.

"Fuck! You are bloody sensational. Cover me. Cover me with you." The words tumbled out before Riley allowed thought to interfere.

Dylan grinned and did exactly that.

Chapter Twenty-Two

Monday morning, Dylan swallowed the dregs of his mug of tea and shoved the last of his toast into his mouth before grabbing his coat.

"Will we be graced with your company tonight?" his father asked. "You've been staying over there quite a lot the last couple of weeks." His mother gave her husband one of her patented looks.

"What? I'm only asking. It's my turn to cook tonight. I'm planning toad in the hole with veg and onion gravy, which if I remember rightly is one of your favorites. And is it wrong to enjoy spending time with my son?"

Dylan kissed the top of his father's head. "No, of course not, and the answer is yes. Riley's working late tonight so I planned to get a lift to the shop and come home with you, if that's all right. I'll need to pop to Riley's to feed and walk the dogs then I'll be home."

"Working late?" Concern etched his mother's face.

"It's this practice thing. Now Riley's senior partner, he's got to reorganize some accounts and decide whether to promote from within or get someone new.

They're advertising for someone to invest. Not everyone is interested in a practice in the north of England."

"He'll be all right, though, won't he?"

"Oh yeah, Mum. Now, I'd better go."

"Watch the steps. I've salted them, but it's icy out there." His mum poured herself another mug of tea. "I need to be off myself too. We've a delivery at eight-thirty."

As expected, Riley was already waiting. Exhaust bellowed out into the frosty atmosphere. Dylan took more care down the steps, not wanting to end up on his arse. Once inside, he kissed Riley, loving he could without worry.

"Did you sleep well?" he asked.

"I missed you," Riley replied, putting the car into gear.

Warmth flooded into Dylan's chest. "Correct answer, but Matt and I had to go through the details of what we need to do on Saturday with Dan and Max. You are still all right to go with me, aren't you? It'll be our first official out event in the village."

"Wouldn't miss it for the world. How should I dress?"

"Smart-casual, whatever that means," Dylan said.

"Usually no jeans."

Dylan chuckled to himself.

"What the hell are you thinking now?" Riley asked.

"Oh, nothing. Well, maybe you turning up in your underpants. Still, it's a pity you won't be able to wear those black jeans I made you buy. I want to bite your arse when you wear them."

The car swerved slightly. "Shit. Don't say things like that when I'm driving. And I'm damn sure biting my arse wouldn't go down well at a christening."

"Naming ceremony," Dylan corrected. He reached for the radio and began to sing along.

Two hours later, sitting at his desk, Dylan felt a tap on his back. He turned to see Oliver standing behind him. "The boss wants to see you in her office in ten minutes."

"Okay, did she say why?"

"Not to me."

Dylan saved his work and locked his computer. He'd been at the town hall just over three months now. He liked the place and the people, though he'd still not managed a Friday night out. He needed to rectify that. Shaking with nerves, he attempted to casually stroll to Barbara's office.

"Come in."

Dylan opened the door and stepped inside. "You wanted to see me?"

"Yes, and for goodness sake, don't look so worried. I like to have a meeting with anyone new after three months to check how they're getting on." She pulled out a file from the cabinet while he sat. "So, tell me, how do you think it's going so far?"

"Um, well, I think. Everyone has been friendly and helpful. I understand the systems, though it would be beneficial to do something different. I know checking the tax amounts is important, but I'd like to do something more challenging."

"Well, as it happens, I'm putting together a team who will be assessing the value of the council's assets. With cuts to our money from the government, the powers that be have decided to do an audit of all our buildings, paintings and other sources of income. I wondered if you'd like to help. It'll mean working with a team and calculating the value. We haven't done an inventory for a while and some assets will have changed in value. From what I remember on your CV it said you used to work in an antique shop."

"My dad owns one in Clitheroe, but he hardly deals with major treasures."

"The process is the same. You can mix this up with your usual tasks and after Christmas we'll see about moving you around."

"That would be great. I'm glad you consider me reliable enough to take on the task."

She took off her glasses and rubbed her eyes. "You came to us with brilliant qualifications which could have taken you to accounting firms in London or into a bank or stockbrokers, but instead you're here and we want to keep you. Having you get bored is in no one's interest. You've the potential to rise in this job, Dylan, and I want to help you do that."

A slight pang of guilt made him swallow. "Thank you." He couldn't wait to tell Riley. "I'd better get back to my desk." He turned and hurried out of the door.

* * * *

Riley brushed his shoulders for nonexistent bits of fluff then checked his hair in the mirror for the umpteenth time. "You're sure this is all right?" he asked when Dylan re-entered the room.

"Fuck me. That's a Hugo Boss suit you're wearing, isn't it? I'm sure I saw something similar in a magazine." Dylan stood and stared.

"Yeah, but it's a few years old now. You're sure I shouldn't wear black or gray?" His stomach churned with nerves. He wanted to make a good impression with Dylan's friends. The last few years had taken their toll, but he'd kept himself in trim and had picked out the odd gray hair. *Maybe I should dye it now.*

Dylan wrapped his arms around him then kissed him hard. "Now, stop panicking. These are our friends and you look a million dollars. The blue in the suit and tie brings out the color in your eyes."

"You're sure? Have you got the present?"

"It's on the table in the kitchen. We can pick it up when we leave."

Riley took a step back. "You look good, too. Is that a new suit?"

Dylan did a twirl. "It is, but this one is off the peg from M&S. Now, come on. Dan will kill me if I'm late."

Dylan took Riley's hand as they strode into the village hall now decked out with streamers and balloons. One end of the room had trestles already laid out with food and drink. Elsewhere there were tables and chairs and a space in between for dancing should the mood take anyone later. Maxine rushed by. Dylan held up the present. "Where do you want this?" he asked.

"On the table over there."

A hand clapped his back.

"You got here then." Riley turned with Dylan to find Matt and Katie stood behind them.

"Obviously," Dylan said. "You managed to find a suit then. Katie, you look gorgeous. I'll never understand what you see in this idiot."

Katie grinned. "Now, that would be telling, and a lady never tells. Should we offer to help or something?"

Maxine passed by, again accompanied by two other women.

"Max's sister and mother," Dylan whispered in Riley's ear.

Maxine halted. "Just sit down for now. Dan's changing the baby. Why do they always have to do the biggest toilet when it's not convenient?"

More people arrived. Dylan led Riley to a table. "I'll get us a drink. I've a feeling we might need one."

Gradually the room filled. Riley recognized a few older villagers, people from his youth who he hadn't spoken to for years. Tony arrived with Lori and sat at the next table. Dylan immediately rose to get them a drink. Tony nodded at Riley. He rubbed his hands on his trousers, sure this day would be a long one. Every so often someone glanced their way. Word had obviously spread.

"Stop it," Dylan said, placing a hand on his bouncing knee. "People are curious, that's all. We are the only gays in the village, well, except for Mandy and Sandra over there."

Riley covered Dylan's hand with his own. "It's just I've got this horrible feeling the party will turn into the most horrible school reunion ever." Just as he spoke, a large man emerged out of a crowd of new arrivals and lumbered toward them.

"Bugger me, it is you. Riley Ormerod as I live and breathe. I thought you were away down in London. What you doing back here? You remember me, don't you?"

Riley was unlikely to forget the person who'd called him names and pushed him around the football field and elsewhere at any opportunity. What he had forgotten, however, was the obnoxious git was Maxine's uncle. He stood and held out his hand.

"Of course I remember you, George. And I live here now. I'm senior partner in a solicitors practice in Preston. I came back when my father was ill." By now Tony had turned around. Their gazes met. Tony clearly recognized Riley's tormentor as well.

George took his hand. "I heard about your dad. Cancer, a bad business. Took my mum last year. We must catch up later."

Not if I have any say in things, we won't. Riley sat back down. It was ridiculous to be so affected by someone he hadn't seen for so many years.

"You all right?" Dylan asked. "You're white as a sheet."

"When we were young, George took great delight in bullying me. Called me all sorts of names. Any time the teacher wasn't looking, he'd hit me. He was so much bigger than me. I can imagine his reaction when he finds out he was right after all when he called me gay as well as other things."

Dylan grinned at him then winked. "Well, maybe we should snog the faces off each other, so everyone gets to know at once."

The tinkling of a fork against a glass interrupted them. "Showtime," Dylan said. Dan and Maxine stood at the front with the baby in Dan's arms and Maxine holding the hand of their two-year-old son.

"We'd like to welcome you all to our naming ceremony for this little one. If the supporters could join us."

Dylan rose along with Matt and two others. "We wanted to have a party to celebrate the arrival of this little one, but neither of us are church-goers, so Max and I decided to have this ceremony. Matt and Dylan are my oldest friends and, along with Lucy and Mel here, have agreed to be involved in her life, which basically means buying her presents and babysitting as far as we're concerned. So, without further ado, raise your glasses to welcome Violet Louise Outhwaite to the world."

Riley raised his glass along with everyone else.

"And now we've done that, eat, drink and be merry, and thanks for all the presents."

While Dylan was off socializing or practicing carrying the baby around, Riley got a chance to talk to Tony. He placed a pint in front of him before taking a chair. Tony gazed toward his son.

"He's always been good with kids."

Riley turned to look. Dylan held the baby in his arms, swaying to the music playing in the background. *He thinks I'm depriving Dylan of the chance to be a father with me being older?*

"We talked about it — children."

Tony stared at him with wide eyes. "Really? And did you decide anything?"

"We didn't rule out the possibility. Forty-two isn't too old these days when you consider how old some fathers are. I like children, too. I just never thought I might have any. We'd need to investigate further how to go about it. I wouldn't mind adopting. We have a lot to offer between us, and if Dylan does decide to set up on his own and work from home, he'd be there and can plan his hours. Now I'm senior partner, and the firm is prospering, we can afford a family in a few years. I'm in this for the long term, but it's a lot to think about, Tony, and we've only been together for a brief time. With the best will in the world..."

Riley glanced over to where Dylan had finally handed Violet back to her father. Their gazes met, and he smiled, warmth pooling in his stomach. Did he want that? A house, children, pets and a man who loved him? The ache in his heart gave him his answer.

"And marriage? Is that on the cards?"

Riley turned back to his friend. "Wow, you don't believe in subtlety, do you?"

"He's my son. He may only be twenty-two, but he's always been strangely conventional. He used to watch the video of our wedding over and over. He won't remember, but when he was five he asked if boys could marry each other. We knew then, so when he told us he was gay, it wasn't exactly a surprise. We worried but, as I've said, he's much more level-headed than his sister. For some reason unknown to me, he wants you, and I'm not prepared to lose my son, or my best friend, over that."

Riley sipped his fizzy water. "I'm glad. It would have torn him apart to lose you."

"Life's too short for stupid grudges."

A noise behind him interrupted their conversation. "Sooo, this is where you are."

George. Riley's heart sank. "We haven't exactly been hiding," Tony replied through gritted teeth. From the slight slur in the man's voice, Riley guessed George had already consumed a few.

"Good to see young people having kids, like Dan and Maxine, isn't it? How's that lad of yours, Tony?"

Tony bristled. Riley almost moved a hand to touch his knee but stopped himself in time. "He's one of the baby's supporters, or didn't you notice him standing there when Dan made the announcement."

"Ah yes. Always good for a girl to have a gay uncle. Isn't that what they say? I assume he's still a poof, then."

"And you're still as offensive as you always were." Riley got his words in before Tony rose to the bait. "What is it you want, George? It's not like we were friends in the past. You were a bastard then and from what I've seen and heard you still are. I hear your wife left you a few years back, and your kids don't visit. I've no doubt they couldn't wait to get away from you."

George breathed in, expanding his chest, and glared at Riley. "At least I've got kids. Couldn't find anyone in London prepared to put up with someone as lily-livered as you then? Or are you a poof as well?" Riley willed away the red flush of heat rushing into his cheeks.

"That's it. You are, aren't you? Well, well. Seems I was right all along. You'd better keep your lad away from him, Tony. God knows what he's picked up in London, or should I say who?"

Tony scraped his chair back and stood up. "Outside, you bastard. This isn't the place for me to punch your lights out." George stood as well. Before Riley could intercede, Dylan appeared out of nowhere with Dan by his side.

"I think you should leave, George," Dan said. "We only invited you because you're Maxine's uncle. We heard what you said."

"You're going to choose this poofter and his pal over a relative?" George spluttered.

Dan placed himself in the man's space. "You bet I am. You're like something out of the dark ages. No wonder your Miranda left you and Cheryl and Jemma moved as far away as possible. They were too embarrassed to admit you were their father when you marched with a right-wing group and appeared on TV spouting your brand of poison. Now, before we throw you out, go."

George slammed down his pint, sending liquid flying over the table. He stormed across the room and slammed the door behind him.

"We were handling it," Tony protested, rubbing his hands together.

Dylan stepped forward. "We know, Dad," he said quietly. "We didn't want a scene, that's all, and Dan hates him anyway."

"I wanted to punch him so hard," Riley growled.

"Not worth sullying your fists with," Dylan said grinning. "I wouldn't want your knuckles bruised, or fingers damaged, now, would I?"

Tony placed his hands over his ears. "No, not in front of me. We made a deal."

Dylan kissed Riley's cheek, there, in front of anyone who had glanced in their direction. "I'll get us some food, Dad." He leaned into Riley.

"Are you all right?"

Riley nodded. "I'm fine. Your dad and I were having an interesting discussion before that pillock turned up."

Lori appeared with Sue and her husband. "Look who I found." She glanced at each of them. "Did I miss something?"

Tony threaded his arm through hers. "No, love. We're off to get something to eat if you care to join us." He turned to Riley and Dylan. "We'll get some for you two as well, okay, and leave you to talk."

Riley sank back down into his seat and Dylan moved a chair so they were thigh to thigh. "You and Dad have been talking, eh? I don't know whether to be worried or happy about this development. Care to share?"

Riley took several gulps from his pint. "Your dad invited me for Christmas dinner and I said yes." Here wasn't the place for anything more. Maybe once he'd sorted the house and taken over at work, they could discuss the future.

Dylan took hold of his hand. "I can't tell you how happy I am you and Dad have buried the hatchet and not in each other's head. Will you dance with me later?"

"I'd love to. You can foxtrot, can't you?" Riley skewed his head to one side, questioning.

"Ha bloody ha. You're not that old, and, as it happens, I can foxtrot and waltz. People will most probably stare."

Riley gulped down the lump of fear rising in his throat. "Of course, they'll stare because I'll be dancing with the most handsome man in the room."

Dylan put his fingers in his mouth and made a retching noise. "I can't believe you said that."

Riley put a hand either side of Dylan's face, not caring who saw them, and kissed him. Dylan's shocked expression was worth it. "Why wouldn't I say it? I can't remember ever feeling this happy. Things have finally started to go right for me — for both of us."

A moment of worry sneaked into his mind. There was still the practice to consider. Even with Patrick leaving, he hadn't yet managed to come out there. Then there was the retirement dinner. Should he have fronted it up and turned up with Dylan regardless? Too late for that. He'd made his decision. Dylan would understand, and Katie would forgive him asking her not to say anything. He just needed a little more time. He touched the wooden table superstitiously then stood and took Dylan in his arms. Whether people were staring at them or not, he didn't care. He only had eyes for the man in front of him.

Chapter Twenty-Three

By the time it reached five o' clock at the end of the next working week, Dylan couldn't wait to get home. The day had been fraught. He'd arrived late after there had been an accident in icy conditions on the motorway. Friday morning was usually less busy for reasons unknown, but this morning, they'd spent an hour not moving. Yes, on the plus side. this had given him more time with Riley, but all Riley had done was fret about being late for an appointment. He hadn't even kissed him goodbye, just bundled him out of the car at the town hall and sped off.

Other than car journeys, he hadn't managed to see much of Riley all week. He'd been like a cat on hot bricks and he'd practically bitten Dylan's head off when he'd suggested an evening away from working late at night.

'I'm sorry.' Riley had apologized immediately. *'There's so much I need to do and with the bathroom fitters...'* Dylan had soothed things over, telling himself things would settle down, but he'd missed Riley every evening when

he'd been forced to get a bus to Clitheroe. Of course, the bathroom fitters had managed to let the dogs out one day. Fortunately, Isabel had secured them again and Riley hadn't sacked them on the spot. On top of all this, today Dylan had a meeting with Barbara Wilson, his boss, about the new audit and his stomach was already doing cartwheels, but at least he wouldn't have to face a long bus journey on a cold and dark Friday night. He had plans for the evening which he hoped would take Riley's mind off everything else.

Despite such plans bolstering his mood, by the time he arrived at his desk, he was wound tighter than a drum. After sprinting up the next flight of stairs to his meeting, Dylan found his line manager and the three others in the team waiting for him.

"I'm sorry, there was a crash on the M65," he said, breathing heavily.

Barbara had glanced over her glasses at him. "I'm sure it couldn't be helped. Let's get going, shall we?"

Nerves seized his bowels, but he took his seat, wishing he'd had time to get a coffee and a visit the loo. In the end, despite his worries, the meeting had gone well. They'd managed to create a plan ready to get going on the audit after Christmas. He breathed a heavy sigh of relief, flited quickly to the toilet, then returned to his desk and a welcome mug of coffee.

This time of year, the council began its annual spending audit along with projections for the next year and more long-term planning. Finance was tight with national government cutting funds. Rumors of library closures, as well as a reduction in funds for social welfare, were rife in the local papers.

He stared at the figures in front of him. The council had several libraries and museums supported by council tax. They couldn't raise the tax enough to pay for them all. He hated this aspect of his job. No matter how often he told himself he was simply performing a statistical exercise, Dylan knew his figures would affect people's lives. Others would make the decisions, but that didn't stop him feeling guilty.

Later in the morning, he lifted his head at the sound of shouting coming from Barbara's office. He glanced over at Lucy, one of the other accountants in his open-plan office. He nodded at the commotion. "What's going on?"

Lucy stood and hurried over to him. "Someone's leaked details of the cuts to the local paper. A councilor got it in the neck at a meeting last night and complained, so now they think it's someone from here. No doubt they'll interview everyone. You haven't said anything, have you?"

Dylan shook his head. "No. I don't know anything anyway, and even if I did, I wouldn't dare." He rubbed his tired eyes. "Before I started work here, I'm not sure I realized how much doom and gloom would go with this job. Everything we do deals with cutting costs and services."

Lucy shrugged. "That's local government for you. At least we don't have to *make* the decisions."

An office door slammed, shaking the glass. That afternoon, everyone had their turn at being interviewed in an atmosphere of doubt and recrimination. He came out feeling guilty, even though he'd done nothing. No doubt the person would be caught and disciplined at some point. After all this kerfuffle, as he prepared to leave, his phone rang.

"Hello, you. Please tell me you're on your way to pick me up and take me away from all this madness." The pause before Riley answered suggested the opposite might be true.

"What is it?" Dylan asked.

"Something's come up. I won't be able to give you a lift tonight. I'm going to be late and tired..." *And grouchy obviously.*

"That's okay. I'll see to the dogs and wait up for you. I suppose it can't be helped, whatever it is." Yes, he was fishing. Something felt off, just as Riley had been out of sorts all week.

"No, don't stay. Why don't you go home? I'm sure Tony and Lori would love an evening with you. I'll just be knackered. It's been a long week."

Home? I thought I was going home. And you still haven't told me what you're doing tonight. "Okay, I'll take the dogs out then pop over there and see you tomorrow. I hope your meeting, is it, goes well."

"I'm sure it'll be fine. You need to get off or you'll miss your bus. I'll see you tomorrow."

The call ended before Dylan had a chance to reply. He stared at it, then noticed the time.

By five o'clock it was dark and dismal when he stepped outside to make his way to the bus station. Rain had soaked the pavements, but at least it wasn't cold enough to freeze. He hurried along with others on their way home. Once safely on the bus, he called his father to let him know the change of plans. He'd be waiting at the station for him. His father had suggested he come home to dinner rather than be on his own, but he needed to walk the dogs, and he wanted to be there when Riley came home, despite what Riley had said. All right, he hadn't quite moved in officially, but he'd thought that day was getting closer. Now, he wasn't so sure. Reaching into his bag, he pulled out his headphones and settled down to listen to some music.

* * * *

A light drizzle covered the windscreen as his father pulled up at the house. Dylan sighed, knowing he'd have to walk the dogs in the rain.

"You all right?" his father asked. "You've been quiet. Are you sure you don't want to come with me? Your mother would be pleased to see you."

So much of him wanted to say yes, but he needed to face Riley. Secrets festered. "I'll be round tomorrow," he replied. "I've got to walk the mutts. Then I'm planning to catch up with my viewing while Riley isn't around. I'll be fine."

"If you're sure."

No, Dylan wasn't sure. In fact, he was anything but sure. Still, he opened the door and stepped out into the cold, damp night.

The yapping started as soon as he turned the key in the lock. "Okay, okay," he called. "Anyone would think you'd been starved and left alone all day." He'd waved his dad off and entered the house to find two excited dogs. He knelt and fussed them before leading them into the kitchen, making himself a mug of coffee and feeding them. Queenie arrived a few minutes later and jumped onto the table. Dylan stroked her head, drank slowly savoring the taste of the warm liquid then, once he'd finished, grabbed the leads from their hooks and set out once more into the dark.

After fifteen minutes, both he and the dogs had had enough. They returned home and settled onto the sofa. His phone rang, and he picked it up hoping to find

Riley on the other end, but that wasn't the name on the screen. He pressed the green button.

"Matt, to what do I owe this interruption to my exciting evening alone on the sofa?"

"I'm bored. Wondered if you fancied some company. I'm on my way home from a job. Thought I might grab a curry and beer for two if you want, seeing as our partners have left us high and dry and are out on a jolly tonight."

Dylan sat up. *What the fuck?* He gathered himself together. "A curry would be great. I'll see you soon." He didn't say anything else.

By the time Matt arrived, Dylan's imagination had reached overload. *Why didn't Riley tell me the truth? What else is he keeping from me?* So many questions. Matt placed the bags on the kitchen table while Dylan sorted plates with shaking hands. His friend had obviously expected him to know about whatever was going on.

Matt handed him a loaded plate. "Chicken biryani for you and beef madras for me. I've rice, chips and naans as well as a six-pack. Should we eat in here?"

"Nah, let's take it into the living room," Dylan said.

Once seated, Matt opened the bottles and handed one to Dylan. "I bet they're not having curry at Melcote Manor tonight," he said.

So that's where they are. So much for a meeting at work. "No, I doubt they are. That place is definitely too posh for curry."

"I'm a bit miffed really, but Katie said only people who worked there were invited to the leaving do for Riley's partner. Still, I wouldn't have known what to say to anyone with them all having gone to university."

Reality smacked Dylan between the eyes. "Did Katie say specifically that partners weren't invited?"

Matt put down his spoon. Dylan could practically see him trying to work things out. "Bugger me. You didn't know, did you? He didn't tell you."

"No," Dylan replied letting the knowledge sink in. "He didn't."

"Now I come to think about it, she didn't exactly say anything about partners. I told her I was working today and wasn't sure when I'd be finished, and that I was worried about fitting in, especially as you weren't going. I sort of assumed it was a workers' only affair."

Myriad of emotions battled for dominance—fear, hurt, anger, resentment. In the end, anger won. "Riley's not out about being gay at work," Dylan said quietly, through gritted teeth.

Matt glared at him. "Do you think he deliberately told Katie not to bring me? Fucking hell, he made her lie to me, didn't he, to protect himself as well as keeping you in the dark? That's harsh."

Dylan nodded and uncurled his fists. "I suspect so. I mean I get it, but why didn't he just tell me? I would have understood he couldn't just turn up with a partner, especially a much younger male partner. He didn't have to lie to me like I'm some stupid teenager whose feelings might be hurt."

"I guess you lot never stop having to come out."

Dylan frowned. "I honestly didn't think it would be such a massive thing now. He's going to be senior partner in the firm, and he was out in London. He's been in a terrible mood all week and now I know why. I thought he'd accepted me being younger than him. Maybe he hasn't. Maybe he's just embarrassed or ashamed. Maybe I'm being an idiot to think, now Mum and Dad know, everything is all right."

"Mate, I don't know what to say. You need to have this out with him. Don't let this fester. It might not be about you. Perhaps this bloke who's retiring is homophobic or something, and Riley's just waiting for him to go."

Dylan swallowed several mouthfuls of beer and stared at the food cooling in front of him. "Could be. He did work with Riley's father. Maybe Riley didn't want to challenge him, either. He never told his dad. I can't imagine living like that, always worrying about saying the wrong thing or using the wrong pronoun. Riley cut his father out of his life rather than tell him the truth," he said, not quite believing his own words. *He's not going to do that with me. I won't be hidden away.* He picked up his plate. "Come on, let's eat up and watch a film. There must be something on Netflix." He needed to think exactly what he was going to say.

A couple of hours later, Matt yawned. "I'd better get off. I don't want to be here when Riley arrives, and Katie said she'd ring when she got home." A smile danced over his lips.

Dylan grinned. His friend had it bad. He punched him in the arm. "You're smitten, aren't you?"

"I may be. I've no idea what she's doing with me. I'm meeting her family this weekend. Her mum's doing better, but they all know it's only a matter of time. It's hard on them. The way she copes. She really is amazing. Don't say anything, but I'm thinking of proposing. I know she can't leave home with her mum being as she is, but I don't mind a long engagement."

"Wow, you don't believe in hanging around, do you?"

"Until tonight I'd have said hark at the pot calling the kettle black. You've fancied Riley for years, and you're practically living with him. Sort this thing out, Dylan. So, he made a mistake. No one is perfect. You too could get down on one knee, maybe at Christmas or New Year. You always loved a romantic gesture."

Matt knew him too well. "I'll see what he has to say before making any rash decisions."

"Just don't cut off your nose to spite your face. You've waited long enough to get him."

Matt was right, of course. After he waved him off, Dylan sat on the sofa and patted the cushion. Both dogs joined him immediately. All he had to do now was wait for Riley to come home.

* * * *

Riley was the first to arrive at the restaurant. He'd booked a table in an alcove off the main room to give them some privacy. The maître d' fussed around, checking the presentation and decorations.

"Everything looks wonderful," Riley said. "The rest of the guests will be here soon. Please show them to the table when they arrive."

"Very good, sir."

His phone beeped. He checked it and found a message from Dylan telling him not to work too hard and that he'd be waiting for him. Guilt smacked him between the eyes and he sank down on a chair staring at the words.

Damn! Had Dylan guessed? He held his head in his hands. *I've been such a coward. I'll tell him the truth when I get home. He'll understand. He will understand.* He'd allowed his fear to take control. He'd told himself that after Patrick had retired, he'd tell the others. Before he could put his thoughts into any order and reply to the text, people began to arrive.

Riley fixed his smile and greeted everyone. Patrick, the senior partner, took his seat at the head of the table with Riley and Mary Whewell either side. They chatted for a little while until others appeared. Another wave of guilt hit him when Katie arrived.

"You look beautiful," he said, to make conversation. She muttered a reply and took her seat, clearly unhappy about the circumstances.

The arrival of Ruth and Kathleen and their partners led to more conversation. Afzal arrived soon after, accompanied by a handsome man introduced as his partner. Riley shook hands with both. He caught Katie's glare, clearly indicating her annoyance at being there on her own. He attempted a smile. She didn't respond.

They'd chosen their food orders in advance, so once everyone was seated, starters were placed in front of them.

"What do you do?" he asked Zahid, Afzal's partner, sat next to him, simply to make conversation in between mouthfuls.

"I'm a psychiatrist at Preston General. I wasn't sure whether to come tonight. Afzal insisted, though."

Riley gripped his fork and swallowed the food. His appetite had all but disappeared. Was it wrong to imagine Afzal and Zahid would have more problems being together than him and Riley?

"I'm glad you came," he said.

Zahid hesitated as if he was trying to work out how Riley would react. Afzal might have indeed taken a risk bringing his male partner, but he'd been brave when Riley hadn't.

"We don't get to go out together much," Zahid continued. "His family don't know about him, or us. It can make things awkward, and with him being younger than me..."

Riley could imagine. He also realized how little he knew about the personal lives of those around him, so careful had he been about his own. He needed to change. "Yes, it must be difficult."

"I only agreed to come because Afzal was right, as always, and my parents have always encouraged me to be proud of who I am."

Riley nodded and let the last of his beautifully presented seafood salad slide down his throat. He glanced across at Katie, who was deep in conversation with Mary and Afzal. "I would guess coming out wasn't easy for you."

"I was lucky. I'll not say they were happy to begin with, but they've come around. Having me in their lives is more important to them than anything else. Anyway, I have three brothers to carry on the family name, and as I'm the youngest, I got away with much more than they did."

"Are your parents doctors as well?" Riley asked.

"We all are, in different fields."

"Wow, I bet you have problems deciding who carves the turkey at Christmas." He paused, realizing what he'd said. "I'm sorry — stupid remark."

Zahid leaned toward him. "I'll let you in on a secret. We have Christmas dinner complete with sprouts, watch the Queen's Speech and *Doctor Who*, and Mum wouldn't miss *Strictly*, believe me." He chuckled. Afzal glanced over and smiled. Riley felt like he was seeing the reserved man he'd worked with for a year in a whole new light.

"He's handsome, your man," Riley said.

Zahid smiled. "I know."

Maybe it was the man's training, but Riley found himself at ease talking to Zahid. He hoped they'd accept an invitation to dinner with him and Dylan, if there was still such a thing as him and Dylan. Later, while they ate their main courses, Patrick told the group of his retirement plans.

"As some of you know, Mary and I have a little villa in Tuscany, so before Brexit cuts us off, we intend to retire there and drink as much Italian wine as we can."

"Sounds like an exciting prospect," Riley said.

"Well, I know the firm is in good hands. Your father was a great solicitor and his son is the same. Your arrival back with us came at a crucial time and you brought in clients. While others have shut down, we've done well. I'm sure you'll find someone to take over from me and bring some new blood and money into the place. Someone who'll continue to nurture young talent." He nodded at Katie. "Whewell and Ormerod may be no more soon, but I'm sure the firm will continue to prosper under your leadership, Riley. And now, I think it's time for a toast. Raise your glasses everyone to Whewell and Ormerod. Best wishes for the future."

Riley raised his glass, clinking it with those nearest. There had been some interest in the partnership already and he wanted to interview each person to make sure they fitted.

Over the next couple of hours, wine flowed, more wonderful food arrived and was eaten, and the company buzzed with laughter and conversation. Riley listened to stories from the past, old clients, difficult cases, successes and failures, the wide and varied lives of solicitors in a northern city dealing with everything from conveyancing to murder over the more than thirty years Patrick had worked for the firm. Excusing himself, Riley hurried to the entrance to collect the flowers for Mary and the leaving present they'd bought for Patrick. He jumped at a tap on his shoulder and turned to find Mary behind him.

"Is everything all right?" he asked. "You're not feeling ill, are you?"

"I'm fine. I told Patrick I was heading for the loo. Can we sit for a minute?"

"Of course." Worried, he led them to a couple of seats at the edge of the reception area.

"You may think this is presumptuous of me, but a life-threatening illness can loosen your tongue. You've always been a private man, Riley, which isn't a bad thing, but Patrick has always worried about you, especially after your father died. Patrick had a great deal of time for Arthur, who was a great support in his youth. He's also a great admirer of you and your abilities. But anyway, I'm getting off the point." She took a breath. "I have a great friend, Barbara Wilson, who works in the town hall."

Butterflies released into Riley's stomach. He gripped the arm of the chair but didn't reply.

"I was rather hoping you might not be alone here tonight. Barbara mentioned seeing you giving a lift to a young man in her team. She also mentioned she'd seen you kissing. Why didn't you bring him, Riley?"

He slumped into the chair. "Simple answer is I let myself be afraid. I wasn't sure how Patrick would react. Dylan and I haven't been together for very long and…" He hesitated. "And he's a lot younger than me."

Mary placed a hand over his. "Oh, my dear man, Patrick knows you're gay."

Riley jerked his head back. "He does?"

"People gossip, and the law can be a closed shop. He talked to a few friends from London who mentioned it, as well as telling him what a great solicitor you are. Many of them wanted your contact number to recruit you themselves. Patrick sees you as the son we never had. He hoped you'd trust him enough to tell him."

Riley swallowed hard, pushing down the lump in his throat. "I didn't tell anyone here. I didn't want my father to know. I overheard him making some homophobic remarks to Patrick many years ago. While I was so far away from him, I could keep my two worlds separate. Dylan's sort of blown that apart."

"Does Dylan know you're here?"

Could this woman read minds? He shook his head. "I've been stupid. I've already decided to go home tonight and confess all. He deserves that much from me. I was a coward. I thought he'd be upset and annoyed with me."

Katie appeared and hurried toward them. "Patrick was worried when you didn't return," she said.

"I'm sorry, my dear. I needed a few words with Riley here." She turned back toward him. "You must bring your young man to dinner before we go."

Riley nodded, catching Katie's confused expression. He let Mary head back. "Katie?"

"Yes, Riley."

"I'm sorry about tonight. I've been an idiot. Please forgive me. Age doesn't always make you wise."

She touched his arm. "I know you're my boss, but just sort this out. Dylan will forgive you. He knows how hard this has been for you."

Riley walked back to the restaurant, determined to confess all as soon as he got home, hopeful Dylan would indeed forgive his foolishness.

Chapter Twenty-Four

Riley paused at the door. He'd been such an idiot. He'd left the party after hugging Patrick and Mary with Patrick's words still ringing in his ears. Life was indeed too short. He turned the key in the lock and walked in.

"I'm home," he called.

"We're in here," Dylan replied.

"I'll make us some cocoa." He pottered round in the kitchen then carried the mugs to the living room. Dylan lay on the sofa with the dogs at his feet. Riley placed the drinks on the table and nudged Dylan over until his head lay in Riley's lap. He stroked Dylan's hair. Somehow, all the words he'd rehearsed all the way home had disappeared.

Dylan gazed up at him. "Good evening?"

Idly, Riley ran his fingers through Dylan's hair, which glowed bright in the light of the fire. He rested his other hand on Dylan's hip.

"About that."

Dylan tensed then shifted until he was positioned with several inches between them. "Yes," he snapped back.

Riley panicked. His stomach churned, making him nauseated. He willed the meal he'd just eaten down and rubbed his sweaty palms down his trousers. It was almost as if Dylan was waiting for his confession. *He knows.*

Pull yourself together. The air felt thick. He needed to get his words out. He touched Dylan's hand, but he pulled away. *Okay.* Riley cleared his throat and began.

"I owe you an apology — no, more than that, much more. I might have led you to believe that I had a meeting tonight. I didn't."

"Oh, do tell."

Clearly, Dylan wasn't going to make this easy for him, and he had no right to expect anything else... "Tonight was Patrick's retirement party. I should have told you. You should have been there with me. I have no defense except stupidity."

"Thank you for telling me now." Dylan's tone was flat.

Needing to fill the silence, Riley continued. "You have every right to be angry with me. I promise it won't happen again. In fact, they already know about you and we have an invitation to dinner with Patrick and Mary. *She* admonished me for not bringing you tonight. She works with someone called Barbara Wilson."

Dylan stood, scattering the dogs onto the floor. "I know," he said. With everything going on in their lives, that nugget of information had somehow slipped his mind.

Riley stared. "You know? Why didn't you tell me?"

"Truth? I forgot. She told me she'd seen you giving me a lift. It was when we weren't together."

"Please, Dylan, sit back down."

Relief flowed through him when Dylan sat. Riley took his hand. "Can you forgive me? I know I was wrong. It's just… I was afraid."

"Were you afraid of them knowing you were gay, or afraid of them finding out about me?"

Riley had promised to tell the truth. "A little bit of both, I think. All my life, I hid myself from my father and I wasn't sure how Patrick would see me if he knew. I'm not as brave as you, and I can't help worrying how people will see us."

"I don't care about people, Riley. I care about my parents, my sister, my best friends and, most of all, you. I care about how *you* see us. And just for your information, Matt came here tonight. He told me where you were. Katie told *him* the truth. She couldn't lie to him."

Riley's blood turned to ice under Dylan's gaze, despite the heat from the fire. He shivered. Out of nowhere, panic set in. He struggled to control his breathing. His heart galloped. He started to shake. He'd ruined everything. *Oh God, no. He's going to leave me, and I'll be all alone again.* Tears flowed unchecked down his face. "I'm so sorry."

"Riley. Riley." Arms wrapped around him. "Breathe with me, Riley. Short in through your nose and long out through your mouth."

For a minute, he couldn't. He babbled in between breaths. Finally, Dylan's words cut through. He took a breath in then out, gradually slowing until Dylan lifted his chin and gazed at him.

"Enough, Riley. You're going to listen to me, okay?"

Riley nodded. He couldn't do anything else. Dylan handed him the mug. "Here, take a drink." He did as he was told and waited.

"You *should* have told me where you were going tonight. I'd have understood you not wanting to announce your sexuality by taking me to a dinner. You didn't trust me enough, though, and that's what hurt the most."

Riley opened his mouth, but Dylan pressed a finger to his lips. "You get this one chance, Riley. From now on, you and I are a team. We face everything together, or not at all. For too long, you haven't allowed yourself to live. You've hidden your feelings. Well, not with me. I love you, with all your faults and insecurities. If anyone wants to take issue with the gap in our ages, that's their problem. We stand together, or not at all."

Dylan leaned forward and pushed him back on the sofa. He pressed his lips to Riley's who then opened his mouth to let Dylan plunder him with his tongue. Dylan ground on top of him then stopped. An inch away from him, he whispered, "You know what the best thing about arguing is, don't you? Makeup sex. And you look so hot in that suit."

Riley gulped, and his cock stirred. He didn't reply.

Dylan leaned back and gazed at him. "I want you to take me upstairs, bend me over anything and take me still wearing your suit while I'm naked. I want you to fill me and make me scream your name."

Jeez, his breathing increased so rapidly, he had to concentrate to calm it down. Could he? It had been so long since he'd fucked anyone. He'd never...not with. He didn't even want to think of that man's name, not now. He sat rooted to the spot.

Dylan stood and held out his hand. "Are you okay?"

"I'm fine," Riley managed. "I think. I have no problem with the suggestion even though I haven't for a while."

Dylan grinned. "It's like riding a bike. Same thing goes in the same place. I need to feel you. I want to wake up tomorrow morning knowing I've been had."

Once in their bedroom, Dylan undid his shirt button by button and pulled it out of his trousers. Riley watched from the bed totally transfixed. The room didn't offer a variety of options as to place and position.

Socks flew past him. Dylan gradually undid his belt followed by his zip and slipped his trousers and briefs down in one swift movement, leaving him buck naked. He wrapped a hand around his cock and began to stroke.

"See anything you like?"

Riley nodded, surprised his tongue wasn't lolling out of his mouth or his cock tugging him forward. He swallowed, to wet his desert-like throat. "The mirror," he croaked. Dylan glanced over his shoulder at the wardrobe door.

"Hmm, I like your thinking. That way I'll be able to see you, too." He scooted over the bed moving to and fro until he'd found the perfect vantage point. His pale skin shone in the lamplight.

Riley said nothing, simply closed the space between them and sank to his knees behind Dylan. He spread his arse cheeks and licked a stripe down. Dylan groaned and squirmed under his touch.

"Please," he whispered. Riley lapped at his hole, tasting his familiar shower gel and something muskier. He had the feeling Dylan had left nothing to chance. He curled his tongue, pushed at the opening and placed his hands on Dylan's hips to pull him closer. Dylan's moans sent blood coursing to his cock. He toed off his shoes while keeping up his momentum, licking, lapping, probing until Dylan had loosened under his attention.

"Need you to fuck me, or I'm going to come from your tongue. Please, Riley, so empty, need you now."

Riley lifted his head, glanced sideways to see Dylan gazing at him in the mirror. "You sure you want me this way?" he asked.

"Take off the jacket, loosen your tie and undo the shirt but leave it on, hanging open, and pull out your dick."

As Dylan lay over the side of the bed, his eyes never leaving the striptease Riley provided, Riley almost pinched himself to check he wasn't dreaming.

"Oh yeah. Looks good on you with that smattering of hair. Now for the main attraction." Dylan's gaze didn't leave Riley's face as Riley reached in and freed his cock. He stood rigid and already dripping with need. A wave of doubt swept over him until Dylan grinned at him and wiggled his arse. Riley reached for a condom and the lube in the drawer.

"No condom. I got tested in September and last week. You told me you've been tested, too. I don't want anything between us. I told you, it's you and me from now on. I'll be fine. Lube yourself and edge in, make me feel you and do me dressed like that. You look like some rampant billionaire executive."

Riley chuckled. "You have some imagination." He covered his cock with lube and moved into position, letting the head touch flesh. Taking hold, he pushed in agonizingly slowly, desperate not to hurt Dylan.

"Oh God, yes, keep going. You feel so big but awesome."

Riley kept pressing forward, loving the tightness around him until his cock was buried so deep none remained visible. "I'm in," he said. Dylan pushed back to be certain as they each gazed at the image of their joining in the mirror.

"Fuck me, we look good like this." Riley kissed the back of Dylan's neck then pulled out and slammed back in. He loved watching his cock appear then disappear.

"You look so good under me. I'd forgotten how amazing this felt, being inside someone, feeling such heat. You're so beautiful."

"Less talking, more fucking. Harder," Dylan cried. Riley wasn't sure he could. They grunted and groaned in tandem as Riley sped up angling so he hit Dylan's prostate with each push. He grabbed hold of Dylan's hips, knowing he would leave bruising, wanting to leave his mark. Dylan pushed back meeting every thrust.

"Oh fuck, yeah just there, so bloody good. Make me yours. Damn, listen to me talking bollocks. Going to touch myself. Don't think it'll take much."

Dylan lifted himself enough to grab hold of his discarded briefs then his cock. With a couple of strokes, Dylan came. Rippling muscles gripped Riley as tingles ran down his spine. Seconds later, his orgasm ripped out of him and he filled Dylan's arse with warmth until he couldn't pump out anymore. He fell forward still inside Dylan as he attempted to catch his breath.

"You can do me again," Dylan whispered. "Not straight away, though. My poor arse needs to recover from such a delicious pounding."

Riley felt conspicuous being nearly fully dressed. "I need the loo and to clean my teeth, not to mention get undressed."

Dylan beamed at him. "Me too. We can share."

Ten minutes later, they lay in bed under the duvet. "You know, the dogs have been awfully quiet while we... I hope they're behaving themselves downstairs."

Dylan snuggled next to him. "Maybe we frightened them with all the noise. I sort of miss them sniffing and snoring."

As if by magic, the door flew open and Bonnie and Millie pushed their way in. "They must have heard you," Riley said, picking up Bonnie, who couldn't manage to jump like Millie. After a fuss, the pair settled into their usual positions at the end of the bed.

Dylan stroked Riley's chest. All was back to being right in his world. "You know, we should have a dinner party here for everyone from your practice. It might be easier to introduce us as a couple on home turf. What do you think?"

Warmth pooled in Riley's chest. He loved how Dylan used 'us' and 'we'. He yawned. "You're right, as always. Now, what shall we do tomorrow?"

"I did say I'd see Mum and Dad, but I'll put them off. Let's drive up to the Forest of Bowland, take the dogs, feed the ducks at Dunsop Bridge, find a pub for lunch, then come back and watch *Strictly* like an old married couple."

Riley tucked himself around Dylan and pressed a kiss to the back of his neck. Dylan wriggled back next to him.

"Is it wrong I love the sound of that?"

Dylan yawned. "Need to sleep. You've worn me out. Love you, Riley."

Riley blinked away a tear. "I love you too." And he did, so much more than he'd ever imagined possible.

Chapter Twenty-Five

Sunday morning, Riley slipped out of bed, leaving Dylan asleep. He tiptoed out, the dogs at his heels, intending to feed them, let them out into the garden and make breakfast to take back upstairs. A leisurely morning reading the papers followed by a brisk walk and lunch had become standard for them even though they'd done a lot of walking in the Forest of Bowland the day before.

Outside, it was still dark but not as cold as it had been. The sun wouldn't be up until after eight if they saw it at all. Bonnie and Millie snuffled around the garden before each had a quick pee and trotted back in for their breakfast, trailing muddy pawprints. Riley grabbed both in turn and wiped their feet and the floor before starting on creating bacon butties. He hummed as he cooked, imagining how much different this Christmas would be. Queenie watched him from the table, sniffing the air, hoping for a morsel or two. Riley glanced around as the door creaked open to be greeted by the sight of a bare-chested Dylan in pajama bottoms, rubbing his eyes.

"You're up. I was going to bring you breakfast in bed."

"I missed you." He patted the dogs and sat at the table. "And I need tea."

Riley reached for the kettle and switched it on just as the papers rattled through the door.

After a morning of Riley and Dylan reading the news, completing the crossword and taking a leisurely joint shower, the dogs bounced around, whining at the door.

"We'd better give these two a walk," Riley said. "I know it's not Christmas yet, but I bought them each a little something to wear on these chilly days."

The dogs danced around him as if they knew. Queenie had already taken herself off to the bed hanging over the living room radiator and she'd not even bothered to go out.

Riley removed the plastic wrapping and held up each coat. "Now, who wants to be a fairy and who an elf?" he asked. Dylan turned from washing up at the sink and sighed. Riley grinned sheepishly.

"I couldn't resist and it's cold out there."

"You couldn't get them something in tartan?" Dylan said.

"The wings are only little, and Bonnie will look so cute." Riley pulled the garment over the pug. "There, don't you look gorgeous." Bonnie spun around as if showing off. "And now for you, Millie. Yes, we're going walkies." They bounced and yapped. Dylan cuddled Riley from behind, resting his chin on Riley's shoulder.

"Totally embracing the gay," he said. "I'll get our coats and their leashes."

Riley knelt and fondled the heads of both dogs while Dylan grabbed their leads and attached them to the halters they still wore.

They walked for miles through the countryside. The trees had lost their leaves now. In a couple of weeks, it would be Christmas then the New Year. So much had happened in twelve months. His life had been transformed. Dylan slipped his free arm through Riley's as they each held a dog lead.

"What are you thinking?" Dylan asked.

"Just about my life this time last year and how much things have changed."

"For the better, I hope."

Riley kissed Dylan's cheek. "You're fishing, and yes, of course for the better. I have you, and these two, and your dad back in my life. Work is brilliant, and I've updated some of the house. I can look toward the future with optimism. It's been a while since I've felt able to. But, even though you've forgiven my stupidity, I still keep worrying I'm going to wake up and find it's all a dream."

"I can pinch you if you want," Dylan said. The dogs pulled on the leads and yapped at the approaching man and dog. Riley instinctively wanted to move apart. Remembering Dylan's words, he pushed his arm through Dylan's instead and held it there.

"Morning," the man said, nodding his head. "At least the sun's out."

"Morning, Mr. Fielding. Are you feeling better, now?" Of course, Dylan would know him. He knew everyone in the village.

"Can't complain, Dylan, lad. Your parents okay?"

"Both fine, thanks, and Mrs. Fielding?"

"The cold doesn't suit her. We're off to Florida for Christmas."

"Sounds wonderful. Will Kevin be joining you? He works over there, doesn't he?"

"Yes, he and Juan have a house in Orlando. We'll be staying with them. I can't wait to get some sun." He gazed at Riley.

"You're Arthur Ormerod's son, aren't you?"

Riley nodded. "Yes, I am."

"Good man, your father. I was sorry to hear about him. Couldn't go to the funeral as we were away. I hear you've taken over his practice. Word travels fast around here. Well, I'd better get off or the wife will think I've got lost. Good to see you, lad. Say happy Christmas to your parents for me." The man pulled his dog away from sniffing Bonnie and Millie then walked off down the path.

"His son was a couple of years above me in school," Dylan said. "Camp as a row of tents. He works at one of the big theme parks. Strange thing about villages is they look after their own. You always get a few bigots, but I suppose I've been lucky."

Although Riley didn't always believe it, he had to admit society had changed and mostly for the better. "We had the AIDs crisis when I was a teenager. Lots of adverts warning about dangers and the papers full of stories of gay sex scandals. It wasn't a time to be out and proud, believe me. Then there was clause twenty-eight and being told you aren't normal. The idea of being able to get married seemed like a fantasy back then."

Dylan raised his eyebrows. "Well, I'm glad to say it isn't now. Shall we head back home?"

"Yeah, let's do that and give the pub a miss. We've soup and bread to eat and more films to watch."

They strolled home hand in hand. A pool of warmth spread throughout Riley's body despite the cold. He wanted to sing, or whistle a happy tune, or even skip with joy. That feeling lasted until they arrived back at the house. In the drive sat a car. The door opened, and a man climbed out. Riley gulped and shivered, not from the cold. He made to move away from Dylan, but Dylan grabbed his hand. Nate stood in front of the car, dressed immaculately, as always.

"I've come a long way," he said. "Aren't you going to introduce me to your new friend?"

Dylan stepped forward before Riley could utter a word. He held out his hand. "I'm Dylan Hargreaves," he said.

Nate glanced at him then shook the outstretched hand.

"I'm guessing you're Nate. Sorry, I don't know your surname."

"He's mentioned me, then."

Dylan stood his ground while Riley floundered, attempting to get his breathing under control. Why was Nate here? What the hell did he want? All sorts of answers skittered through his mind. He needed to say something. This man had no power over him anymore. The dogs barked and pulled on their leads. Bonnie growled low in her throat. He knelt and patted her. "There, there, girl. Nothing to be afraid of." He meant the words for himself as well as the dog.

"It's okay, Dylan. I'll deal with him. What do you want here, Nate? It's hardly your natural habitat." Riley attempted to keep his voice low and level. Dylan didn't move, but Riley noticed his hands clenched behind his back. He needed to be strong.

"Maybe we could go inside. It's not the weather for standing out here."

Riley didn't want him to set foot in his house, but he gestured to the door. Dylan opened up. "I'll give the dogs a clean," he said, taking their leads and pulling them to the small utility room. Riley wanted to comfort him, to reassure him. All the color had leached from Dylan's face. Instead, he watched Dylan hurry away then showed Nate to the kitchen. He didn't want him going any further.

"Sit down," Riley said. "I'll make us a coffee, and you can tell me why you're here before you go on your way."

He reached for cups then turned around, still leaning against the counter and doing his best to appear relaxed. Nate had removed his scarf and hung his overcoat on the back of the chair. Riley took off his own outer layer, conscious of wearing jumper and jeans underneath. Nate wore a suit which probably cost an average month's wages for most people. He sat with his hands clasped, leaning on the table.

"This is cozy," he said, glancing around. "Interesting choice of color. Is that jade green? And beech worktops give it a country feel. Your father, I suppose."

"No, me. I had it fitted a couple of weeks ago. It suits the house and *my* taste. I wanted a natural feel." *Damn, I'm defending myself already.* "I'm improving the place room by room." Dylan reappeared with the dogs, his face still deathly white.

"And pets as well." Nate's nose wrinkled. Even those few words dripped with sarcasm. Riley had a light-bulb moment.

For what might have been the first time since he'd first met the man he'd spent twenty years of his life with, Riley saw him for what he was — pathetic and needy. He hoped Millie would rub against those designer trousers, leaving her hair behind. He turned to pour the coffee and flashed what he hoped was his warmest smile at Dylan.

"We have a cat as well," Dylan said, taking the seat opposite. "Riley and I chose them from the rescue center. Beds, girls." The dogs immediately wandered to the corner but remained staring at the intruder in case he made a move. Riley stirred the drinks, certain Nate would hate the instant coffee he'd chosen to make rather than using the machine. "Did you travel up this morning? It's a long journey from London."

"No, I had a meeting in York yesterday, so I thought I'd drop in today to see how you were faring here in the back of beyond. I saw the advert for a partner at your firm."

Riley placed the mugs on the table and sat between the two men. He noted Nate had said nothing about the death of his father — no condolences on his loss.

"Riley needs a junior partner, now he's senior partner," Dylan said. Riley lay his hand over Dylan's in the hope he wouldn't keep feeling the need to jump into the conversation as well as to send a message to both men. It didn't work.

"The practice has a great reputation locally," Dylan continued. "In fact, we were both out for dinner with the people in the firm the night before last to celebrate Patrick's retirement. We had a wonderful evening, didn't we, Riley?"

Nate turned to face Riley with a smug look. "Oh, I see. He *works* for you."

Riley's hand itched with the need to punch Nate right on the nose and wipe that look from his face. *Of course, you would think the only way I'd have someone like Dylan was if he was trying to get in the boss's good books.* Dylan opened his mouth and closed it again, after glancing at Riley.

He unfurled his hand, took a sip of the coffee, and met Nate's gaze. "No, as a matter of fact, Dylan's an accountant in local government."

Nate leaned back. A slight rise of eyebrow revealed his surprise. "Finally came out then, did you? I thought you'd be in the closet forever, knowing how backward people are around here. You two must be the only gays in the village. Quite brave, really."

Riley didn't rise to the bait. "Do you know, I've no idea if anyone else in the village is gay? It doesn't matter. Dylan's been out since he was a teenager."

"Never been in," Dylan muttered. "And we're not in the middle of nowhere. We have the internet, hot and cold running water, indoor plumbing *and* central heating. *All* the mod cons."

Riley noted how the color had come back into Dylan's face. He needed this man gone.

Nate sipped the coffee and pulled a face. Riley resisted the temptation to roll his eyes. "For fuck's sake, enough of this. Why are you here, Nate? I don't imagine for one minute this is a social call. You didn't even text after I left. Oh, and how's love's young dream? Still together, are you?"

Nate smoothed his features quickly, but Riley noticed the reaction. He'd hit home. Nate nodded at Dylan.

"From the look of *him*, it seems I'm not the only one with a taste for younger models. How old is *he*?"

"*He* can speak for himself," Dylan said, pulling himself up straight. "And for your information, I chased Riley, not the other way around. Age doesn't matter to me."

Nate laughed. Riley's skin prickled.

"Oh, for fuck's sake, Riley." He waved an arm around. "This is priceless. Do you expect me to believe all this is real? Are you that naïve? Do you think the pair of you will go on playing happy families together? How long do you expect him to hang around? He must be half your age."

"Pretty boy left you then, has he?" Riley stuck out his chin, hoping he appeared determined. "What? And you thought you'd turn up here and I'd be ever so grateful, I'd go back to London with you with my tail between my legs, to act as your skivvy, grateful for the crumbs of affection you throw at me? You expected to find me all alone, didn't you? Rattling round in some rundown old house, but here I am happy, with someone, making a life without you."

Nate leaned forward. "We both know you're talking nonsense. He's a gold-digger after your money. This place must be worth a bit even up here, and no doubt your father left you a decent amount. I bet he wants to set up on his own with your financial backing. He'll bleed you dry and leave you. He can't give you what I can when you're stuck here in this backwater."

Riley squeezed Dylan's hand. He'd thought every one of Nate's words himself. Believing Dylan had feelings for him hadn't been easy, but everything Dylan had said and done had proved him wrong. A few months ago, he might have given in and gone back to Nate out of pure loneliness, but not now. Even if he didn't have Dylan, he had other people, and his gorgeous pets. He had a life he himself had chosen. He glared at Nate, meeting his gaze.

"That's where you're wrong, Nate. Dylan gives me something you never gave me. He gives me himself. Even after twenty years, I didn't know the real you. I only had this unrealistic image of you I'd created, and you certainly didn't know me. If I asked you to name my favorite book or film, you wouldn't have a clue. You don't want me as a partner — you never did. You want someone to run your life for you, to cook, clean and wash your smalls then occasionally bend over and make the appropriate noises. For too long, I mistook what you gave for love. I told myself I was lucky to be the one you came home to, when you came home. There I was, successful in my own right, and yet, with you I was the same twenty-one-year-old I'd always been, still incredulous you had offered your beneficence to me, a boy from the north, unsophisticated and unproven. I know better now. I've packed twenty years of learning into the last eighteen months. I don't need you or want you. You're the one who needs me. I have everything I've ever wanted."

Riley turned to Dylan and took both his hands. "I know I fought against us at the start, Dylan, and I've made some mistakes, but falling in love with you was the easiest thing I've ever done. You let me be me, and I like the person I am now. You see, Nate, with you nothing was real. I only feel sorry for you now."

Out of the corner of his eye, he saw Dylan smile. Nate rose, pushing back the chair. "You think he'll stay when you're an old man? You're kidding yourself. He'll be off with someone else."

Was there a tear in Nate's eye? Had his replacement done that to him, told him he was too old? Nate had passed fifty recently. His forehead remained smooth, no doubt with the aid of Botox, and not a gray hair existed, but the color no longer matched his skin tone.

"Age has no relevance when you love someone," Dylan said quietly. "And no one knows what the future may hold. And I *know* Riley's favorite film and book."

Riley thought of the hours they'd spent talking in the car going to work and coming home. He'd never talked so much to Nate in twenty years. He and Dylan had laughed and sung in those forty-minute slots, sharing so much more than a car.

"And I know Dylan's favorites, too."

"So that's it. Just because you know such things, you choose to stay here dealing with petty people with their petty cases." Nate's frown almost wrinkled his forehead.

Riley squeezed Dylan's hand once more. "I choose happiness. I choose love. I choose people who don't care about how they present themselves every minute of the day and night. I choose laughter and joy. I choose this big old house in this village. I choose living and working with people I like and respect, and who feel the same about me. I choose life, as all those T-shirts said in the eighties — real life. *I choose.* Go back to London, Nate. There's nothing for you here."

Nate didn't say anything more. He grabbed his coat, turned on his heel and walked out. They heard the slam of the door and the roar of the engine as he pulled out of the drive.

Riley stood, finally letting go of Dylan's hand. He kissed the top of his head. "I'll get the soup on then, shall I?"

"Yes, please. I'm starving. I'll butter some rolls. Let's eat on the sofa. We've a certain film to watch, and it's exactly the right time of year for it."

Dylan lay with his head in Riley's lap as George Bailey ran down the street shouting to every building. The dogs snored in front of the fire while Queenie had curled up in her hammock. All was right with his world. He stroked Dylan's hair.

"You all right?" he asked. Neither had said anything about Nate's visit.

"I'm absolutely wonderful. I have to admit, when I saw him here, I panicked."

Riley shook his head. "I meant every word. He never stood a chance." He leaned down and kissed Dylan, letting warmth spread from that connection all over his body. He sat back up, pushing back the desire to do more than kiss.

"It'll be New Year soon," Dylan said. "We've so much to look forward to. Now I've someone to explore with, to visit all those places on my list and to share what I've always wanted. Does that make me sound like the female lead in some old-fashioned romance?"

"Maybe just a little," Riley conceded. Dylan's smile brought a lump to Riley's throat.

"Being here makes me happy. I still have things to do, a business to establish."

On the screen, Clarence the angel got his wings and Riley reached for a tissue. As the titles ran, Dylan turned to face upward, reached his hand to the back of Riley's neck and pulled him down into a kiss. They met open-mouthed, hungry for each other.

"Damn. Your fingers are freezing," Riley hissed.

"Cold hands, warm heart," Dylan replied. "I'll make us a coffee to keep us warm while we W A L K the dogs."

Riley glanced out through the window overlooking the garden. Large flakes of snow had begun to fall. He rose, maneuvered around the animals and stood next to the glass. Dylan crossed the room to stand behind him.

"Maybe we'd better just let them out in the garden," he said. "You'd better go now, or you'll not get home while it's still light." Dylan rested his chin on Riley's shoulder and wrapped his arms around his waist. He smiled at their reflection.

"I don't need to go home, Riley. I'm already here."

Epilogue

Four months later

"You're going to do what?" His sister, Kayleigh, glared at him.

"You heard right," Dylan said. "I'm going to propose. I've bought a ring and I'm going to get down on one knee on his birthday, the day after tomorrow."

"But you're only just twenty-three. That's no age to settle down."

"And Riley will be forty-three."

"So you're acting in haste because he's so much older than you. You haven't known him that long."

Dylan shrugged. He'd hoped for approval from Kayleigh. If she disapproved, he'd have no chance with his parents. "I've known of him for years and *known* him seven months. We've been living together for nearly four months now." He paused. "I want us to be married when we have kids."

"Oh. My. God." Kayleigh leaned forward. "You're serious about this, aren't you?"

"Deadly. I love him, Kay. I've loved him since I first saw him all those years ago. I thought he'd remain a fantasy for me to — you know — but then he appeared in my life and I went after him. We fit. And…I've been looking into ways we could have a child. I could work from home, setting up my own business. A summer wedding would be wonderful. Please be happy for me."

"I want to be happy for you. I am happy for you. I'm surprised, that's all. I mean, I like Riley, but he's Dad's age and Dad's best friend. You say you don't worry about that, but what about when you're both older? If you have kids, you could be left a single parent."

How many times will I have to have this conversation? He hoped being married might at least stop them. "I can't live my life worrying about what might happen, Kay. His mum was way younger than his dad and she died when he was nine, leaving his dad a widower for thirty years. Anything could happen. And I've had this argument with Matt and Dan. Right now, I know this is right for me. He's right for me. In some ways I feel older than him."

She snickered. "Well, you always did have an old head on young shoulders. I mean who announces they want to be an accountant when they're ten? You used to have spreadsheets for your pocket money, for goodness sake, and I bet you know to the penny how much you have in your accounts."

Heat rushed into his face. "I may do, but that's beside the point. I'm going to ask him on his birthday and that's all there is to say. Would you like to see the ring?"

"Go on, then." This time she smiled.

Dylan opened his briefcase and took out the box. "I bought something in platinum. It's narrower than a wedding ring to give him room for both on the same finger. The stone is small but stylish, and it's set in the metal." He opened the box.

"Sapphire. It's a lovely shade of blue."

"The nearest I could find to his eyes. I wanted something different."

"It's lovely." She wiped a tear away. "I can't believe it. What about the wedding? I hope you'll be having a bridesmaid."

Dylan put the ring back safely. "Groomsmaid," he corrected. "No bride, remember? And I've no idea about the ceremony. Nothing big and ostentatious, but I want people there. And sometime in the summer if we can." A shiver ran down his spine. "Bloody hell. I'm going to do this."

Kayleigh moved near enough to wrap her arms around him. "I wish you all the joy in the world. And you're right, you never know, so grab on to the happiness you have. I sort of envy you in a way, but I'm in no hurry to follow you into matrimony. I have so much I want to do. Degree first then the world's my oyster. I've never been certain like you."

Dylan pulled back. "No, you've always had more wanderlust than me. Go out and shake the world, sis."

* * * *

Summer had come early as it sometimes did at Easter in Britain. "Are we mad?" Riley asked, as he pulled up at the pay kiosk to the safari park.

"Don't blame me," Dylan replied. "You wanted to come for your birthday."

Riley's cheeks flushed. "I've never been and this time of year there are babies to see. I wanted to do something fun, though they'll probably think it's strange, two adults without children. We should have borrowed one." *Maybe sometime we won't need to.*

Riley resisted the temptation to pat the pocket where he'd stashed the ring. Today was the day. All he needed to do was seize the perfect moment to propose. It had taken more than three months of them living together for him to finally believe this was real, that Dylan loved him enough to want to spend the rest of their lives together.

"How many tickets, please?"

Riley shook himself and noted the woman leaning forward. He moved forward to reach her then took the money from Dylan. "My treat for your birthday, and get a brochure as well."

The woman took their money and handed over the tickets and booklet.

On the slow journey round the park, they laughed and oohed and ahhed. Laughing as the monkeys jumped on every car, some carrying little ones on their backs. Oohing at the size of the rhinos up close. In the lion enclosure, they stopped with many others until a lioness, feeling somewhat frisky, offered herself to one of the lions who immediately fulfilled her desire. Cars around them moved off in a hurry.

"She knows what she wants," Dylan quipped.

"Well, he is a fine fellow. Look at that mane. I wonder if big cats have a hook on their penis like domestic ones."

Dylan glanced over again. "She seems happy enough, I have to say."

The tour ended at the elephants' enclosure, opposite a large picnic area. They parked and climbed out to get a better view of the newest arrival. The tiny baby elephant could still stand under his mother. Riley took more photos, including one of Dylan with the animals in the background.

They moved off again and parked their car then wandered around the small animal enclosures. The place was crowded by now with children on holiday nagging their harassed parents.

"I'm starving," Dylan said. "Pub lunch then home again? And I'm cooking tonight. We can open your presents then."

Warmth pooled in Riley's chest. Last year, he'd spent his birthday on his own with no presents. So much of his life had changed. This man had brought excitement and surprise back into his life and he wanted to keep the feeling he woke up with every day — that anything was possible.

They arrived home a few hours later, took the dogs for a walk then collapsed on the sofa to open his presents. "You've spent too much," he said, gazing at the pile in front of him.

"I couldn't decide," Dylan said. "So I got a few things."

Riley unwrapped a book, a box set, aftershave and socks. "I thought socks were for Christmas," he said, holding up the pair decorated with pugs. "I half expected to get some sort of sex toy."

"Maybe I have more to give you," Dylan said, winking. He pushed the paper aside and clambered into Riley's lap to straddle and face him. Riley's body reacted immediately. As he gazed at Dylan's shining eyes and grinning mouth, he thought this was the perfect time. Dylan kissed him, pushing his tongue forward until they kissed open-mouthed. Eventually, he pulled away, sucking on Riley's bottom lip, while

Riley worked his fingers into his pocket and dug out the box. He held out his open palm.

"There's something I wanted to ask you..." He stopped as Dylan lifted his hand and opened his palm, too.

"Snap." A small box, identical to the one he held, lay in Dylan's hand. "I wanted to ask you something, too. I had a speech prepared and everything, in case you wanted to say I was too young, or you were too old, or something stupid like that."

Riley shook his head. He'd already had those arguments with himself in the small hours of several mornings. "I planned to say sometimes you instinctively know what's right regardless of anything else. I love you, Dylan Hargreaves, and I want to spend the rest of my life with you."

"And I love you. So, who gets to pop the question as we both have rings?"

Riley chuckled. "It's a bit of a dilemma. We could toss a dice, or pick a card, or play rock, paper, scissors or I could simply say, would you marry me and make me the happiest person in the world. I think that works."

Dylan grinned at him and Riley's heart skipped a beat. He wanted this so much and as soon as possible. It struck him Dylan hadn't yet replied.

"You haven't said anything."

"I wouldn't want you to think I was easy," Dylan replied. "I'm giving your offer due consideration."

"I sort of assumed, as you have a ring, too."

Dylan went to open the box.

Riley stopped him. "Wait a minute, I just need to go into the kitchen."

"O-kay."

Riley woke the dogs and picked up an annoyed Queenie from her hammock. Bonnie and Millie followed him back into the living room. Dylan greeted him with a wide smile. Sometimes, he couldn't quite believe this was all real.

"I thought it only appropriate that we should have some witnesses," he said, sitting back down on the sofa. The dogs sat as if waiting for some treat.

Dylan nodded and opened his box. "Riley Ormerod, in the presence of these witnesses, would you do me the great honor of agreeing to marry me as soon as possible?"

Riley opened his box as well. "Dylan Hargreaves, there's nothing I'd love more."

Want to see more from this author? Here's a taster for you to enjoy!

The Call of Home: Choosing Home
Alexa Milne

Excerpt

"Morning, sir, and welcome to Moray Lodge How can I help you?"

Seth Pritchard tried not to grimace. He hated feeling so weak, but spying the chair in reception, he made for it and sat, stretching out his leg in the hopes that taking his weight off it for a moment might help—it didn't.

"Are you all right, sir? Can I get you anything?"

Seeing the concern on her face, he raised his stick in explanation. "Sorry, I think the plane ride and drive from Inverness may have been a bit much. I'm Seth Pritchard. I've booked the cottage for six months, and I need the keys."

"Of course, Mr. Pritchard." She returned to the desk and pressed a few buttons on the laptop in front of her. "Here are your keys. My name is Caitlin, and you'll see me around the place. If you need anything, press one on the phone in the cottage and it will come straight through to here. To get an outside line, you need to press nine. The cottage has a reasonable mobile signal, depending on your service provider. There's a file with all the instructions on the coffee table in the property. I hope you'll enjoy your time with us."

He stood and pain shot through his leg once more. "Thank you," he managed, taking the keys from the beautifully polished surface of the reception desk.

"Do you need any help unloading your car, Mr. Pritchard?" Concern clouded her features. "We're setting up for lunch, but I could send someone over later."

As she spoke, a couple entered the area and stood waiting.

"I'm fine," Seth said. He knew he sounded tetchy, but he'd had enough sympathetic looks to last a lifetime. "Don't worry. I'll have a rest then get myself sorted later."

He limped outside past the couple and around the back of the hotel to where he'd left his new car next to the small cottage. After opening the driver's door, he sat with his legs on the ground and breathed in. The smell of the sea made him feel better. It was different here, cleaner somehow, but also more pungent than the Bristol Channel. He turned his face up in an attempt to capture any warmth from the bright sunlight, then he closed his eyes and listened to the waves crash onto the rocks. The sun disappeared behind a cloud and he shivered in the cold February breeze. At least it wasn't snowing.

He leaned over and pulled his shoulder bag from the passenger seat. His suitcases could wait. All he wanted to do was wrap a heat pad round his knee, take two painkillers and lie down.

The lock needed jiggling, but once he'd mastered the technique, Seth entered straight into the open plan living room-come-kitchen. The space was surprisingly large, painted in neutral colors, with windows on two sides. Although he'd seen photographs on the Lodge's website, they often gave no idea of size and scale. Happily, he noted a desk under one window where he could work. He dropped the bag on the sturdy piece of furniture, sat on the chair and stared at the view. It was beautiful. The winter sun made patterns on the constantly shifting water. He guessed there would be frost in the morning after another bitterly cold night. The current high-pressure system locked over the country would keep things dry and sunny, but cold.

Seth removed his laptop from the bag and gazed at his surroundings while automatically rubbing his knee. One door led off the main room, which he supposed could only be the bedroom. He tucked a hot pad in his pocket, then, bracing himself, he stood once more and pressed his stick to the floor. At least the carpet provided purchase to cross safely. Laminate floors were a nightmare if the stick got wet, and he'd almost fallen more than once when he'd forgotten to wipe the rubber ferrule at the end. He opened the door to the bedroom. The furniture inside consisted of a large, high bed, which would make life easier, a chest of drawers, a triple wardrobe and an armchair. He liked the shades of blue in the bedding, carpets and curtains. His injury made him assess every piece of furniture, something he'd never considered before the accident, to make sure he could get off it without too much pain. The open door to the bathroom revealed it contained a large shower at one end as well as a bath.

Finally, he sat on the edge of the bed, took out the hot pad and wrapped it around his knee. He downed a couple of painkillers, then swung his legs around to lie on what appeared to be a comfortable bed and closed his eyes.

* * * *

"Shit. What the hell?" It took him several moments to remember his location. The alarm clock told him he'd been asleep for nearly three hours.

"Hello, anyone here?"

"Yes," he shouted. "Give me a minute." Seth pulled the wrap from around his leg and moved carefully, testing his knee before he stood up. The first step after sleeping was always painful. He moved it gingerly. It was stiff still, but bearable. He grabbed his stick and went to meet his visitor.

He entered the room to find a tall, dark-haired man in jeans and a jumper standing with his back to him, scanning the view out of the kitchen window. He turned and Seth took a sharp intake of breath. The man facing him smiled, showing straight white teeth and dimples on either side of his face. Heat rushed unbidden to Seth's cheeks and his body stirred in response to the way his visitor scrutinized him from bottom to top, then he moved forward and put out his hand.

"Hi, I'm Zac McKenzie. I own the Lodge. Caitlin told me you'd arrived. I hope everything is all right for you."

Seth noticed the quick glance at his stick, but he had no intention of explaining why he needed it. He'd come up here to put a few hundred miles between him and his past. No one knew his current location and he intended to keep things that way. He doubted anyone other than his mother would be worried, but after so long in a hospital bed, he couldn't face his mother fussing around him, or the piteous looks and tedious teasing from his stepfather and brothers. He knew it was his fault, what had happened to Anna, cosmic karma for all the lies, so he'd made his plans and had left his family a note.

"Everything is fine, thank you."

"I've brought over sandwiches and a few bits and pieces for later, although you're welcome to book in for dinner whenever you want. There's milk and butter in the fridge, and tea bags, coffee and bread. Tesco delivers if you want to make an order for your own food, or you can give us a list and we'll add it to ours. Mina, our chef, will always have extra, and we can freeze meals for you if it's easier."

"Thank you, you're very kind. For now, I need to get my suitcases and unpack." Seth wanted this person gone as soon as possible. His concerned glances unnerved him.

A look of doubt crossed the handsome face in front of him. "Would you like me to fetch them while you rest your leg? No point in making things worse."

Seth took his keys from the desk, sat and reluctantly handed them over. "That would be helpful. It's still achy after the journey."

"No problem—I know what leg injuries can be like. I'll get your luggage then make us each a coffee. I bet you could use a drink by now."

Seth hated being so useless, but he'd become accustomed to accepting help when offered. The medical profession had warned his leg, secured by several steel pins and a new knee, would never be as good as it had been. He'd been lucky to keep it at all. It had been touch and go to begin with and had taken months in traction to get him to his feet and able to walk any distance. But he was better off than Anna—at least he *could* walk.

Zac returned carrying a suitcase in each hand. "I'll put these in the bedroom, shall I?"

Seth got up and moved to the kitchen area. "It would help if you could put them on the bed."

While Zac went into the bedroom, Seth put the kettle on.

"The mugs are in the top cupboard," Zac said, coming back into the room. He reached into another and took out a jar of coffee then pulled out a drawer containing cutlery.

"Milk?" he questioned.

"Yes, please," Seth replied. He glanced at the package on the work surface. His stomach rumbled loud enough for his host to hear.

"Why don't you sit?" Zac said. "The seat on the armchair has been raised as you asked. I'll make us a coffee and put these sandwiches on a plate. I hope you like BLTs. The bacon is produced locally at McNaughton Farm, and Mina makes all our bread from scratch."

"Sounds good." Seth sat and leaned his stick against the side of the fireplace. The mantle surrounded a gas fire, but the central heating blasted out enough warmth for now. He noted the reading lamp above the chair, which would make life easier. He glanced over to where Zac was preparing the food and couldn't help himself. Zac certainly filled his jeans nicely, and the dark blue jumper fitted his upper body just as well. Strands of dark hair curled at his neck. When he turned, Seth noticed a scar along his forehead and his nose showed signs of having been broken at least once. His handsome face, with its strong jaw and creases around the eyes, had that lived-in look. Seth guessed Zac was around forty to his thirty.

Idiot! Stop it. You came here to get away. Nothing good comes from these feelings.

"Here you go," Zac said, putting the food and drink down on the coffee table. "I hope you don't mind me joining you. If I'm here, I'm out of shouting range and can't be called to do one task or another. I like to stay out of the way when Mina creates. She can get scary with her fiery Italian personality, but she is an amazing chef."

Seth reached over, picked up the sandwich and took a bite. The taste of salty bacon hit his taste buds, prompting a loud and appreciative moan as he chewed. "Wow, this is good."

"The bread is flavored with tomato and herbs. In the summer, we grow our own salad vegetables and they taste even better. So, Seth—at least I can pronounce your name correctly. Welsh names, like Scots and Irish, can be tricky to get your tongue around."

Seth instantly had to knock back a thought about what else Zac could wrap his tongue around then caught the look of mischief in his landlord's eyes. *Is he flirting with me? Does he know? Is it me?* He shook his head.

"I've known the odd Welshman over the years," Zac continued. Again Seth couldn't help but notice Zac's eyebrows rising over his twinkling brown eyes. Known or *known*, he wondered, moving his legs together. He needed to change the subject.

"Have you always been in the hotel business?" he asked.

"No, I've been here for about five years, although I was born nearby and my parents live at Hopeman, a village along the coast. When I bought the Lodge it had been closed for a few years. The council used it as a care home for a while, then it was offices. I refitted the whole place. Each room has a different Scottish theme and design. It's been a labor of love. I lived in here when I first bought the place, and now I have part of the top floor in the main building."

"So what did you do before coming here, then?" Seth drank the excellent coffee and stretched his knee again to stop it from stiffening.

"I played professional football."

"Oh, should I know you? I've always been more of a rugby fan, I'm afraid." He scrutinized his landlord's face. His stepbrothers would have had football on the TV twenty-four-seven, so he'd been exposed to lots of games over the years.

"I retired six years ago with a back injury, but I was captain of Scotland and Glasgow Rovers. I guess I was well known at the time."

Realization hit Seth between the eyes. "Hang on a minute — Magic McKenzie, that's you, isn't it? Didn't you score the winning goal for Trentino when they beat Manchester United in the Champions' League?"

Zac's cheeks flushed red and he grinned. "Yeah, that was me — stupid nickname." Seth noticed the way the skin around Zac's eyes crinkled when he smiled and, *oh my*, his smile lit up a room.

Zac rose from the sofa and picked up the plates. "I'd better be on my way before Mina sends out a search party. No doubt she has a few jobs for me to do before tonight's service. We're nearly full, but can fit you in if you want to eat with us, or I'll get someone to bring something over for you until you get organized."

"Is Mina your wife?" *Fuck. Idiot, where did that question come from?*

There was the smile again. "Mina, good God, no. She'd eat me alive and spit me out. No, her husband plays in goal for Inverness Cally Thistle. We met when we both played in Italy. No, me... I'm not the marrying kind, not anymore."

Seth watched Zac close the door then leaned back in his chair. So much for coming to the back of beyond to escape his problems. It looked like he might simply have found a whole lot more.

PUBLISHING

Sign up for our newsletter and find out about all our romance book releases, eBook sales and promotions, sneak peeks and FREE romance books!

About the Author

Originally from South Wales, Alexa has lived for over thirty years in the North West of England. Now retired, after a long career in teaching, she devotes her time to her obsessions.

Alexa began writing when her favourite character was killed in her favourite show. After producing a lot of fanfiction she ventured into original writing.

She is currently owned by a mad cat and spends her time writing about the men in her head, watching her favourite television programmes and usually crying over her favourite football team.

Alexa loves to hear from readers. You can find her contact information, website details and author profile page at http://www.pride-publishing.com